The Bear's Forbidden Wolf

Weres & Witches of Silver Lake
Book 4

Vella Day

When forbidden love can turn deadly…

Part Wendayan, part wolf shifter, Ainsley Chancellor has spent her life fighting who she is. She carries the tainted blood of her Changeling Clan, but she refuses to embrace their evil ways.

But when she comes face-to-face with the sexy and totally off-limits, Jackson Murdoch, she feels her inner wolf yearn to be with his bear—a desire like she's never felt before. However, mating with him would end in his ultimate demise.

Distrusting Changelings his entire life, Jackson, a bear-shifter, can't deny the pull he feels for the irresistible wolf, but that doesn't mean he has to accept her.

When tragedy strikes, Ainsley and Jackson are forced together. As their need intensifies to an all-time, undeniable high, can they keep their hands to themselves and defeat the Changeling Clan before it's too late?

Beneath the calm and shimmering surface lie intrigue, power, magic, and danger.
Welcome to Silver Lake—where appearances can be deceiving, and what you see isn't truly what lies below.

Chapter One

F OR THE FIRST time in years, Ainsley Chancellor felt safe. Her wolf, who hadn't been let free in way too long, was jonesing for a run. Ever since moving to Silver Lake, Tennessee two weeks ago, she'd been eyeing the hills on the edge of town. The problem was that her roommate told her Changelings roamed the area, and they were the last people she wanted to run into. It didn't matter she was one herself. Her Clan was pure evil.

Happy to be off work, Ainsley unlocked the front door to the apartment and dropped her canvas purse on the linoleum kitchen counter. After grabbing a bottle of water from the fridge, she headed over to the red leather sofa—which doubled as her pullout bed—to enjoy a few minutes rest after her long day. Her feet hurt from standing since nine a.m. and her bones ached. Twenty-seven had never felt so old.

As an acupuncturist, not only did the work require a lot of concentration when placing the needles in her patient's body, she spent much of her time assuring each of them that she could help manage the pain. While she loved her job, hitting the precise spot took concentration and energy—energy she hadn't had today.

Her roommate and coworker, Blair Murdoch, came in a few seconds later, waving a stack of envelopes. Ainsley didn't know how she always looked so good, especially in the not-so-stylish uniform they had to wear: blue slacks with a white shirt bearing the Silver Lake Wellness Center logo on the pocket. Blair's long auburn hair that always looked perfect brought out her green eyes and porcelain skin.

"You got mail!" Blair said.

Ainsley's pulse shot up. After she'd interviewed for her job last month, she'd moved to Tennessee and ended up staying with Blair. Mail was the last thing she expected. She prayed her brother hadn't learned of her whereabouts. Nothing good could come of that. "Maybe it's from the university."

"Nope. Stamp's from Scotland. It was forwarded from Atlanta." Blair handed her the letter.

Hearing the location had her heart pounding. When she checked the return address, her pulse slowed. "It's from Shamus!" How had he found her?

"Who's Shamus?"

A wonderfully kind friend who I should have kept in touch with better. "Shamus and I go way back. In fact, he's a bear shifter."

"Ah, like me." Her roommate kicked off her tennis shoes, set down her purse, and then disappeared into the kitchen. The refrigerator door banged opened. "I thought you said bears and wolves didn't get along over in Scotland," she called out.

"They don't get along the way they do here, but Shamus was my best friend since the fifth grade—until I met you, of course." She and Blair spent the last four years in Georgia as roommates—two as undergraduates and then as graduates. "He kind of protected me against a few jerks who didn't treat me well."

Blair returned with a yogurt cup and a bottle of water in hand. "Protected you?"

Ainsley picked up her own bottle of water and drank from it. "Let's just say he stood up for me. And I stood up for him too. I told you our town was a lot like yours in that the humans didn't know about shifters." But that was all she'd said. Now that she'd succeeded in disappearing—hopefully where her family couldn't find her—it was time to come clean. "Where I lived, the bears had come to the area long before the wolves did, but eventually, the Changeling werewolves grew in number and decided to take what they wanted. Don't get me wrong. There were good wolves that lived there too, but the bad ones seemed to be more prevalent. I'm sure I mentioned that my stepfather was the werewolf Alpha to the Changelings which made him the biggest ass of all."

"You did. That must have been hard on you."

"It was, which is why I'm across the pond now, far away from my family."

"Got it. So then what happened?"

"The land that belonged to the bears was valuable in that it had the same kind of stone that helped the Changelings stay strong. Basically, we pushed the bears out." During their four years together, Ainsley hadn't wanted to discuss her evil Clan. She was too embarrassed to let anyone, except Blair, know what she was. Now that Ainsley was safe in her new town, it would do her soul good to let it all out.

"That pushing out stuff sounds like what the white man did to the Native Americans a long time ago. I hate to say it, but your Changelings sound exactly like ours."

"Genetics don't change because of geography."

"True." Blair peeled off the yogurt lid and dipped her spoon in. "How did you deal with it? I know you haven't wanted to talk about it, so I'll shut up if you want."

"No. It's time to air the dirty laundry, so to speak. Actually, it's way past time. Because I don't think my family will find me here, it's safe to finally give you the lowdown. I should have told you all the sordid details long ago, but I didn't want you to think badly of me."

"I never would have."

Ainsley wanted to believe that, but she'd never been willing to take the chance and tell Blair everything. "You wouldn't have been scared thinking that I might...oh, I don't know—rip out your throat in the middle of the night or something?"

Blair moved next to her on the sofa and set her food down. "I knew from the moment I met you that you had a good heart."

Heat rose up her face. People didn't compliment her very often. "Thanks. So what do you want to know?"

Facing her, Blair sat cross-legged on the sofa then brushed back her hair from her face. "A billion things. Like did your parents make you do terrible things against your will?"

That was a legitimate question given how bad the Changelings were. "No, but that might have been because I was a female and young. They kept me pretty much in the dark about their ways."

"That's good, I guess."

"I always attributed my father's Wendayan genes for keeping the evil lurking inside me at bay. It wasn't until I was maybe thirteen that I overheard my brothers talking about some things they'd done—and it wasn't pretty. It made me realize what Shamus had been saying all along about my Clan was true. At first, I thought he was just jealous of my family since we had money and his family didn't, but he was trying to open my eyes."

"What did you do when you learned your brothers weren't nice people? Did you go to your parents and tell them?"

Ainsley held up a hand. "That's a big fat no. I never liked my stepfather, and my mom wasn't much better once she married him. Remember, they were both Changelings. One didn't complain to either one of them and expect sympathy."

Blair blew out a breath. "I know you said you didn't have a real good home life, but I didn't know it was rather loveless."

She shrugged. "I didn't know better. At least my real dad was great—until he died." Ainsley looked off to the side, refusing to get all teary eyed. She was stronger than that. "The one good thing to come out of being raised a Changeling was learning how to fight."

"Fight? How is that a good thing? When I grew up, I learned that I could count on my brothers to always be there for me."

"You're lucky. My two brothers went through the training with me, but I don't remember them coming to my rescue—ever. Teaching all of us to do battle was my family's way of keeping the wolf population strong."

Blair unfolded her legs. "Who did you have to fight? Other wolves, I hope. Heaven forbid, if you had to go against a bear."

"Just other wolves. They broke us into female and male groups at first, but since I had an affinity for battle, I moved up in the ranks rather quickly." Ainsley hadn't told anyone this before, but she didn't want to have any more secrets. She was tired of them. The burden on her soul had already taken a big toll. "I had a special talent that I used, but only if I had to."

"Special talent?"

She inhaled, fearing this might be the one thing that made Blair pull away. "Remember my dad was Wendayan?"

"Yes."

"When I was maybe five, he was standing right in front of me laughing, and a split second later, he was gone." She snapped her fingers. "Poof."

"Was he a magician?"

"Close. As you know, all Wendayans have some kind of magic. My dad could disappear—though only for a short time. Mind you, he was still there. It was just that no one could see him. If I reached out, I could feel him."

Blair sucked in her breath. "Really? I've never heard of anyone being able to do that."

"I didn't know anyone could either until I saw him do it, but apparently, I inherited that talent too."

"Are you shitting me? Show me!" Blair clapped her hands.

Ainsley shook her head. "I haven't tried it in years. Besides, it really wipes me out."

"How come you never told me?" The hurt in Blair's voice cut her.

Ainsley looked around, trying to come up with a good reason. "It was something I did in Scotland. I came to America for a fresh start, which is why I haven't practiced." She leaned forward. "I tried to tell you many times, but then I chickened out. I thought you might think I was some kind of freak. It was bad enough that I belonged to a group that was your Clan's sworn enemy, but being able to disappear made me even more of an anomaly."

Blair clasped Ainsley's hands. "I never would have thought less of you. Your magic doesn't define you. I just never thought a shifter had magic—unless she or he had mated with a Wendayan."

"Mixed breeds are a strange lot."

Blair glanced to the side, as if trying to assimilate all the new information then nodded to the letter. "Are you going to open Shamus's letter or what?" She grinned. "Do you think he's writing to profess his undying love?"

"Hardly." Ainsley was happy that conversation was over. In truth, it went a lot better than she could have hoped. As she ran a finger along the edge of the envelope, she spotted the date stamped on the outside. "Crap. He mailed this over three weeks ago." She ripped open one end then shook out the letter. When she spotted his beautiful penmanship a warm, fuzzy feeling filled her. Ainsley held it up and smiled. "Pretty, right?"

Blair whistled. "A man wrote that?"

"We were schooled in calligraphy, but Shamus in particular enjoyed writing. He's such a gentle soul." She held up a finger. "Don't get me wrong. When provoked, he would fight and do a damned fine job. In fact, even though he worked in a bank over in Scotland, he helped train other shifters so they'd be prepared if and when they had to fight the Changelings."

"Wasn't that a conflict of interest between you two, since you're one of them?"

"Not really. Shamus could see through to the real me."

Blair picked up her yogurt cup. "You sure you aren't hiding some big romance from me?"

"No. I've told you everything. As for Shamus, we're just really good friends—friends who haven't seen each other in eight years. Now do you want to hear what he wrote?"

Blair leaned forward. "Absolutely. I love juicy stuff."

Ainsley shook her head but failed to keep the smile from her face. *"Dear Ainsley, I hope this letter finds you well. First, I must apologize for not writing sooner, but it seems you forgot to give me your address in America."*

Blair cocked a brow. "Ainsley?"

"I told you. I needed a clean break. My parents, as well as my two stepbrothers, were well aware how much he meant to me. If they thought Shamus could find me, then they might have used him to get to me, and I couldn't take that chance."

While her parents had helped finance her college and had the address of the dorm where she lived the first two years, they'd never written. After she moved in with Blair, Ainsley didn't send them a change of address.

"I'm sorry. That must have been tough to lose him—or rather lose contact with him."

"It was, but he was always in my thoughts."

Blair nodded to the paper in her hand. "Finish reading."

She located her place. *"I had a dickens of a time finding you, lass. But you know me, I don't give up easily. I'm proud to see you're in graduate school. Yes, I pulled in a few favors to locate you. I have some relatives in America, most of whom I've never met, so I thought it was time to connect with my family and visit you."* Her heart pounded.

"He's coming to the United States to see you? I wouldn't call that merely a friendship. You sure you two aren't mates?" Blair asked.

Ainsley shook her head. "No. We've never even kissed." Besides, she'd never take the chance that her genes might taint his if they mated. Her father had learned the hard way what happened when a non-Changeling mated with a Changeling.

Blair leaned back in her seat. "I don't know. There may be more than meets the eye here. Perhaps he was waiting for you to grow up."

Ainsley let out a big breath. She'd heard that a shifter didn't feel the mate pull until they were older. Maybe Blair was right. Eighteen had been too young. "Do you see why I haven't mentioned him before?"

Her best friend laughed. "Did he say when he was coming?"

As she read the last few lines of the letter, she had to think what day it was. "It's today. He's flying to the US today!"

"Uh-oh. Do you think he'll go to Atlanta, thinking you're still there?"

Her stomach dropped. "I don't know." She flipped over the envelope to check the address. Her heart sank. It had been addressed to their place in Atlanta and then forwarded. "I'm hoping he plans to visit his relatives first. I'll have to figure out how to get ahold of him."

"Call Marybeth. She can give him your new address if he shows up at our old place."

"Good idea." Marybeth Randall lived next door to where she and Blair had shared an apartment. Ainsley checked her phone and dialed their friend. When it went to voicemail she told Marybeth what happened, and that if she spotted a six-foot five, redheaded burly man with a funny accent, to give him her new address. She then rattled it off. Ainsley set her phone on the coffee table. "All set."

"I can't wait to meet this Shamus fellow. He sounds really nice."

Ainsley smiled. "He is, but don't get too attached. I doubt he's staying longer than a few days."

"Well, darn." Blair grinned then nodded to the letter. "Is that all he wrote?"

"Almost." She scanned the last two lines. "He just said that he couldn't wait to see me as it's been too long." She swallowed. "He signed it, Love Shamus."

Blair grinned. Not good.

"JACKSON, COME HELP me take the lid off of the pickle jar," his mother called from the kitchen.

Jackson Murdoch leveraged himself out of his dad's recliner and went in to help his mom. When he saw the three plates of hors d'oeuvres and a ton of desserts, he shook his head. "I know you said my cousin was a big man, but Mom, he's not going to eat all this stuff."

"I'm doing it for my sister, goddess rest her soul. Moira always said her son could eat a horse."

A knock sounded on the front door, and a smile broke out on his mom's face. "He's here." She wiped her hands on her apron then slipped it off. "Well, go answer it," she said, shooing him out.

"You come with me. He knows you better." Jackson had met him one time when he was eight after Aunt Moira had come over to the States with her husband and young son.

"Dan? Where are you?" his mom called out as she hustled out of the kitchen and rushed past the dining room table. Striding up to the front door, she shook her head. "Where is your father when I need him?"

Jackson knew better than to answer.

When she pulled open the door, the cold air rushed in, and his mom gasped. "Shamus? Is that you behind that beard?"

"Hi, Aunt Felicia. Thought I'd give it a try." His grin was wider than the door.

"Come in, come in. It's chilly out there."

"This isn't cold." They hugged, and when the big bear of a man lifted Mom off her feet, Jackson thought he'd have to intervene. His cousin finally set her down and ran his gaze from top to bottom. "It's so good to see ye. Why ye haven't changed a bit. Still a lightweight, I see."

Jackson bet his mom loved that since she was always on a diet.

"Aw. You don't need to sweet talk me." She turned to Jackson. "You probably don't remember, but this is my youngest son, Jackson."

Jackson stuck his hand out to the man who was a good two inches taller and a lot heavier than he was. He wore dark blue jeans, work boots, and a plaid shirt that looked close to bursting. Jackson bet his cousin would be a beast in a fight. "Nice to finally meet you—again." Jackson didn't expect the bear hug that followed.

"Can't wait to get to know ye better too." Shamus looked around. "Where's Uncle Daniel and the rest of the crew?"

"Your uncle will be here in a moment," his mom said.

"And Kalan?" Shamus asked.

"Kalan's still at work." Jackson faced his mom. "You did tell Blair about the visit, didn't you?"

She glanced to the side. "I don't remember. When Shamus wrote us a month ago to say he was coming, Blair hadn't moved back here yet. I told your dad to let her know."

Jackson held up a hand. "I'll give her a call right now."

"Before you do, bring in Shamus's suitcase while I get your cousin something to drink."

"Is your car locked?" he asked Shamus.

"No, but leave the bag. I'll get it later." Shamus faced his aunt. "Now where's that drink ye promised? I'm a might thirsty."

His mother smiled. "Come with me. I figured after that long flight, you'd be hungry too."

"Ye can count on that," Shamus said with a grin.

Jackson liked his cousin. He was open and honest. What a shame they hadn't reconnected sooner. As Jackson headed through the living room toward the sliding glass door that led outside and to his dad's workshop, he dialed Kalan.

"Is the guest of honor there?" Kalan asked.

"He is."

"And?"

Jackson chuckled. "You'll like him. Too bad he's some kind of banker. If he had any law enforcement background, I know you'd try to recruit him at the sheriff's department. Half the criminals in town would take one look at him and run. The man is huge."

"Good MacLeod stock."

"You got that right. Are you going to make it to dinner?" Jackson asked.

"On my way there now."

"What about Elana?"

Kalan let out an audible sigh. "I'm afraid my mate will be absent tonight. She's creating some arrangements for a wedding and has to set it all up. She'll come over if she finishes early."

"Great."

When his mother had first announced that their cousin from Scotland was coming for a visit, Jackson hadn't been overly excited to meet him. Shamus was kind of scrawny as a kid with bright red hair. Jackson always pictured him growing up to be some stuffy, conservative man. Boy had he been wrong. Now that he'd met him, Jackson wished he'd found the time—and the funds—to take a trip to Scotland to meet all of his relatives.

Just as he was about to step outside to find his dad, his father exited his workshop and headed his way. Mom must have telepathed him.

Dad stomped his feet on the outside porch before coming in. "Shamus is here?"

"Yup. They're in the kitchen."

Seconds later, his mom came out of the kitchen carrying a tray of hors d'oeuvres, followed by Shamus who had two large trays.

"There you are, Daniel. Take off your coat and join us." She waved both of them over.

His father strode toward them and gave Shamus a hug. "I swear you've grown since we last saw you, boy."

Shamus laughed. "Only in me belly." He patted it.

Jackson joined them. "Kalan is on the way. I was just about to call Blair to let her know."

His mom and dad started in on Shamus, asking him a ton of questions. Not needing to disturb them, he stepped into the living room and called his sister.

She answered on the first ring. "Hey, stranger."

He laughed. "You're the one who's busy working all the time. Listen, I think Dad might have forgotten to mention that one of our cousins from Scotland was coming to town."

"He never said anything about it. Have I met this person?"

"When you were seven." Only their parents had flown over to Scotland two years ago when Aunt Moira had passed away, but none of the kids had joined them. "He just arrived."

Blair covered her hand over the phone. His sister must be speaking with Ainsley, who used to live over in Scotland. "What's our cousin's first name?"

Did it matter? "You don't remember?"

"We have a lot of cousins."

That they did. "His name is Shamus. Mom wants you to come over now for dinner and meet him." His sister didn't respond. "Blair?"

"I think we may have a problem."

Chapter Two

FROM THE WAY Blair's face paled, something bad had happened. Ainsley waited until her friend hung up before asking. "What is it?"

"What's Shamus's last name?"

"MacLeod."

"Wow. I just found out that your Shamus is my cousin."

It was as if ten people with guns had come at her at once. Ainsley held up her hands, her blood curdling in her body. "Are you sure?"

He was a bear shifter, so she supposed it was possible, but what were the odds?

"My mom's sister is Moira MacLeod."

Crap. "That's his mom. Poor Shamus. Your family can't know that he's come here to visit a Changeling. They'll never understand."

Blair blew out a breath and stabbed a hand through her hair. "You're right. This isn't good, but you aren't the typical Change-ling."

"That doesn't matter. Do your parents know that I'm one? Or rather that I'm a half Changeling?" Blair promised she'd never mentioned it to her folks, understanding that they wouldn't react favorably.

"After we went out to lunch with Mom last week, I told her. I'm guessing that means Dad knows too, but he's never said anything to me, so he must be cool with it. They both know how close we are and trust my judgment."

"What about your cop brother?"

Her nose scrunched up. "I may have forgotten to mention that fact to Kalan or Jackson. They'd just finished working a case in which two Changelings stabbed a Wendayan and took his magic. Fortunately, the security firm that Jackson works for was able to retrieve it, but Kalan was injured in the fight."

Guilt swept down. Even though she had no connection to the Changelings in the US, it didn't mean she didn't feel bad when their malicious acts touched someone good. "I bet that pissed off everyone around here."

"You can say that again. Once Jackson and his team stole back the magic, the Changelings tried to take a different Wendayan, but she managed to escape."

That caught Ainsley's attention. "She must be one powerful witch."

"She is, especially when she mated with another Wendayan and inherited his powers too."

"That's cool."

Blair stood. "My parents have asked that I come over for dinner right now. The whole family will be there, so I gotta change."

Ainsley wanted to see Shamus, but not under these circumstances. "Can you pull Shamus aside and tell him I'm in town?"

Blair leaned over and hugged her. "I sure will."

Her roommate stepped into the bedroom and returned five minutes later wearing a cute pair of jeans and a pink sweater. She then gathered her things. As soon as Blair headed out, a sense of doom descended. Someone would end up being hurt because they knew her, and she prayed it wasn't Shamus.

"SO TELL US Shamus, how did you defeat those bastard Changelings?" Jackson's dad asked as he broke off a piece of bread from the loaf then slathered on too much butter. If he weren't a werebear, Jackson bet his dad would have some serious health issues.

"It was a might hard, I'll tell ye that. Owen Chancellor—he was their leader—thought he had the edge, but—"

"Owen Chancellor?" Kalan asked.

"Kalan, wasn't that Izzy's stalker?" Jackson asked.

His brother glanced at him. "Yes, but what are the chances there are two Scotsmen with the same name who came over here?"

Shamus smiled. "I'm betting it was the same person, and I'll tell ye why I think that. After we defeated him and his useless Clan members, his parents gave away his title-to-be to the younger son, Alex. Since he's mated and a tad smarter, Alex was elevated to be next in line as Alpha."

Jackson chuckled. "I bet being stripped of his title put oil in Owen Chancellor's blood."

"It did. That embarrassment caused him to look for a powerful wife. I heard through the grapevine that his search lead him to America to find her."

Jackson glanced over at Kalan, whose jaw had tightened. If his glass hadn't been plastic, he bet his brother would have crushed it.

"But he failed," Kalan said, his voice sounding like he'd swallowed gravel.

"Thankfully. I wouldn't have given a hoot one way or the other, but ye see, I was always a little sweet on his sister."

Blair knocked over her glass of water. If Jackson hadn't been gazing in her direction, he wouldn't have seen that she'd done it on purpose.

His sister jumped up. "I'm sorry. I'll get something to clean it up with."

His mom used her napkin to keep the liquid from flowing too far, but it wasn't enough. Jackson stood. "I'll help too."

While Blair protested, he needed to ask her what the hell was going on and rushed into the kitchen after her. Fortunately, from the dining room, no one could see them. With the excellent shifter hearing, he'd have to whisper. "Why did you tip over the water? I know bears have the reputation of being clumsy, but you have never been like that."

She looked over her shoulder, probably to see if their mom was coming in. "My roommate Ainsley is Ainsley Chancellor—Owen's sister. But she's nothing like him." Her words spilled out. "Nor does she know he's dead."

Jackson didn't hear much past the part about how his sister had roomed with a Changeling for four years. His heart was pounding too hard. "Are you crazy? You knew she was one of them, yet you told no one? And worse, you're rooming with her now!"

"Shh. Keep your voice down. You don't know anything about her." She blew out a breath and looked at the ceiling, as if she were trying to figure out what to say. "I'm not going to defend myself or Ainsley. I'm sorry that you're too pigheaded to listen. Shamus is her dear friend, and he wouldn't have protected her since fifth grade if she had been evil. Just so you know, Owen is her stepbrother. They're not even related."

He pounded a fist on the stone countertop. "But she's still a Changeling." It didn't matter that two Changelings had risked their lives to help Kip's brother retrieve his magic. Those two were an anomaly.

Footsteps sounded. "What's going on in here?" Their mother grabbed a hold of each of their arms like she used to do when they were little. So what if he towered over her by a foot, she still had the ability to make him quake a bit.

"Did you know that your daughter's roommate is a fucking Changeling?" Jackson ground out, not caring if his voice traveled or if his mom took offense at his language.

Her grip loosened. "As a matter of fact I do. Ainsley is a lovely girl. And she's only half a Changeling. The other half is Wendayan."

"But—"

"I'm ashamed of you, Jackson Murdoch, judging someone before meeting her."

"You should know," Blair said, "that Ainsley is a dear friend of Shamus's."

"Is that so? What a small world. By all means invite her over to dinner. There's plenty of food."

He could see his sister's mind spinning, trying to come up with a reason not to. "Ah, I don't know if that's a good idea."

His mother's chin tucked under. "Why not?"

Her shoulders sagged. "Okay, I'll call and ask her, but she might not want to come."

"That's fine," their mother said. "It's important that she understands she's welcome in my house." She looked straight at him. "Some family members might not be soon."

Blair glared at him too, but he wasn't backing down. "Don't tell Kalan or we'll have a war on our hands," he said.

Their mother lowered her hands to her side, but her lips remained pinched. "I raised both of you better than that. Come back out to the table and act like adults."

With that, she stepped out. Without another word, they gathered wads of paper towels to clean up the water spill. Jackson kept his focus away from his brother and Shamus while trying to quell his anger as he helped soak up the mess on the mahogany table. Even as they blotted the water, Shamus never stopped his story telling, seemingly oblivious to the discussion in the kitchen or what they were doing.

"Good, you're back," his dad said as soon as Shamus took a breath. "Shamus was describing the massive defeat against the Changelings." His father returned his gaze to his cousin. "So did Owen take this mate home then? Not that I'm looking for a happily ever after for that scumbag."

Jackson was sure Kalan had told their father about what had happened to his best friend's mate's. Dad must have forgotten.

"I'll answer that, Dad," Kalan said. "No, he didn't. I told you about Izzy's stalker. Don't you remember?"

"Her stalker?" He glanced off to the side. "Was he the one who got tangled up in a vine?"

"That's him, yes. After Izzy shunned him, he ran off the road at

Gulver's Gap and tumbled down the mountainside where his car burst into flames. I figured he committed suicide because he was heartbroken."

That was a line of crap, but Jackson wasn't about to bring that up in front of everyone.

"Blair has some good news for you, Shamus," his mother said.

If his sister could have turned any whiter, she'd be lighter than a piece of paper. Blair pasted on a smile, though most likely Shamus could see it was fake. "Yes. I couldn't believe it when you said Owen's name, but my roommate is Ainsley Chancellor. She just received your letter maybe half an hour ago."

Shamus slapped a hand on the table. "Good goddess, woman, ye need to bring her here. I came across the pond to reconnect with her. Why didn't ye say something sooner?"

Answer that one, sis.

"I honestly didn't think *her* Shamus was you."

"Well, call her for me, will ye?"

Blair pushed back her chair. "Right away."

His sister stepped into the living room not only for some privacy but probably to regain control of her emotions. No doubt, later tonight, Dad and Kalan would blame her for tainting their house with a Changeling.

"So how long have you known Owen's sister?" Kalan asked Shamus with a hard edge to his voice.

"Since we were young. I got to know her before I learned what horrible creatures Changeling's were."

Kalan leaned forward on his elbows. "Didn't it bother you when you found out that she was one of them? I mean her brother was one sick dude. He stabbed my best friend in the gut and left him to die."

"Is he okay?"

"Fortunately, he got help in the nick of time. He's a werewolf, so he healed quickly."

"I'm sorry. I, for one, know firsthand how bad Owen Chancellor is, or rather was. He always tormented Ainsley, which was partially why I needed to protect her. The bears and wolves didn't get along well back in Scotland, and even the good werewolves made fun of her."

Sympathy swelled, but Jackson couldn't get past the fact that she had defective genes. "How did she escape being like the rest of them?" Jackson asked, not convinced she had.

"Her dad was a powerful Wendayan. He died when she was young, so she was basically left alone," Shamus said. "Me Mum took a liking to her and tried to do right by her."

That could have helped. Perhaps Jackson should reserve his judgment until he met her, but while quite a few Changelings appeared to be model citizens on the outside, many wouldn't think twice about stabbing a person in the back.

Blair returned from the dining room, her gaze everywhere but on him or Kalan. "I got a hold of her. Ainsley is thrilled we invited her, and she can't wait to see Shamus."

Well, shit. From the strain around his sister's eyes, she'd had to twist her roommate's arm to accept the invitation, and his gut told him nothing good could come of this encounter.

AINSLEY KNEW THIS was a bad idea to go over to the Murdoch house, but what choice did she have? She wanted to see Shamus, but she also wanted to throw herself on the bed and grieve over the loss of his mother. Thankfully, Blair had warned her first of Moira MacLeod's death. If Shamus had mentioned her passing during dinner, Ainsley wasn't sure she'd have been able to keep it together.

Now she could see that by not keeping in contact with him, she'd lost the chance to see his mom again and tell her how much she'd helped Ainsley grow into the person she was today.

She swiped a tear from her cheek.

Suck it up, Ainsley.

She was made of sterner stuff than that. Her Changeling genes helped her push aside her feelings and tuck them away for the time being. Needing to ignore the tragic loss of his mom, she refocused on what she had to do right now, which was get ready to face Blair's family.

While Ainsley had met Mrs. Murdoch, who'd been warm and really nice, the rest of the family might not greet her with open arms. It didn't matter that Shamus had probably told everyone the two of them were good friends. From the short conversation Blair told her she'd had with her brother Jackson in the kitchen, he was quite put off by the fact his sister was friends with her. It didn't seem to matter that she wasn't even related to Owen. She had Changeling blood in her system, and that damned her in his eyes.

And then there was her other brother—Kalan, who was a cop. While Blair didn't give her many details over the phone, she'd mentioned that because of his job, he'd had run-ins with her kind many times. During the last scuffle, Kalan had been severely injured. Not surprising, his hatred for Changelings was off the charts.

Wonderful. Tonight would be *déjà vu* all over again. It would be like walking into her fifth grade classroom where everyone automatically assumed she was the devil incarnate because her stepfather loved to ruin lives.

Ainsley figured she could always disappear if things became too awkward then slip out unnoticed, but that would only prove to Blair's family that Ainsley was some kind of shifting freak.

No. She had to face them, and she couldn't take too long, or they'd think she was avoiding the challenge. She was Ainsley Chancellor, a woman with a thick skin and a temper to go with it. *I can do this.*

She rushed into Blair's bedroom to find something appropriate to wear, as she certainly wasn't about to go to dinner in her uniform. Ainsley's three suitcases were laid out on the floor on the far side of the room. Blair was a saint for letting her crash at her place for as long as she had.

What to wear? The fact Ainsley had purple streaks in her short blonde hair would be enough to turn them off, which meant she had to soften her appearance with something that wasn't flashy. She refused to take out her nose ring, however. It didn't matter that Mrs. Murdoch was a down-to-earth person who didn't seem to mind it. From the way Blair described her two brothers, they were conservative with a capital C.

She hadn't laid eyes on Shamus in eight years, and she couldn't wait to see what he looked like now. Blair's words came back to her about Shamus's motivation for flying all the way to America. Was it because he wanted to connect with his relatives and figured Georgia wasn't all that far from Tennessee? Or did he really come just to see her?

Stop procrastinating. I'll find out soon enough.

She chose a pair of straight-legged black pants and a white buttoned-down shirt that she'd purchased when she first interviewed for the job at the clinic. Because it was cold, she threw on a mohair peach-colored sweater that would complement her tinted hair.

Shamus was a foot taller than she was, so she slipped on her leather boots that had two-inch heels. After refreshing her makeup, she headed out, hoping she wasn't walking into a shit storm.

While she was excited to see Shamus again, she wasn't looking forward to the chilly reception from the others. But that couldn't be helped. She'd learned long ago that she couldn't change people. All she could do was be herself, and maybe she could break down the barrier between them. For both Blair and Shamus's sake, she hoped tonight went well.

As she headed out of town toward the shifter compound, her stomach twisted into knots. Ainsley never had been good with meeting people, in large part, because her mom sure as hell hadn't drilled any social graces into her. If it hadn't been for Shamus's mother's guidance, Ainsley wouldn't have stood a chance at making a good first impression.

One of her strengths was her ability to face her fears head on— and the fear of rejection was a strong one. The problem was that when backed into a corner, her temper often got the best of her, and of all the nights to lose control, this just couldn't be one of them.

When the street sign appeared where Blair's parents lived, she made a left turn, but then had to slow down in order to find the number. As she searched for it, she spotted her roommate's car in the drive three houses away. Relieved she'd made it, Ainsley parked on the street instead of the driveway, not wanting to get blocked in, just in case she had to leave in a hurry.

For Shamus's sake, and Blair's, Ainsley had to be polite, no matter how ugly things might get.

As Ainsley walked up to the front door, she spotted a large group of people through the bay window, sitting around the dining room table laughing. They were probably enjoying something Shamus said. He always had been amazingly charming.

Here goes.

Chapter Three

TO AINSLEY'S RELIEF, Blair opened the front door. Before Ainsley changed her mind and decided it would be better to meet Shamus on more neutral ground, she quickly stepped inside. The entranceway of the Murdoch's home blocked not only the sight line to the dining room, but some of the sound as well.

Blair rubbed Ainsley's shoulder. "I know this will be awkward, but Mom really wants everyone to get along."

"Get along? She's kidding, right?"

"No. She loves harmony. Besides, it's only for one night."

Harmony, hell… "From what you've told me, neither Jackson or Kalan will ever accept me," Ainsley whispered.

Her roommate waved a hand. "Just be charming, and I promise they'll love you. But for goddess sake, don't lose your temper if they say something about your kind."

That would be like asking the sun to rise in the west tomorrow. "I'll try, though I'll probably agree with them."

As her roommate led her to the dining room, Ainsley briefly looked around. The living room was straight ahead and contained lots of dark brown furniture, complete with three comfortable looking loungers, something she could use right about now. Family photos graced the walls and made the place homey. Her stepfather only had pictures of his two sons, but never any of her. A strong longing for a loving family of her own welled up inside her.

Ainsley's thoughts were cut short as soon as she stepped into the dining room. The dark wooden table sat eight, three seats of which were empty. The chair backs were ornate, sculpted with swirls, and the flowered seat covers blended well with the light blue walls and dark wood wainscoting. Everyone stopped talking as soon as they saw her. Well, crap.

Forget them. Concentrate on Shamus. Her gaze shot straight to her old friend, and joy elbowed its way in despite the uncomfortable glares. Without warning, a strange emotion that she could only describe as lust attacked her from all sides. What the hell was going on? Her chest tightened and nearly cut off her air. Dizziness assaulted her and forced her to stop while she inhaled a few deep breaths. Her vision slowly cleared, and the tension in her shoulders released its death grip. Her heart, however, was beating harder than a stampede of cattle. The pounding had to be anxiety and nothing else. Right?

Stay calm. Don't make a scene. For a few seconds, she was tempted to turn around and run, but that would only make matters worse. More than anything, she had to prove to everyone in the room that she wasn't evil; that the eight years away from her family in Scotland had taught her how to embrace her good side.

When she looked deep into Shamus's kind eyes, her lips started to work again, and she broke into a smile.

"There she is." Shamus shoved back his chair so hard it tumbled. "Sorry." His ruddy cheeks turned beet red as he leaned over and righted it.

Once he moved around the others, he rushed toward her. Seconds later, she was in his arms being swung around, and for the first time in weeks, she laughed. Boy, did that feel good. Shamus could always erase her worries.

"Put me down you big oaf." She lightly pounded on his back with one fist while holding on with her other arm.

Shamus obeyed. "You're a sight for sore eyes, lass." He wrapped an arm around her waist with one hand and fluffed her short hair with the other. "I like the purple, squirt." He squinted. "A nose ring? What have these American's done to me sweet little friend?"

"Sweet?" Now, he'd gone too far, though most likely he was kidding. "I may only be five foot six, but I'm the same Scottish Ainsley you always knew. I still pack a punch too." To prove her point, she jabbed him in the belly. To her surprise, it was hard. "Ouch."

He laughed. "Oh, lass, I have missed ye. Come on in and have something to eat. My aunt has made a delicious meal."

As he led her back to the table, another wave of uncontrollable lust assaulted her, and her wolf wanted to be released. That was more than crazy. Her teeth sharpened, and her bones started to crack. *Stop!*

She'd heard tales about what happened when a person met her mate; it was like the world had tilted on its axis, and her desire was ramped up to a point where she would do anything to have that other person. Never in her wildest dreams, however, had she thought her mate would be Shamus. Didn't he realize it could never be? Mating with her would eventually cause him despair and even death. Poor Shamus.

"Here ye go," he said, offering her the seat across from him, between Mr. Murdoch and a man who she suspected was Kalan, if the sheriff's uniform was any indication. His long, dark blond hair was tied back and he looked like he could use a shave. He'd be a handsome man if it weren't for the clenched fists and his lips pressed thinly together.

Shamus held out her chair and she sat down. Not wanting the Murdoch family to believe she had no manners, she smiled and waved. "Hi, everyone. I guess you know I'm Ainsley. Thanks for inviting me."

Blair sat to the left of her father, and next to her was most likely Jackson who was next to Shamus. To his left was Mrs. Murdoch, then the last empty chair, and finally Kalan who was sitting next to her.

Yup, this was going to be a tough crowd.

She debated shaking everyone's hand, but she feared they'd not extend her the courtesy. Not that she'd care, but it might make

Shamus uncomfortable.

Strong, angry pulses radiated off Jackson whose negative energy was mixed with Shamus's sensual vibes, making it hard to breathe again. *Focus on Shamus.* Soon, her chest expanded and the pain began to diminish—but not enough to help her relax.

"I love your new look, Shamus. You look good with a beard," Ainsley said with as much cheer as she could muster.

He stroked it. "Why, thank ye. Keeps me warm in the winter."

As much as she wanted to study all the changes in her friend, it was Jackson, with his ruggedly good-looking short beard, who drew her attention. His flannel shirt had the top three buttons undone, and wisps of light brown hair filled the open expanse. Oddly, her stomach fluttered at the masculine view. That was not good. Despite it being late fall, his skin was tan, which brought out his emerald green eyes. His short hair hinted he might have been in the military, but she didn't remember Blair telling her that Jackson had served.

Perhaps his most striking feature was the symmetry of his face. His nose was straight, his eyes were wide-set, and his lips were just about perfect.

Stop it. All the lust pouring from across the table came from Shamus—didn't it? Of course it did. From the lines around his eyes and mouth, Jackson was looking at her as if he was waiting for her to shift or something, which would give him an excuse to attack.

"Jackson, stop staring at our guest," Mrs. Murdoch said in a sharp tone.

"Sorry." The moment he looked away, air returned to her lungs.

What is wrong with me? Shamus came all this way to see me.

Blair was right. He must have known all along they were mates and had waited until she'd grown up before he sought her out. That had to be it. Otherwise, it made no sense that her body was going crazy. If she and Shamus were alone, she'd ask him back to her place to have a wild Scottish fling. There could never be any biting or mating. Oh no, that could lead to his death.

"So what have ye been up to these last eight years?" Shamus

asked, as if he were oblivious to her discomfort. He must feel these strange stirrings too, so how was he remaining so calm? Then again, the man always did have control.

Oh, I don't know—avoiding Changelings of all kinds—including my family. Did he really think she'd talk about her life as a Changeling when Kalan and Jackson were probably looking for something to prove she was evil? "As Blair probably told you, I'm an acupuncturist now. So, for the last eight years, I've basically been studying my ass off while working part time for an awesome acupuncturist learning my craft." Crap. She shouldn't have said *ass* in front of Blair's folks. Not wanting to witness more scowls, she kept her gaze on her friend. "When I called Blair a month ago and said I wanted to come for a visit, she helped me get an interview, which landed me a job at the clinic where she works. Wasn't that nice of her?" *Stop rambling.* Ainsley cleared her throat and placed the napkin next to her plate on her lap. "As soon as I find my own place, I'll officially be on my own for the first time in my life." She smiled, but it took more effort than she thought imaginable.

"I know of a place you might be interested in," Kalan said, his low voice gruff.

Ainsley's tongue twisted from the shock. "You do?"

"My mate used to live in the small apartment above her flower shop. Now that she's with me, it's available for rent."

Jackson sent a glare straight at his brother that looked as it if could cut him in half. Mrs. Murdoch shot Jackson a stern look, and he glanced away again. That man had serious issues, though she did understand where the animosity was coming from. To tell the crowd that she disliked Changelings as much as they did, however, would probably sound like a lie, mostly because they were brought up to believe everyone of her kind was evil.

"I'd love to take a look at it. Thank you."

Shamus grinned. "If Kalan can set it up, how about I come with ye? We could check it out together."

She almost laughed at his protective nature, but she shouldn't be surprised. He'd always looked out for her. From Shamus's quick turn of his head toward Jackson, Jackson might have kicked him under the table.

"What was that for?" Shamus said. "Can't a man make certain his friend isn't being taken advantage of?"

As if someone had dumped a bucket of ice water on his head, Jackson's shoulders slumped. What she wouldn't give to know what that was all about. "Sure. In fact, I think it's a great idea."

Kalan glanced at his mother then turned back to Ainsley. "Tomorrow, I'll call my mate's former landlord to see if he can set up a showing."

For some reason, Kalan must have decided not to go to war with her, for which she was grateful.

Wanting to take the focus off herself, she asked about Shamus's banking job and whether he enjoyed it.

He shrugged. "I can take it or leave it. What I'd really like to do is start me own financial investment firm."

Excitement soared through her. "Why don't you? You'd be perfect. You're honest and smart."

His cheeks turned pink again. "I need a bit more experience, as well as some capital, but I'm working on both."

She wanted to ask if he was happy, but she figured his mom's death had to have dampened his love of life. "I'm really happy you're doing so well."

"Thanks. I know this might not be the best place to ask ye, lass, but did ye know Owen is dead?"

His words stole her breath. "My brother is dead? For real?" Only because it was inappropriate to show joy over another person's death did she fight her smile.

"Aye. In fact, I'm told he died right here in Silver Lake a few months ago."

This was too good to be true. She hoped he suffered, but it would be impolite to say so. "What was he doing here?" Was he looking for her? An unexpected shiver shot out to every nerve ending. Atlanta was a good four hours from Silver Lake.

Shamus reached across the table and squeezed her hand in support. He then nodded to Kalan. "You want to tell her how Owen ended up here?"

Kalan regaled her with the story of a Wendayan named Izzy Berta. Because of her magical talents, which Owen had witnessed while Izzy had been visiting Scotland, he decided he wanted her for his wife. He flew to Silver Lake and stalked her, but then resorted to kidnapping her when she refused to go with him. "Izzy was mated to our Alpha, you see."

A chuckle escaped. "That sounds like him. He always had such a high opinion of himself." She shook her head. "My brother was a fool."

Jackson's head jerked toward her. "You weren't close, I take it?"

She could list numerous things he'd done to her, but she'd promised Blair she'd play nice. "Let's just say, there were good reasons why I went to school in the US."

She would have thought her parents would have told her about her brother's death, though it was possible they hadn't been informed. She looked at Shamus. "Do my mother and stepfather know?"

"I can't say," Shamus said.

Kalan cleared his throat. "They do. Your brother's remains were shipped home."

"Oh." More betrayal. The Changelings had little use for women, but she expected more from her mother. Ainsley always believed it was Owen who distrusted her and wanted her out of the way.

"Ye know, lass, with Owen gone, it's safe to come back home now. I'm guessing Alex will be too busy taking over for your father to bother with ye." He leaned back in his seat and his feet bumped hers. He immediately sat back up. "I'm not suggesting ye stay in the same town as your family. May I suggest Edinburgh? It's big and quite safe."

She'd be near Shamus then. "I like my job here, but I will consider it." Her certification as an acupuncturist might not even be accepted in Scotland.

Mrs. Murdoch cleared her throat, pushed back her chair, and then stood. "Dessert, anyone?"

Everyone but Ainsley had eaten. "I'm still working on my meal, but you go ahead," she said.

Shamus stood. "I'll help clear, Aunt Felicia."

Blair rose too. As much as Ainsley wanted to offer, she didn't want to be in the way. Once those three left, she expected her heart rate to slow and the throbbing between her legs to stop—but it didn't.

Kalan was mated, as was Mr. Murdoch. From what Blair said, her brother Jackson was too much of a carefree spirit to ever settle down, even if he found his mate.

She shoved aside the thought that she and Jackson were paired. Changelings shouldn't mate with other shifters. It wasn't just Wendayans who would be driven mad if they bit a Changeling. Shifters were equally affected. Most likely Shamus's aura was strong enough to reach from the kitchen.

The silence at the table made her uncomfortable. "So what do you do, Jackson?" she asked.

His features softened a bit, but his eyes held a lot of wariness. "I work at McKinnon and Associates as a security expert."

She knew that much from Blair and had hoped he'd elaborate. "Do you spend your days fighting Changelings?" Damn. Ainsley hadn't meant for that to slip out, but perhaps having the elephant in the room out in the open might make things better.

His glare shot straight through her. Guess not. The temptation to disappear was strong—assuming she remembered how—but she wouldn't give him the satisfaction.

"Not always. Some of our cases involve solving crimes the cops either can't figure out or don't have the resources to go after." One brow rose as he looked over at his brother.

"Which isn't very often," Kalan shot back.

Jackson swept his attention toward her. "We're investigators. We do everything from protection to solving a crime to retrieving what's been stolen."

She didn't like the way he said the last four words, but she wasn't about to ask for details. She assumed he was speaking of the Changelings who stole that Wendayan's magic.

Before she could ask Kalan about his job, Blair, Shamus, and Mrs. Murdoch returned with three different desserts.

"Wow," Ainsley blurted. Her mom never baked anything. "The pie looks divine, as does the chocolate cake." The third dessert was some pastry filled with berries.

"Thank you."

Jackson's phone buzzed, and Mrs. Murdoch looked straight at him, displeasure evident on her face. "Sorry," he said. "It's Connor."

She didn't know who Connor was, but apparently he was important. The moment Jackson disappeared, the air became easier to breathe, and her body relaxed. At the thought, her blood pressure shot up. Then reason intruded. If Jackson and she were fated to be together, he'd make sure it never happened. Hell, he'd deny it until long after she was dead.

Chapter Four

JACKSON RETURNED TO the dining room. "I'm sorry, but we have a case that requires the use of the drone."

That was a lie, but he couldn't be in the same room with Ainsley anymore. She was affecting his thinking, and his body was going crazy with need. Only by glancing at his mother or father had he been able to control his hair from sprouting and other changes from occurring. The horror of the signs alone should have been enough to tame his libido, but her scent had invaded his very being.

His damn bear kept calling out to him: *Mate, mate.*

The whole idea was preposterous. He refused to take the bait. Ainsley Chancellor—a Changeling—was not his mate no matter what his bear claimed. The image of the two Changelings, Olivia and Nathan, being cleansed surfaced. It would be nice if that could happen to Ainsley.

"Can't Connor handle it?" his mom asked. She glanced at her watch. "It's late. You boys need to rest sometime."

"Kip is with Teagan tonight, and I told Connor I'd help if he needed me. I'm the one who knows how to use the surveillance equipment."

"Okay, but try not to be long. It might be years before you see your cousin again."

Damn Ainsley for messing up his precious time with Shamus. "I won't be." He briefly glanced around the table. "Nice meeting you, Ainsley."

No, it wasn't, as it had been pure torture sitting there watching her angelic face smile and flirt with Shamus. Underneath it all, she was a Changeling and nothing could change that fact.

"You too." She looked at him, seemingly so pleasant, but her eyes said good riddance.

Jackson nodded and left. The moment he stepped outside, relief poured through him. Maybe his little outburst in the kitchen had triggered a reaction to Ainsley. His hard cock and urge to shift might have been a residual effect from his hatred of the Changelings.

Don't be ridiculous. Hatred would never cause my libido to go berserk.

As much as he wanted to deny it, his bear could still smell her scent. Hell, his animal was sniffing, and he bet he was grinning like a fool.

Jackson growled as he looked up at the sky. "Naliana, why?"

Of course, the goddess didn't answer.

Jackson slipped into the front seat of his Silverado truck. Connor McKinnon had called him, not to ask him to stop by work, but to ask him to fill him in on what he'd learned about their recent case. Jackson was just grateful for the chance to escape Ainsley's allure. Hopefully, Connor, who had a level head, could help him figure out his next move.

Asking his brother for help was out of the question. His own flesh and blood seemed to be taken with her. If Kalan hadn't been, he never would have mentioned the apartment above the Blooms of Hope flower shop—unless he was desperate to get Ainsley away from their sister. Everyone knew that apartments weren't plentiful in Silver Lake.

His sister's opinion would be totally biased when it came to her roommate, and Ainsley had clearly pulled the tartan over Shamus's eyes. The hardest part of this whole attraction thing was that Ainsley Chancellor was stunning. Her short blonde hair, streaked with purple gave her an edgy, sexy look—just the type of woman he was attracted to. Normally, he didn't go for nose rings, but on her it looked good. And her body: it was killer. Her breasts might be small, but those long legs of hers could wrap around a man and make him forget to breathe.

Stop it.

Ainsley was the devil. For all he knew, Owen told her to get a job in Silver Lake just so he'd have someone to help him recruit Izzy. Little did the poor bastard realize that their Clan wouldn't stand for his kind and kill him.

Before he knew it, Jackson had arrived at work. The light shining from the office window implied Connor was still there. Even though his boss and good friend didn't have a mate, he might have an explanation as to why Jackson felt this draw to Ainsley. At the very least, he could come up with some suggestion for how to tame Jackson's bear. He sure as hell wasn't going to give into his inner beast when a Changeling was involved.

Jackson unlocked the back door and headed inside.

"That you, Jackson?" came the call from his office.

"It's me."

Connor exited his office into their large workroom, looking tired. If he didn't slow down, he'd be heading for an early grave.

"You didn't have to come in," Connor said.

Oh, yes he did. "I need your opinion on something."

Connor slipped a hip on the makeshift table at the front of the room. Last month, when they needed to find a way to foil the fucking Changelings, this room had been turned into their war room. Before, the area had been filled with plush leather sofas, chairs, and a large wooden table. Now that table was in a vacated office, and the comfortable furniture was stashed in the back near the coffee machine.

"You don't look so good," his friend said.

Jackson bit back the urge to tell him to look in the mirror. "You wouldn't either if the same thing that just happened to me happened to you."

Connor stood, walked to the back of the room near the coffee machine. It was where they had their hidden stash of booze, and pulled out a bottle of whiskey along with two glasses. "I take it you could use one."

"Oh, yeah."

After pouring each of them a drink, Conner dropped down on the sofa and motioned him over. "Tell me what happened."

Jackson picked up the golden brew and chugged it. "Turns out Owen Chancellor has a sister who happens to be my sister's roommate."

Connor whistled. "Fuck me. Really? Does Blair know she's a Changeling?"

"Yes." He went through their history, including the fact that Ainsley was half Wendayan. "My cousin, Shamus, from Scotland knew her growing up and seems enamored by her. I don't get it."

"What's the problem?"

Jackson looked off to the side, trying to find a way to say it without looking stupid, but he failed. "I think she's my mate."

Connor laughed. Now that pissed him off. "I take it this is a joke?"

Jackson shot up from his seat and paced. "I wish. As soon as she walked into the house, my body went crazy. I swear her scent was sweeter than this whiskey. I sure as hell did not want to be attracted to her, but my bear kept clawing and scraping to get out. It was insane."

"You do realize that if you mate, it will alter your genes? And probably not for the better."

Jackson stilled then relaxed. "Don't worry. I have no intention of getting anywhere near her again."

"You might not, but your bear might take over. Rye said he lost all control around Izzy."

Jackson tossed back his drink then immediately realized it was empty. He sat back down and smacked it on the table. Jackson looked Connor dead in the eye. "So it's true about what this insane attraction means? Kalan hinted at the same thing a long time ago, but I didn't want to believe him."

"Appears so."

"Fuck me. What can I do?"

"Besides move away from here?" Connor leaned back, but this time his smirk had disappeared.

He wouldn't leave his Clan, his family, or his job. "Besides that."

AS SOON AS Jackson left the dinner party, Ainsley let out a breath. While she was happy she could now focus on Shamus, a boatload of worry was settling in. If she and Jackson were mates, it meant she'd live out a lonely life, because the two of them could never be together, even if she wanted to be with him—which she didn't.

"Tomorrow's Saturday," Shamus said. "Do ye have time to go exploring with me?"

That was one question she was happy to answer. "Absolutely."

He looked over at Kalan. "When do you think you could find out about the apartment?"

"The man who owns the place is Len Berta. His cellular phone store is across the street from the Blooms of Hope flower shop. I imagine if you go into his store and ask, he'd be happy to let you check out the place. To smooth the way, I'll give him a head's up in the morning."

That was easy and nice of him.

"Thanks," Shamus said, looking happy.

"Ainsley, you want to help clean up?" Blair asked as she pushed back her chair and stood.

"I'd be more than happy to." Even though Kalan had his claws retracted, she had the sense he was being polite for his mom's sake.

Mrs. Murdoch held up a hand. "Nonsense. Kalan and I will clean up. I know you girls are tired. Ainsley, it seems like you'll have a long day of fun tomorrow with Shamus."

Ainsley genuinely smiled. "I do." She faced him. "How about I pick you up here around eleven? We can check out the apartment and have some lunch."

"Sounds good to me. We have a lot of catching up to do."

With her plans all set with Shamus, Ainsley was anxious to leave. Dread and despair sat heavy in her gut over this whole mate thing. She prayed she was wrong, but her internal sensors were screaming she was not.

Blair hugged everyone goodbye and then walked out with her. They stopped in front of Blair's car, and she faced Ainsley. "I'm sorry about the way Jackson acted. I don't know why he was such a pill."

Tell her. "That's okay, I understand."

"Understand, why he wasn't civil?" Blair asked.

"Yes, and it wasn't just that I'm a Changeling." Okay, that was most of it. A cold wind blew right through her sweater, and she wrapped her arms around her waist for warmth. "How about we head home, and I will tell you everything?"

Blair clasped her shoulder. "Did something happen while I was in the kitchen helping mom with the dessert?"

"Kind of."

Her roommate shook her head. "I can't wait to hear this." She waved and slipped into her car.

Ainsley jogged to the end of the drive and jumped in the Jetta's driver's seat. Glad for a few minutes of quiet to think through her dilemma, she took off, arriving home a minute before Blair.

The short drive only increased her agitation and anger. With all she'd endured in her life, why did she end up with a bear shifter? Not that she wanted another Changeling, but if she had to live with this kind of intense yearning for the rest of her life, she might end up like her dad—despondent and then dead.

As soon as Blair entered her apartment, she set down her purse and headed straight for the kitchen. "I can't wait to hear what happened. You want some wine?"

"Totally." Hopefully, her admission wouldn't drive a wedge between them. With Jackson being Blair's brother, she might have an idea what Ainsley should do.

Blair returned a minute later with two glasses of Merlot and joined Ainsley in the small living room. She sat on the red sofa while Ainsley took the yellow chair across from her.

"Tell me," Blair said.

Ainsley inhaled deeply. "I need to start by giving you a little background on my father."

Blair leaned forward. "I didn't think you remembered much."

"This isn't about our time together. My mom told me later how and why my father died."

Her roommate hissed in a breath. "That must have been a rough conversation."

"More than rough. I still can't believe it. Apparently, my father wasn't aware that when a non-Changeling mated with a Changeling, he would inherit the Changeling's bad genes, which would change his perspective on things. I'm guessing my mom didn't know either."

"How is that even possible?"

"I don't know. Do you understand how Kalan was able to transfer his ability to shift to his mate? I understand she was human."

Blair nodded. "She was, and you're right. I don't understand how all that works either."

"Anyway, according to my mom, when I was about five, Dad became depressed. By the time I was eight, he was so distraught with all the evil thoughts pummeling his body that he killed himself." A sharp pain stabbed her gut, and she crossed her arms.

"I'm so sorry. Were you aware he was unhappy?"

She shook her head. "He was good at putting on a happy face when he was around me. He always told me that I was his light."

"Aw. So you believe that if you mate with a non-Changeling, that person would end up in despair? Or worse, dead?"

"That's what I've been told."

Blair leaned back against the sofa and drank her wine. "I'm glad you confided in me, but why tonight?"

Now came the hard part of the conversation. "Because as soon as I walked into your parents' house, I was so overwhelmed with lust that my pulse started racing, sweat formed on my upper lip, and my inner wolf was clawing for some release."

Blair's eyes sparkled. "You found your mate?" Just as quickly she sobered. "Oh, no. Poor Shamus. Does he know this will happen to him?"

"Probably not." Ainsley swirled her wine in her glass to give her time to think about how to phrase her next sentence. "Yeah, about that; it's not Shamus."

Blair stilled. She placed a hand over her heart. "What are you saying? The only available male at dinner was Jackson."

"I know, but don't worry. I won't get near him again. Maybe he isn't aware that we've been paired, though I don't know how he couldn't know. If he had those erotic sensations coursing through his body, I'm betting he'll be in serious denial, never believing he's been mated to his arch enemy."

Blair clasped a hand over her mouth. "Not only that, if you can't be with Jackson, it means you'll never mate. What will you do?"

"Do? Live my life the way I have been. I can have protected sex with a human without him suffering any consequences, but I'll never experience deep desire or passionate, unbridled love. He can never be my *everything*."

Blair polished off her glass. "That would be horrible. What happens if Jackson knows you're his mate and decides to pursue you?"

"Seriously? You saw his reaction."

"True."

Poor Blair was holding her glass so tight, her fingers were losing color. "Listen, I doubt he'll do anything about it. We can't be together. Ever."

Her roommate slumped against the sofa. "Well, fuck."

"Well said."

Chapter Five

O N MONDAY MORNING, after reading over the list of ailments for her next patient, Ainsley set out the appropriate needles for the job. This weekend had been bittersweet. While she'd been able to spend two wonderful days with Shamus, she understood that she couldn't hog all of his time with his family. He'd asked her to join them for Sunday dinner, but Ainsley had made up some lame excuse why she couldn't go. She felt bad not accepting, but she had no intention of telling Shamus it was because she and Jackson were fated mates—fated never to be, that is.

As much as she had no desire to be with the moody man, her inner wolf had other ideas. It didn't matter if Jackson hated her or not, her animal still yearned to join with him.

Thinking back to Friday night, the one positive outcome from suffering through the meal was that she'd learned about the one bedroom apartment above the Blooms of Hope flower shop. As soon as Mr. Berta had showed the place to her, she'd fallen in love with it. Kalan's mate, Elana, had lived there before her. Apparently, someone had ransacked her place looking for some sardonyx that wasn't there and ended up ruining much of the furniture. Because Elana had moved in with Kalan after that, she graciously offered Ainsley what furniture was left.

Having lived in a furnished apartment with Blair, Ainsley didn't have any pieces of her own and was delighted to take any hand-me-downs. After work, her new sofa and chairs would arrive, and she'd officially be on her own.

While Ainsley was excited not to be a burden to Blair anymore, she'd miss their late night talks. As much as she was thrilled to start her career and get on with her life, Ainsley was also afraid. Blair's family was basically off limits now, and making friends had always been hard since she always feared her identity would somehow leak.

Thankfully, the humans in town had no idea that shifters existed, which meant those at work treated her well.

A knock sounded on her workroom door and one of the nurses popped her head in. "Your next patient is here."

"Send him in." She'd read his file and was curious to see if she could help.

Ainsley stood to greet the man, but the moment he walked in, her heart jackknifed. He was a Changeling. She'd never met a shifter who could tell if another wolf was a one, but she was able to. Ainsley had heard that only those who came from a long line of Changeling blood could recognize a fellow Changeling. She believed she could detect one because her Wendayan half must have been blended in a unique way with her Changeling half. Her good side enabled her to detect the evil tainting her blood.

The man was tall, rather overweight, and had a limp. Besides having pock marked skin, his hair needed cutting. She painted on a friendly face. "I'm Ms. Chancellor."

"Ms. Chancellor. Do I detect a hint of a Scottish accent? We had a man from Scotland by the same last name come here recently. Are you any relation to Owen Chancellor?"

Her heart nearly stopped. As much as she didn't want to be affiliated with the Changelings—here or anywhere—to lie would piss him off. She suspected he already knew the answer. "Yes, he was my brother."

"I'm sorry for your loss." From the lack of warmth in his eyes, he wasn't sorry at all. "I heard your brother lost a brave fight to the Alpha of the wolf and bear Clan."

What was he talking about? "My brother committed suicide and died in a car crash."

His eyes widened. "That's what those fucking holier than thou asswipes told you? They're a bunch of liars."

Not that Ainsley cared how Owen died, she wasn't happy Kalan and Jackson saw fit to keep her—as well as Shamus—out of the loop, assuming the Changeling wasn't lying. In the back of her mind, she had never believed Owen had taken his own life. He was the type to claim the woman was defective, not him. After all, he had believed that all women wanted him. "So he was in a fight and lost?"

The losing part didn't surprise her. Owen never practiced his fighting skills because he believed he was already too good.

"Yes. He was killed on the property where one of our witches lives. I'm not sure what really went down, but we found a lot of blood at the site. The rumors claim that the Alpha did him in because your brother was trying to capture his woman—a woman who was a powerful witch."

Then he deserved to die, but she wouldn't tell him that, nor did she want to discuss Owen. The last thing she needed was for someone at work to learn what her brother had tried to do.

The man's gaze shot straight through her and the hairs on her neck rose, sending her inner sensors to high alert. How did he know that Kalan's Clan had told her about her brother's death or the way he'd died? Were they following her? Listening in on her conversations? Shivers tripped up her spine.

Needing to stop this line of conversation right now, Ainsley picked up his folder. "You're having trouble with your leg, Mr. Ernst?"

His lips pinched as if he'd wanted to test her further. "It's been paining me for months."

"I trust your wolf has been unable to heal it?"

He nodded. "I was born with one leg shorter than the other. It didn't give me any trouble until recently."

Ainsley suspected this visit might be more of a fishing expedition than to receive any health benefit. Some Changeling might have spotted her and been curious why she hadn't sought them out. How they could tell she was one of them was anyone's guess—unless that person was of noble Changeling blood. That thought scared her. "Have you had acupuncture before?"

"No, but I heard it works quite well."

She doubted the word of mouth had spread to the Changeling community. From what Blair had told her, Ainsley was the first acupuncturist in many years to work at this clinic. "Hop up on the table and let's take a look."

For the next thirty minutes, she carefully placed the needles in his lower back and legs. "Have you been to a chiropractor?"

"No. I don't believe in them," he said, face down on the table.

And yet he believed in an acupuncturist? She wasn't buying it, but she did the best she could. Once Ainsley finished with him, she discussed some herbs he could take to reduce the swelling in his lower back. "One treatment isn't enough to cure your pain. I'll need to see you next week."

"I'll think about that," Mr. Ernst said. "Do you make house calls?"

Her stomach tumbled. "I haven't in the past, but I guess I could. Why?"

She didn't want to be trapped in his house with no way to escape. If the two of them battled, she'd lose. Not having practiced her skills had made her rusty though they'd be no reason for him to attack.

"My father is ailing and can't walk." He slipped a hand in his pocket. "Here's the address. Can you come tomorrow morning?"

"I'll have to check my schedule."

"I've left my number. Call if you can make it."

That was rather presumptuous of the man, but having grown up with Owen and Alex, it was best to smile and move on. "I will."

As soon as he left, it was like the air had returned to the room. She washed her hands and stretched, her mind zinging. What the hell had that been about?

LAST NIGHT, JACKSON hadn't been able to sleep, and it was catching up to him. Ainsley's image kept floating in his head. It didn't matter that she smelled liked lavender and vanilla, or that he kept picturing sinking his cock into her, she was off limits. He'd never mate with an evil Changeling, no matter how sweet she appeared or smelled.

What he wanted to know was what had he done to deserve being alone for the rest of his life? He was given one shot at a fated mate, and he got a fucking Changeling. That was the definition of drawing the short straw.

He was the first to admit that at twenty-eight, he wasn't ready to settle down. There were a lot of women left in town to sample, but to be told he'd never have a mate was beyond depressing.

"Did you fix the drone?" Connor asked, coming out of his office.

Jackson looked up. "Yeah. I just needed to recharge the battery."

Connor stood in front of him, his stance wide, looking like a commander. "You figure out what you're going to do about Ainsley?"

He looked around. Not that he needed to hide his issues from their other co-worker, Kip, but some things should be kept between shifters. "Naliana cleansed those other two Changelings—Olivia and Nathan. Do you think she'd do it to Ainsley?"

"*Do it to her?* It's not like taking a pet to get neutered. I think Ainsley has to want to undergo the ritual. Have you spoken to her about it?"

"Hell no. I don't want to get near her."

"Then I guess you're fucked."

That he was.

His cell rang, and Connor held up a hand. "I'll let you get that."

His boss slipped off the table, and as soon as he headed back to his office, Jackson checked the caller ID. It was Tawny, his current woman of the week. While he cared for her, he'd needed some space and hadn't even called her. Now he felt like a cad.

"Hey there." Tall and blonde, she was a local realtor who had provided him with some useful information in the past. They'd clicked and started dating. This past weekend, he hadn't given her a thought, and he blamed Ainsley for that.

"Sorry to call you at work, but you asked me to let you know if there was any more activity on the Donaldson place."

Jackson sat up straighter. Because he'd been unable to concentrate—due to a certain short-haired blonde—he'd been goofing off by doing research on a possible treasure located under the burned out Donaldson building. Most likely it was another hoax, but he'd been intrigued doing the research that dated back over a hundred years. "What did you find?"

"A Mr. John Ernst put a bid in for the building."

He'd never heard of the guy, but he'd check him out. "Did Donaldson accept?"

"No. He said the property wasn't for sale."

"Do you know what he plans to use the land for?"

"No. I've never spoken with him. For now, no transaction is happening, but that's the second bid this month, which I find odd. Usually people don't ask to buy a place that's not even for sale."

Something was happening, he could feel it. "I appreciate you letting me know."

"You're welcome. So you want to do dinner some time this week?"

Crap. His head wasn't in the right spot. Of course, she'd wonder why he hadn't called, but he wasn't going to admit to a human that as a bear shifter, he'd found his mate—a mate he wouldn't touch with the proverbial ten-foot pole. "I have a big case at work."

"Oh, I understand."

Jackson hated to disappoint anyone, but suddenly he wasn't into her like he had been a week ago. "I'll call you, okay?"

"Sure."

As soon as she disconnected, he felt like a real jerk, but he didn't need another woman to mess with his head.

ONCE WORK LET out, Ainsley rushed to her apartment to wait for her furniture delivery. She entered the building from the back alley and traipsed up the steep wooden stairs. The whole issue with Mr. Ernst still bothered her, but she couldn't let her prejudice of Changelings get in the way. If she did, she'd be no better than anyone else. While most of the Changelings tended to be a bit sociopathic, she'd met some who were capable of having feelings. The fact her real dad loved her mother implied Mom had those redeeming qualities at one point. It was only after she'd met Owen's dad that she'd changed.

No sooner had she entered than there was a knock on her door. "Coming."

Ainsley was expecting the deliverymen, but instead it was Elana. She had on a cute pink top and jeans, and only a sprinkling of makeup. Her hair was pulled back and tied with a pink ribbon that had some baby's breath stuck in the side for added interest. "Hey. Come in."

While Elana hadn't come out and asked if Ainsley was a Changeling, she bet her mate had told her. "Just wanted to check to see how the move was coming."

Ainsley had been brought up to be suspicious of everyone, but Elana seemed really open and nice. "Good. The living room set I ordered should be delivered today."

From the way Elana was looking to the side, she wasn't really here to find out if Ainsley's move had gone smoothly.

"Do you have a minute to talk?" Elana asked.

Here it comes. "Sure. Want something to drink?"

Her cheeks stained red. "Water's good."

"You sure? I'm having a glass of wine."

"I'm sure."

Ainsley stepped into the open kitchen a few feet from the small table, fixed the drinks, and then carried them out. "What's on your mind?"

Elana sipped her drink. "This is kind of awkward, but I wasn't sure if you were aware that Naliana, the moon goddess, can cleanse people if they want."

"Cleanse people?"

"Remove their bad Changeling blood."

Goose bumps shimmied up her spine. "That sounds barbaric." All Ainsley could picture were tubes attached to her body sucking the life out of her.

"It's not like that. It's really rather simple." Elana told her about two Changelings, who because of their human ancestors—one parent and one grandparent—didn't want to live the Changeling lifestyle anymore. Naliana was able to rid them of their Changeling genes by having them submerge under water and touch the bottom of Silver Lake.

"How is that possible?" Ainsley asked, thinking her story sounded like a fairy tale.

"Naliana is a goddess. Anything's possible."

"So you're saying it was a miracle?" Ainsley asked.

"It sure looked like it to me."

She supposed if a Changeling could alter another shifter's genes by mating with them, why shouldn't a goddess be able to alter hers? "Did you actually see Naliana do this?"

Ainsley had never even set eyes on a goddess, nor had she heard of anyone who had. Perhaps the gods and goddesses from above didn't visit her kind.

"Yes. She and her husband, James, performed the ceremony at the lake, though I'm not really sure what his role was."

Ainsley was overwhelmed with the possibilities. Even if she were to be cleansed, she doubted that Jackson would believe she was absolved of all the Changeling wrongdoings of the past. He'd still harbor distrust. "Can you get a hold of her for me and ask her what I'd need to do to have this feat performed?"

Elana laughed. "I can't, but my mate might be able to. He and our Alpha, Rye, have spoken with her husband many times. Naliana only returns on the white moon."

Mentally, Ainsley went through the lunar calendar trying to remember when the next white moon would be. "She'll be here in a few days then. Do you think you could ask Kalan for me?"

"I'd be happy to. I think the whole family, including Shamus, would be relieved if you didn't have the stigma of being a Changeling hanging over your head."

"Amen." So that was the real reason for bringing this up—to lift the veil of shame from their family. She wondered if Jackson had mentioned anything to Kalan about them being ill-fated mates. Someone knocked on her door and disrupted her thoughts. "That must be the delivery men."

"I'm excited to see what you bought. I'm kind of lucky—or rather you're lucky—that my parents' hand-me-downs were destroyed in the break-in. I never liked their flowered furniture."

That wasn't her style either. Ainsley opened the door, recognizing right away shifters weren't on the other side. Two men in blue overalls, with sweat on their foreheads, and the moving company logo on their shirt pockets were standing next to her new sofa. "Come on in," she said.

"Those stairs sure are steep," the shorter of the two said.

"Don't I know it?" Trudging up and down all the time would keep her in shape however. "It's a downfall of an old building." The plus side of living there was all the character built into the place. She loved all the nooks and crannies and high ceilings.

The men carried in the yellow tweed sofa and placed it against the stairway wall. Next, they brought in the two matching lime green leather chairs with brass tack elements along with a metal coffee table. The retro look blended really well with the brick on the far wall.

"Thank you." She then tipped them once they finished.

The whole time the men were arranging the furniture, however, Ainsley couldn't keep her mind off the idea that she might be able to become a normal werewolf. As excitement sizzled inside her, she wondered why she'd never learned of this opportunity before?

Most likely it was because no Changeling would want that fact known.

She spun around to face Elana who was running her hand over the leather chairs. "These are awesome. I love the color," Elana said.

"Me too. I wanted something a bit edgy."

"I'm surprised you didn't get purple chairs then," Elana said.

Ainsley fingered her hair. "Good point."

Elana smiled. "I'll let you enjoy your new place. If you need anything, let me know."

Ainsley escorted her to the door. "I appreciate it. Can you tell me where this James person lives? I'm really interested in this cleansing process."

"I've only been there once, and it was dark, but ask Kalan. He knows."

He'd probably think she wanted to spy on the goddess's husband or something. "I will. Thanks."

Or perhaps she could ask Blair to ask her brother if she didn't know. Ainsley still wasn't convinced Kalan trusted her. Heaven forbid, she dare ask Jackson.

Chapter Six

A INSLEY'S ALARM WENT off way too early the next morning. She'd been up half the night wondering if what Elana had said was true. The part that troubled her the most was that even though she might want to be cleansed, would the gods deem her worthy? Elana said there weren't any conditions attached to being cleansed, but that other couple, Olivia and Nathan, seemed to have earned the right by providing insider information into the Changeling's inner workings.

Ainsley knew all of one Changeling, and after tomorrow, she'd know two, but without living among them, she wasn't sure what she could do to help. Even if cleansing weren't possible for her, she still wanted to help take them down.

Her best hope of learning the truth was to speak with James in person—assuming he'd see her and assuming she could learn where he lived. Before that, however, she had to treat Mr. Ernst's father in order to judge if she might be able to worm her way into their culture. If the dad was pleased with her healing abilities, she might be recommended to others. While working on Changelings wasn't ideal, she didn't fear them. If the ones here were anything like those in Scotland, there was a loose ethic among thieves. As long as she didn't mess up, they'd leave her alone.

Last night, she'd brought home her needles so she didn't have to stop by work before heading out. Mr. Ernst had drawn her a map saying that GPS was spotty in the hills.

Once she'd eaten, she gathered her gear and left. It didn't take long to reach Grand View Drive on the north side of town. As she wended her way up the foothills, she imagined what the views would look like in the summer. She bet the foothills would be full of lush trees, interlaced with flowering pink and white mountain laurel. It would be breathtakingly gorgeous.

Unfamiliar with these roads, she drove slowly, careful to watch for unexpected drop-offs where no guardrails existed. She was partway up the mountain when a light colored object, seemingly out of place off to the side of the road, caught her attention. She slowed. Having excellent eyesight, she detected something sticking up from the leaves that looked like a foot, though she figured it had to be a log stripped of its bark. Because no one was behind her, and because she'd left plenty of time to get lost, she pulled over to check it out.

The moment Ainsley slipped from her car, her heart pounded, though she didn't know why. As she stepped onto the leafy area by the side of the road, she saw what had attracted her attention. It *was* a bare foot. Holy shit. Flies buzzed around a bloodied nude body that was angled downward and out of sight from the road. A tight band immediately squeezed the air from her lungs. She blinked, not believing what she was witnessing.

As if in slow motion, she had to fight with herself to take those last few steps to reach him, and a scream lodged deep in her throat. The horror closed up her windpipe, and for a few seconds, she couldn't breathe. Ainsley dropped to her knees next to the body.

"Shamus?" Not that she expected him to answer, but she could hope he was still alive.

Oh my goddess. His red beard was matted in blood, and his throat had been ripped out. Wolves must have attacked him, but why? Why harm her dear sweet Shamus? Never in her dreams did she think something could best him. Given the number of bite marks covering his arms, legs, and torso, he must have been attacked by four or more wolves.

Her chest hurt as a giant sob bubbled up. Ainsley reached out and touched his knee to make certain this wasn't a mirage. When she met with resistance, sobs wracked her body over the loss of her dear friend. Out of breath, Ainsley dropped her butt onto her heels and cried.

As much as she wanted to cover his body with leaves, disturbing the crime scene would lessen the chance of finding the identities of the killers. There had to be something she could do though. Leaving him here was out of the question, as was calling the cops. A human witch hunt would ensue for each and every wolf.

Kalan! He was a shifter and a deputy, only she didn't have his number. Blair did though. Hopefully, her best friend wasn't with a client. If so, she wouldn't be able to take the call. Ainsley swallowed a few times to stop from sobbing, but she failed to control the tears. If Eve, the clinic's receptionist answered, from the sound of Ainsley's shaky voice, she'd know something was terribly wrong. Ainsley wasn't sure she could explain to a human why she wasn't calling 911.

Wait a minute. Elana could get ahold of Kalan. Still in shock and having a hard time functioning, Ainsley fumbled in her pocket for her phone then wiped her nose and cheeks with her sleeve. As she located the Blooms of Hope phone number in her cell, her finger shook. With a press of a button, it rang.

"Blooms of Hope, Elana speaking."

"Elana, it's Ain…Ainsley." She swallowed the next sob. As objectively as she could, she explained what happened, but her voice warbled, and then a fresh set of tears erupted.

"Calm down. Did you say Shamus was dead? Are you sure?"

"Y…yes. Can you contact Kalan?" She gave her directions to the location.

"I'll call him right away."

Because Ainsley didn't have blood on her, hopefully Kalan wouldn't think she had anything to do with the murder. Knowing she couldn't leave her friend, she called Mr. Ernst and asked if she could reschedule. Thankfully, he didn't ask too many questions. Even better, she'd managed to pull herself together for those few seconds while she spoke with him. Given Shamus's location in the hills, it was possible the Changelings had done this to her dear friend.

She leaned over his body. "Shamus, why were you even here?"

Time seemed to stand still as she stared at the remains of what once was such a wonderfully vibrant man. What seemed like seconds later, someone placed a hand on her shoulder. "Ainsley? I need you to move away from the body."

Without looking, she knew the voice belonged to Kalan. Four other shifter signatures were behind her. Drying her eyes with her sleeve again, she leaned back on her heels and pushed up, but her legs gave way. Kalan caught her before she landed on her knees.

"Help her to my car, please."

Ainsley's senses shot up, and the urge to shift nearly felled her. Jackson was there.

"Come on, Ainsley," he said. This time his voice was raw with emotion and not accusatory.

While Shamus had only met Blair, Kalan, and Jackson one time when he'd visited as a child, Jackson seemed quite distraught over the family's loss.

He helped her into the back seat of a cruiser then slipped in next to her on the other side. "Can you tell me what happened?" Jackson asked.

She would have waited for Kalan, but he seemed busy with the coroner. "Poor Shamus. Why would someone do this?" A sob erupted and Jackson rubbed her back.

"Take your time and start from the beginning."

Of all the times for him to be nice, she wasn't sure she wanted him to be approachable when she was in such a state of despair. It was easier when he was shooting daggers at her. "I had an appointment with Mr. John Ernst's father to do some acupuncture."

"John Ernst?" The sharpness of his tone took her by surprise.

She finally looked up at him. "Yes, he's a Changeling, but then again so am I. It was a job, okay?"

"Sorry. I'm devastated too. How did you find the...Shamus?"

She sniffled. "I happened to see something that looked like a foot sticking out off to the side of the road, so I stopped. Once I was near, I saw it was Shamus." The terrible image brought a fresh wave of grief.

"Did you notice anyone nearby?"

She shook her head. Out of the corner of her eye, she watched Shamus being loaded onto a gurney and had to turn her head away from the gruesome scene. "Why kill him? They couldn't have known that he fought the Changelings in Scotland," she said as fresh tears streaked down her face.

"The forensic team might be able to tell us more. Kalan said Shamus told Mom that he was going for a morning run."

"In the hills?" She'd lived in Silver Lake only two weeks, yet even she knew who lived in them. Then again, she was a Changeling and could sense them.

"My mother said she assumed he'd stay around the lake and didn't think to warn him."

Nothing was making any sense. "Listen. I'm really tired. I've told you everything. Is it all right if I go?" Ainsley had calmed down a bit and didn't think they suspected her of foul play.

"Kalan will want to speak with you first."

She bet he would, but she wouldn't be able to provide him with any more information. "I didn't see anything. I called Elana the moment I found Shamus." Her lips trembled.

Jackson reached out and clasped her wrist. "Kalan isn't accusing you."

Her mate's heat nearly singed her skin, and Ainsley pulled away. Now that the shock of Shamus's death had sunk in, her anger festered. "I want to find out who did this."

"So do I, but this is a job for Kalan and the other Clan members. I doubt he's going to report it to his department since shifters were involved."

She jerked toward Jackson. "He'd cover up a murder?"

Jackson scrubbed a hand down his jaw. "No. He will find out

who murdered our cousin and punish the offenders."

The acid in her stomach receded a bit. "How can he? The man won't be tried without a body—a body that was clearly murdered by wolves." Jackson stared at her as if she'd lost her mind. "What are you looking at?"

"Are you going to tell me that the Changelings in Scotland don't cover up crimes they've committed?"

No, I'm not. My brother did it all the time. It was one more reason to leave there, but Kalan isn't a Changeling."

"True, but don't worry. The Clan will mete out their own brand of justice."

His logic finally sunk in. "You mean the killer or killers will be in a fight to the death?"

The corner of one side of his mouth lifted for a second. "I'm glad you understand."

She was about to say the wolves wouldn't stand a chance against bears, but then she remembered Shamus. For once, she was speechless. "I want to help."

Jackson shook his head. "No way."

That pissed her off. "I've known Shamus a lot longer than you have, and secondly, I can fight. After all, I am a Changeling. John Ernst knows I'm Owen's sister. I might be able to find out things— things a regular wolf couldn't."

"Back up. How did you know John Ernst was a Changeling?"

"I can tell."

Jackson leaned back. Her senses had stopped reeling, which gave her a chance to actually see the man who the crazy gods had paired her with. His eyes were slightly bloodshot, though she doubted he'd been crying. More than likely stress or fatigue had caused it. His blue chambray shirt and camouflage jacket brought out his tan skin and beautiful green eyes.

"How? No one else can."

For the first time since she'd met him, Ainsley had the upper hand. She debated how much to tell him, but if he could introduce her to James, she'd sell her soul. Sweetening the pot would go along way to getting what she wanted.

"From what my brother told me, only those from families who come from a long line of Changelings can detect others. I can tell one from a regular wolf because of my unique Wendayan mix." She had other talents too, but she decided not to mention them since they weren't pertinent to the case.

"So not all Changelings can tell if someone is or isn't a Changeling?"

"Right."

"Impressive."

For the first time, he seemed to take what she had to say seriously.

The door opened, and Kalan poked his head in. "You okay, Ainsley?"

Okay was a relative word. She had to admit being with Jackson had distracted her from her consuming grief. "As well as I can be for losing my dear friend. Thank you for asking. How are you holding up?"

"Working hard to keep it together. Mom will be devastated. When her sister passed away, she was a mess for weeks."

"I'm sorry."

Kalan slipped in the front seat, started the engine, and then dialed up the heat before twisting around in his seat. "I'd like to ask you a few things."

For the next ten minutes, he pummeled her with questions, but she couldn't tell him what she didn't know. "I want the killer or killers dead as much, if not more, than you do."

"Ainsley can tell if a wolf if a Changeling," Jackson said.

"Is that so?" Kalan said. She was able to detect a hint of pride.

"Yes."

"Are you a good actress?" he asked.

She glanced at Jackson, but he appeared as confused as she was. "Why?"

"Because if you know who's of your Clan and who isn't, I'd like you to sniff around the Changelings and see what they know about Shamus's murder."

This was her chance. "Absolutely." She told him about John Ernst and her appointment with his father.

"It's too dangerous," Jackson said.

That pissed her off. "You don't own me. Hell, if the Changelings kill me, you should be happy that you wouldn't have to deal with me anymore. If I'm dead, then I can't disgrace the Murdoch name."

From the strange frown marring his handsome face, Jackson actually appeared concerned she might be killed. The only explanation she could come up with was that he *had* recognized that they were mates. If he believed that, then she'd have to convince him as well as the Murdoch family that she deserved the honor of being cleansed. Not only that, Ainsley wanted justice for the murder of the sweetest man that ever lived.

"I don't want to give the Changelings any more victories," Jackson said.

That implied she'd lose against them in a fight. She shook her head, doubting that was his only concern. "While I've avoided being around shifters for a long time—your sister being the exception—I can handle myself around them." Now might be a good time to tell him about her ability to become invisible, but she wanted to save that surprise for later; the fewer people who knew about it the better. Though, if she did disappear from their sight, she'd love to hear what these two thought of her while she was still in their presence.

"If you learn anything from John Ernst, will you tell us?" Kalan asked.

"Of course. I'm on your side. I want Shamus's killers brought to justice too. Now, can I go?"

Jackson placed a hand on her arm, and her senses reeled again. Really? Sexual energy had no place while she was mired in grief and anger.

"Sure, but keep in touch," Jackson said.

A ton of sassy remarks shot to her lips, such as she didn't have his number, but it wouldn't do any good to let them fly. With her emotions swirling out of control, no telling what she'd say. Ainsley pushed open the cruiser door, and as much as she didn't want to look at Shamus lying wrapped in a body bag on the gurney, she couldn't help it. The stench of blood permeated the area, and her stomach roiled once more.

Move. And for goddess's sake, don't cry until I'm out of their sight.

Chapter Seven

A S SOON AS Ainsley left the scene, Jackson slipped into the front seat of his brother's cruiser. His internal sensors were still going crazy. From the moment Ainsley stepped into his parents' house, he'd been disoriented, unsettled, and completely frustrated. Then when he'd spotted her kneeling over Shamus's body, his bear wanted to protect her from the hurt, but his human part had enough sense to talk him down, knowing she might not be what she appeared on the outside. His bear insisted she was good through and through, but he refused to listen.

Jackson had to keep his distance from her, at least until Naliana cleansed her, assuming she would and assuming Ainsley wanted to go through the process. The difficult part between now and then would be to not let his hatred for Changelings shine through and taint his actions. Ainsley claimed she wasn't a true Changeling, but her kind wasn't known for being truthful.

If it hadn't been for Shamus's strong endorsement of her—as well as his sister's—Jackson wasn't sure he could keep an open mind. He kept reminding himself that even if her Wendayan genes were strong enough to counterbalance the Changeling blood in her, she was still half Changeling. Once more his bear tried to convince him that Naliana would never be so cruel. The only way to know for sure was if he could find her and ask her himself.

Jackson glanced over at the scene to calm his erotic thoughts. Two shifters, both of whom were members of the crime scene unit were taking photos and gathering evidence around where the body had been. Kalan, he knew, wanted to wait around until they were done before leaving. Their cousin deserved the best.

"You were really nice to her," Kalan said with much surprise in his voice. It was clear his brother wanted to know what had changed between them.

"No need to be a jerk. She has to be hurting too. She cared a lot for Shamus."

His brother twisted in his seat. "I've never seen you like this. She's gotten to you somehow. Sure, she's pretty, but you see pretty all the time. What gives? You hate Changelings with a passion."

As much as Jackson didn't want to admit that she was his mate, he couldn't hide it from his brother any longer. Kalan would be angry enough when he found out he'd already confided in Connor. "As hard as it is to say, let alone believe, Ainsley is my mate." He held up a hand. "Don't tell me it's fucked up, because I know it is."

A tic formed around his brother's eye. "Are you shitting me? I admit she doesn't exhibit the usual bad behaviors of a Changeling, but they can be deceptive. Are you sure?"

He remembered how Kalan had been in denial about being mated to a human. "The second she walked into the house, her scent invaded my body. When I'm anywhere near her, my dick gets hard. Hell, I had to fight not to shift at dinner. So you tell me. Aren't those the signs?"

"They are. I'm guessing the phone call requiring you to go into work was bogus?"

He nodded. "I didn't know what else to do. I've been sick about the whole situation ever since. I'm just hoping she wants to be cleansed."

"Let's hope. You know you can't bite her before then, right?"

That's what Connor had said. "I have no intention of even being alone with her, but I'm at my wits end. Last night, I kept picturing sinking my cock into her. Is that messed up or what?" Jackson dropped back his head and blew out a breath.

Kalan's phone rang. "Yeah? Where? Were his clothes inside? No, don't. We need a plan. Thanks." He disconnected. "They found Shamus's vehicle off Ridge Road. His clothes were tucked behind a tree about a hundred feet down the path, implying that's where he shifted before he started his run."

"I'm guessing they wanted to follow the trail to see if they could find out where he'd been killed?"

His brother's brows rose. "You should work for the department."

"No thanks. I like the freedom I have."

"We won't know whether the body was moved until Doc Williams finishes the autopsy."

Or until the actual murder scene is found. "He wasn't killed where Ainsley found him, and here is my reasoning: First, there aren't any hiking trails near that road. Secondly, I don't know how or if anyone even realized that Shamus was related to us; but it's almost as if they are sending us a message to stay out of their nest."

Kalan stabbed a hand through his long hair. "Fuck. Do you think this is retribution for us stealing back the Wendayan's magic?"

Jackson shrugged. "That or Shamus was in the wrong place at the wrong time."

"Which was why I suggested Ainsley try to find out."

"My gut reaction was to say no, but the more I think about it, it would give her a chance to help—something she seems to want to do."

The coroner and his team took off in their black wagon as the two CSU techs packed up and headed out in a separate vehicle. Kalan then stabbed a key in the ignition and turned the engine over. "Have you asked her if she even wants to be cleansed?"

That question had kept him up all night. "I haven't, but she seems willing to help us. From what she's said, she doesn't care for the Changelings. Hell, she seemed almost happy her brother was dead." Kalan didn't look at him. "What?"

"I need to come clean. My lovely mate told her about the process. I didn't ask her to. She did it on her own."

Then why ask me? Jackson's pulse fluttered. "Why the hell didn't you tell me before?" If his brother hadn't been driving down the mountainside, he would have punched him.

"I wanted to know your intentions toward Ainsley."

Fuck if he knew.

DRIVING BACK TO town took all of Ainsley's effort. The image of Shamus's body was burned into her brain, and she wasn't sure if she'd ever recover. From the horrific memory, another sob erupted, and her hands nearly slipped off the wheel. Even her foot had a hard time keeping a steady pressure on the accelerator.

After an eternity, she passed the supermarket and then the gas station where she'd filled up yesterday. As horrible as this pain was, she needed to use the ache, welling deep inside her, to propel her to find Shamus's murderers.

Her swirling mind turned even darker. Why attack a bear? Shamus never would have instigated a fight, especially against a wolf. Sure, he fought Owen and a group of Changelings in Scotland, but that was because her family was brutalizing his Clan.

No. Most likely his death was random. But did it matter? Murder was murder. The Changelings had done this to him, and Ainsley might be the only person to find the truth.

Before she was even aware of where she was, her new second floor apartment came into view. She drove into her spot in back, parked the car, and sat there until she'd gathered enough energy to push open the door. Then with a heavy heart, she trudged inside and up the poorly lit stairwell.

She was totally disappointed with herself. Yes, she had every right to grieve, but she needed to draw on her inner strength. If she waited until the pain subsided, all evidence of the kill would be long gone.

She fixed a hot herbal tea, more for the calm it might bring than because she was thirsty. Music from Elana's flower shop floated upward, but even the upbeat sound didn't settle her frustration. Nothing could help other than finding Shamus's killers.

Most likely either Kalan or Jackson had called Blair to let her know the tragic news, but Ainsley wasn't ready to talk about it. Right now, she needed a few moments to herself. She'd told Mr. Ernst that she had to break the appointment with his father, and the last thing she needed was for him to learn the real reason. She couldn't let any Changeling know of her relationship to the victim or she'd never find out anything.

In her most cheery tone, she dialed the Changeling's number and paced to help her think better.

"Ms. Chancellor," Mr. Ernst said.

Damn. He must have programmed her number into his phone. "I want to apologize for missing the appointment this morning. I'd like to reschedule when it is convenient for your father." She was rather pleased with her smooth delivery even though her stomach wanted to vomit the words.

"How about tomorrow?" he asked.

That worked for her. "Would eight a.m. be okay for your father and you? That would give me a chance to work on him and still make it back in time for my job."

"That would be perfect."

Her hands shook so hard it was difficult to swipe a finger across the screen to disconnect. As soon as she ended the call, she rushed over to the sofa and dropped down, her legs barely able to hold her up any longer.

She glanced at the clock mounted on the brick wall. It was just after twelve noon, and she should head back to work, but she feared she might become distracted when working on a patient. On the other hand, maintaining a normal routine would be the only way to convince any Changeling that she believed in their cause. Changelings didn't grieve.

However, running into Blair would renew her pain. Hopefully, Kalan had called her already. Even though Blair barely knew Shamus, she would still be distraught.

Other than self-pity, Ainsley couldn't think of any reason to stay home. Sucking in all of her objections to crawl into bed and cry, Ainsley grabbed her purse and headed back to work.

Though she believed she'd be able to stay calm while being among those who were healing, it wasn't to be. The moment she spotted Blair's red eyes, Ainsley nearly lost it.

Her friend was talking with Eve at the front desk. While Ainsley didn't detect any Changelings in the building, word might leak if Ainsley broke down in front of everyone, but she couldn't walk on by without saying something. Ainsley wrapped an arm around her friend's shoulder. "I'm guessing Kalan told you?"

Blair spun around and hugged her. "Yes."

Not wanting to discuss the details in the open, she led Blair back to her room. Ainsley didn't have a client for another hour, so she could have some undisturbed time with her friend.

Three rust-colored padded chairs sat along one wall across from the table where she treated her patients. Ainsley guided Blair to those seats now. The only time more than one chair was used at the same time, was if Ainsley needed to discuss her procedure or nutrition plan with the family.

"You saw him?" Blair asked.

"Yes." Giving only the minimum detail, Ainsley described what she was doing on the road. "I freaked out when I saw him."

"Why didn't you call me?"

"I wanted to, but I figured you might be treating a patient, and I don't think I could have kept it together long enough if I had to speak with Eve first. I couldn't call the police, so I asked Elana to contact Kalan for me."

Blair nodded. "That was smart. Kalan said that Jackson came to the crime scene. How did that go?"

Blair seemed to have accepted the whole concept that she and Jackson were mates. "He was surprisingly nice."

Her brows rose. "I wonder what made him soften. I'm surprised he didn't accuse you of harming Shamus." Her lips curled in disgust.

"I thought he might too, but I had no blood on me, and the marks indicated many animals were involved."

"Given you don't know any other Changelings, he probably figured you were innocent," Blair said.

"That, and I had no reason to harm him. As far as not knowing any Changelings, I have met one. He came to the clinic yesterday." She explained how she was on her way to treat his father in the hills when she'd spotted the body. As her mind shot to the image of the foot sticking out from the leaves, all of a sudden, a powerful blast of lust descended upon her. Ainsley gripped the chair, forcing herself to push back her desire. "Jackson's here."

As if Blair had been lost in thought for a moment, she jumped up. "I wonder what he wants. Come with me."

"Why?" Blair must not understand how hard it was for Ainsley to be around Jackson. Her inner wolf wanted him, but she did not. He was judgmental, and while he was rough and tumble sexy, he wasn't always nice. Right now, she needed nice, which was why she was talking to his sister and not him.

"I bet he's here to ask you some more questions."

"I just left him."

A knock sounded on the door. Damn. Eve poked her head in. "I thought you might be in here, Blair. Your brother wants to see how you're holding up." She looked over at Ainsley. "He asked to speak with you too."

Her brain froze, as did her mouth. There had to be something she could use as an excuse not to see him. If he came into her room, the sexual tension would be worse. Her mind spun, but she came up blank. "Okay."

She and Blair followed Eve back to the front desk. The moment she saw him standing at the reception desk, her wolf nearly clawed a hole through her stomach. Sure, Jackson looked good in his camouflage jacket, faded jeans, and boots, but now wasn't the time for such a reaction. *Stand down, dammit.*

As soon as he caught sight of both of them, he trained his gaze on his sister, and Ainsley couldn't help but feel the small mental slap from the dismissal. Rationally, Jackson should care about Blair first, but he could have at least acknowledged her. Or was he having the same reaction to her wolf as she was to his bear?

He embraced his sister, and the love that poured from his eyes melted her. Neither Alex nor Owen had ever looked at her like that.

"How are you doing?" he asked Blair.

"I'm upset, of course, but Ainsley is the one who is suffering. I barely knew Shamus. How is Mom holding up?"

"Kalan is with her now."

Ainsley's internal sensors finally clicked in. Another Changeling was here. "Excuse me," she said.

Having her kind wander about wouldn't do anyone any good.

"Ainsley, hold up. I'd like to talk to you for a minute," Jackson said.

The Changeling was close by, and she didn't want him to see them together. Her only chance of finding a clue to Shamus's death was to distance herself from Jackson. After all, his company had been responsible for breaking into the Changeling bunker and recovering some of the Wendayan magic that had been stolen. "I'm sorry. Now's not a good time."

"Then can I stop over to your place tonight after work? I have some things I'd like to discuss with you."

Be alone with Jackson? Hell no. It would be too hard.

Tell him yes, her inner wolf urged. She wished she had the skill to shut her up.

Ainsley pressed a hand to her stomach and pushed inward, hoping to quell her inner beast who had never acted up like this before. "What about?"

He looked around. "I can't discuss it here."

Ah, then why ask to see her in the first place? "Sure, now excuse me."

As quickly as she could, she stepped away. Before she reached her room, a Changeling emerged from the physical therapy area and looked straight at her. Well damn.

Chapter Eight

GOING OVER TO Ainsley's house might be about the dumbest thing Jackson had ever done, but he didn't have a choice. She was the only one capable of finding out who'd killed Shamus. Everyone in the Clan was depending on her—just like many had depended on Olivia and Nathan before they left town.

He also needed to have the discussion about the whole mating issue. At the moment, his human side wasn't ready to be with a Changeling. Even if he wanted to be, he couldn't. One bite and his genes would be tainted for life, and from what he understood, not even Naliana could undo that damage, if he let his bear take over.

It would be hard to stay in control being so close to her, but he needed to suck it up and threaten his bear if he misbehaved. Those few minutes at the clinic had tested his resolve to the max. Ainsley not only looked adorable, but her scent continued to alter something inside him. The more he was with her, the harder it was to contain the animal within, but for Shamus, he had to see her.

He slipped his hand in his pocket and fingered the envelope his dad had given him for Ainsley. It was from Shamus.

Jackson parked behind her building and gripped the wheel tight, stealing himself against the sexual draw that was about to tug on him from the inside out. Being in a small space with her would be pure torture, but this was about retribution for Shamus's death, not his comfort.

For the last hour, he'd debated bringing her a piece offering—

like flowers, chocolate, or a nice bottle of wine, but he didn't want her to think this was a date. Having her remain distant toward him might be the only way to maintain his sanity.

Get going.

With his shoulders pulled back, Jackson stepped up to the intercom that Mr. Berta had installed on the back door of the brick building. Elana told him that the rear door was left open during shop hours, but now that the store was closed, this entrance was locked.

He pressed the worn button. A few seconds later, Ainsley answered then buzzed him in. Their discussion needed to be factual, appealing to her sense of justice—assuming she hadn't been faking her grief this morning. If Elana was right, Ainsley wanted to be rid of her evil Changeling ways and was all in favor of having Naliana help.

As he trudged up the dimly lit, steep steps, his heart pounded, and the rapid beating wasn't from exertion. That damn mating pull was doing a number on him. Grabbing onto the handrail, he pictured Shamus's prone body and his libido calmed.

I can do this.

Jackson interviewed people for a living, drawing out secrets they had no desire to share. Speaking with Ainsley shouldn't be any different—just more strenuous.

He knocked. When she pulled open the door, Ainsley didn't make eye contact as she motioned him inside, and he was grateful for small favors. She'd changed out of her work uniform and thankfully had on a baggy rose-colored top that went well with the streaks in her hair. She hadn't applied any makeup since the last time he saw her, but she still looked pretty. It was the low slung jeans that hugged her body too well, outlining every lickable inch, along with her bare feet, that was making his animal claw at his gut for release.

Touch her, his bear urged.

Jackson clenched his fists to force a barrier between him and his inner demon. "Thanks for letting me come over."

"Sure. You want some tea?"

He needed something stronger than that to get through this

conversation without doing something stupid. "Got a beer?"

She shook her head. "Whiskey okay?"

A woman after his own heart. "If you'll share one with me."

He swallowed a groan. Now why the hell had he said that? He was here on business. If she hadn't rushed into the small kitchen right away, he would have told her not to bother. Keeping her back to him, she fished out two short glasses then retrieved a bottle from one of the top cabinets.

"Shit," she said as she poured the drinks.

"Need help?"

"No I just spilled some." Her level of frustration seemed higher than was warranted.

A minute later, she brought out two drinks and set them on the small table wedged between the kitchen and the living room. She then sat down. Jackson pulled out the hard seat across from her, and when he sat, his knees practically touched hers.

He was close. Too close. His gaze locked onto hers, and then his teeth sharpened. A few bones cracked. Damn. Her flowery scent was undoing his resolve one cell at a time.

"How are you holding up?" he asked with so much sympathy, it even surprised him that he cared whether or not she was okay.

"I'm still upset, but I'll make it through. I have a job to do. And your mom?"

She must not believe that he was upset about his cousin's death, but he was. Shamus was family, and family meant everything to him, but he'd leave that discussion until later. He didn't need to defend his honor. "Distraught. Losing Shamus has brought back all the memories of when my aunt died. Shamus was my mom's last bit of connection to her. Not only is she grieving that loss, she's trying to come to terms with Shamus's violent death—as we all are."

Ainsley nodded. "Your mom is a nice lady. She and her sister shared a lot of the same kind-hearted traits."

His heart pinched. Ainsley had to be good inside if she could see that his mom and aunt were amazing women. "Thank you."

Her grip on her glass was so tight that her nail beds had turned white. Ainsley drew the glass to her lips and chugged half the contents. "What did you want to talk to me about?"

He'd rehearsed this a million times, but nothing ever sounded right. "I'm not sure where to begin."

"How about the fact that we're mates, and I'm a Changeling?" Her lip curled as if she found the mating distasteful too.

His gut clenched. "You don't pull any punches, do you?"

"I see no reason to."

A trickle of relief wormed its way into his body and helped release the tension strangling his gut. Now that she'd pointed to the big elephant in the room, he wanted to address it head on. "Elana told me she mentioned the chance to have Naliana help rid you of your Changeling genes." It would have to happen if they had any chance of being together.

She slammed the glass on the table and leaned closer. "My Changeling genes? It's more than that. Why don't you come out and say it. You hate that the goddess has paired you with me—someone who is evil and deceitful." She held up both hands and glanced to the side. "Sorry. That was rude. I'm on edge."

"I get it. It's okay." The sad part was, that he did think that. It didn't matter that Ainsley had never exhibited any of that bad behavior. The way she sincerely grieved over Shamus's death implied she was a good person. "It's not important what I think or what is happening between us. We need to find Shamus's killer. We can discuss our mating issues once justice is served."

She leaned back in her seat, the dark circles emphasizing her beautiful forest green eyes. "I agree, but we can't ignore what is happening between us."

"Trust me, I'm not."

"Do you think you could put in a good word for me with James? I want to be cleansed."

So she knew about him. He sipped the smooth whiskey. "I was at the last cleansing ceremony, but I can't say I'm on a first name basis with James. However, Rye and Kalan might put a good word in for us."

"Us?" A bit of color flooded her cheeks.

"Fuck. I know I've been an ass, but cut me some slack here. It's hard as hell even being in your presence; my words get so jumbled."

Her lip curled. "I disgust you that much?"

"What? Hell, no. My body craves you, but you and I both know I can't even touch you."

The briefest of smiles crossed her face, acting as if she enjoyed seeing him squirm, though given his actions, he couldn't blame her. "Fair enough."

"What does that mean?"

"My wolf is antsy for some action too, but I won't let her out for that very reason. Trust me when I say, I do understand what you're going through."

"Good." Though he doubted she understood his level of desire, but at least he didn't have to deal with a woman clamoring to be with him. As long as she could control her wolf, he'd be good. He tossed back the rest of his drink. "Oh. I almost forgot." He fished the envelope out of his pocket. "Shamus gave this to my dad to give to you in case he wasn't around to protect you."

Ainsley stared at the envelope. Her name was written in beautifully scrolled penmanship. With trembling hands, she opened the envelope and a necklace fell out. What the heck? Small red onyx stones were evenly spaced on the top portion of the gold chain. Attached was a larger sardonyx stone. "It's beautiful, but why give it me?" she asked. She peeked inside the envelope and withdrew a letter. Silently she read it.

"What does it say?"

"I'll read it. *My dearest Ainsley. If ye are reading this letter, then something has happened to me during one of my many battles. Please don't grieve for me. Your friendship has brought me comfort on my darkest nights, and now it is time for me to be with me mum.*" She stopped reading. "Excuse me."

Ainsley rushed over to the kitchen, grabbed the tissue box, and when she returned, she blew her nose.

"I'm sorry. Shamus must have really loved you."

She nodded and picked up the letter. "*This necklace belonged to me grandmother. Did I ever tell ye she was a wizard?*" Ainsley glanced up at Jackson, but he had no idea and just shrugged. "*She wore it until she died, and it was passed down to me mother. It is a protection necklace that has a very strong spell on it. Wear it always because I am no longer there to help ye. I will always be watching over ye from above. Your loving friend, Shamus.*" She sniffled. "That is the nicest thing anyone has ever done for me, but shouldn't it go to your mom?"

He was impressed that she would be willing to give up something so valuable. Didn't she think she deserved it? "No, it was meant for you."

She clasped it around her neck then fingered the gems. "It's beautiful."

"It is." But he wasn't looking at the necklace. Ainsley glanced away as if lost in thought. The emotion in the room was high—too high, and he needed to talk about something that would flip the switch from sad to angry. "This makes me want to find who killed Shamus even more. How do you want to do this?" he asked. Her eyes widened. "What's that look for?"

"You're acting like we're a team here. I'm surprised you're even asking my opinion," she said with a strong grasp on the large dangling stone.

He stabbed a hand over his short hair. "In my line of work, I, along with the help of the good men I work with, decide how we're going to proceed, but there are two extenuating factors that made me ask what *you* want."

One brow arched, showing off just how stunning Ainsley Chancellor really was. "Factors? You've really analyzed this, haven't you?"

He wished he understood what she wanted from him. He was doing the best he could, given how his traitorous body was warring with all of his past prejudices. "This is important to me. I don't want to mess anything up."

"Mess up this mate stuff, or mess up finding out who killed Shamus?"

Ainsley didn't give up. Ever. "Both."

Her shoulders lowered. She pushed back her chair, rose, and strode over to the kitchen. Seconds later, she returned with a nearly full bottle in hand. "What do you suggest? I've an appointment tomorrow with Mr. Ernst's father to give him a treatment. I can try and ask questions to see what he knows, but I doubt an old man who can't even get around inside the house, would be aware that there'd been a murder."

He shook his head. "Coming right out and asking wouldn't be wise. Given the fact that Mr. Ernst is a Changeling, he could have been one of the attackers. I think you need to take your time and develop a trust with them. Maybe find other jobs—one of which might pan out as far as providing information."

She refreshed their drinks. "I could, though it might help if I could give something in return. Help prime the pump so to speak."

"They might wonder where you got your information, and we can't have them think you're in bed with the Clan—figuratively speaking, of course." He leaned forward. "Can the Changelings tell you're part Wendayan?"

"Not that I know of. As for the Changelings thinking I'm a spy, don't worry. People like to brag. I'll just say I overheard a few things and wanted to know what they meant."

He downed more of his drink. "Makes sense. All we know so far is that Shamus's rental was found near Ridge Road. Two of Kalan's men located his clothing about one-hundred feet down the path behind a tree. I doubt any Changeling would know that, however."

"So he was going for a run, like he said." She sipped her drink slowly, but from the way her eyes were roaming around, her mind was spinning.

"Yes. After that, we know nothing."

"Hmm." She lowered her glass and tapped the side with a delicate blue painted nail. "We should take the same trail to see if we can find any clues."

That would be too dangerous, but if he voiced his concern, Ainsley would balk. Instead, he decided to redirect her focus. For effect, he snapped his fingers. "I think we should speak with James about what to do next."

She lifted her drink to her lips, but he could still detect the smile she seemed determined to hide. "How can he help?"

Jackson filled her in on as much of the background information he had about Olivia and Nathan, the two Changelings who were sending information to James. "I'm thinking he knows who's important and who to question for answers."

"I say let's go and ask him."

Her fearless attitude was unlike anything he'd seen before. "Let me call Rye and see what he suggests. One doesn't just barge in on an immortal."

"If James is as powerful as you claim, he'll know why we're there."

Okay, she had him there. "I guess it couldn't hurt."

She polished off her glass and stood. "How about I follow you?"

He wasn't sure that was a good idea. "When you came to dinner at my parents' house, did you feel any effects from being near the large amount of pink quartz at the bottom of Silver Lake?" The last thing he needed was for her to become dizzy and drive off the road. "It affects Changelings negatively."

"I might have been dizzy, but I think it was being around you that caused it. Besides, I have this." She lifted up her shirt, and he nearly roared. She wore a red onyx belly button ring. "This will help, but it's not very large." She fingered the necklace Shamus had given her. "This will help too, but Elana warned me that if I shifted, I might not be able to remain in my animal form for long."

"True. Your belly button stays on during the shift?" The image of her shifting and then returning to her naked human form forced him to look away.

"Yes. Same for my earrings."

"Okay then. How about you follow me to my house, and I'll drive the last mile to James's place. There aren't any street lights, and it wouldn't be good if you got lost."

Jackson wasn't quite sure why he wanted to torture himself by having her sit next to him when he drove, but he still didn't quite trust her.

"That's fine."

From the way she pursed her lips, it was anything but fine, but she seemed to be hanging on by a thread and probably didn't want to get into an argument.

Chapter Nine

A INSLEY WAS EXCITED and fearful at the same time to be visiting the immortal. What if James told her that his wife, Naliana, wouldn't even consider cleansing her? Sure Ainsley still wanted to find Shamus's murderers, but even if she did, her life after that would be rather bleak if she had to live her life as a Changeling.

As a young girl, she dreamed of having the perfect mate, hand-picked by the goddesses just for her. Because she'd never wanted to be mated with a Changeling, she'd set her heart on a human, knowing her genes wouldn't taint his if they were careful.

Not that she was disappointed with having Jackson as her mate—far from it. He was strong, handsome, and protective, but he lacked one thing: he didn't like her. If she couldn't be cleansed, she'd have no hope of finding love.

Jackson's house was a mile deeper into the shifter cove than his parents' place, which might be why she was feeling a bit lightheaded. That, or the day's events were finally catching up to her. The farther she drove into the forested area, the faster her heart beat and the quicker her strength weakened. With one hand on the wheel, she fingered her sardonyx pendant, but perhaps it wasn't enough to block the effects of the area, or else her wolf was trying to sabotage her for some reason.

Less than five minutes later, Jackson pulled down a long drive-way. The nearly full moon helped to illuminate the hard packed ground, but she still slowed to make sure she didn't hit a pothole and break an axle. The front porch light shone on the area around the house, allowing her to get a good glimpse of his place.

She just stared. It was perfect. The one-story log cabin wasn't large, but the chairs on the front porch made the place cozy. Nestled in the trees, his home looked secure and peaceful.

Jackson parked his truck, and she pulled up next to him, not wanting to block his exit.

Before Ainsley had the chance to slip out, Jackson was by her door to help. When he touched her shoulder, streaks of heat shot straight through her. "I'm good. Thanks."

He let go. "Thought you could use a hand. You were driving a bit erratically."

Was that true? Maybe. "I don't like driving at night." Okay, that was totally lame, especially with her excellent night vision.

"Come on then."

Drawing on her inner strength, she managed to slip into the passenger's side, though she didn't know why it had to be so damn high. Jackson jumped in, put the truck in reverse, and headed out the way he came.

"You know where this man lives?" she asked.

"More or less. His house is on the north end of the lake, away from everyone. Apparently, he owns hundreds of acres, purchased back in the eighteen hundreds, or maybe it was the seventeen hundreds. I'm not sure."

She hadn't realized he was that old. "Can he even walk?"

Jackson chuckled, and the rich sound seeped into her skin, helping to ease the pressure on her chest.

"Very well in fact. I believe he was granted immortality when he was about sixty."

"Why was he granted that?" She'd never heard of immortals even existing on earth.

"Lore has it that Naliana was about eighteen when the gods and goddesses of the realm decided that the earth needed someone to make sure the shifters and Wendayans didn't mess up the order of things."

"You mean to make sure they didn't scare the humans to death."

He glanced over at her. "I suppose that's one way of putting it. Anyway, Naliana came to earth to live among the humans, wolves, bears, and other shifters. She was supposed to learn about the culture in order to help decide which shifters would be best suited for each other. Then she'd get them together and move on."

"I take it something went wrong?"

"You could say that. She met a human by the name of James, and they fell in love. What was supposed to be a two-year stint on earth lasted forty."

She sucked in a breath. "That's so romantic. I think Elana told me that Naliana only comes down to earth but once a month, on the white moon. Why's that?" Ainsley couldn't believe she was actually having a normal conversation with the man and really enjoying it.

Jackson turned onto the main road that rimmed the lake. "Supposedly, James became ill with a fever that not even the Wendayans could cure. Naliana pleaded with the other gods for help. They told her that because she'd refused to return to the heavens when they'd ordered her to, she would have to sacrifice if she wanted him saved."

Pain and sorrow sliced through her. "What did she have to do?"

"The gods promised to save James and make him immortal if Naliana returned to the heavens, guiding shifters and witches around the world from above. She was only allowed to take a physical form once a month on the white moon."

"Ah, so that's why she stays away for so long." Ainsley would love to meet her. "I'm not even sure the Changelings have any type of goddesses looking over them. If they do, I don't think they're very attentive."

Jackson chuckled. He then pulled down a long drive and came to a stop. "That is a shame. Ready?"

"Yes." She was more than ready, though she would have enjoyed hearing more about Naliana and how the Clan lived.

Once more, Jackson helped her out. Even as she neared James's house, she couldn't make out much of its shape, other than it was built out of stone, which she suspected was as old as James himself.

After the first knock, James answered. It was almost as if he knew who was there and what they wanted. "Come in."

Ainsley stood to her full height of five-foot six, but she felt tiny next to Jackson and even James. As much as she didn't want to get sidetracked by looking around, she couldn't help it. A fire blazed in the stone hearth, casting a warm, yellow glow over the room. The furniture was sparse but functional.

"Can I get you some of my homemade ale?"

"Yes please," they said in unison.

James smiled then disappeared down the hallway.

Jackson looked over at her. "Kalan tried to describe this place to me, but he didn't do it justice. I feel like I've been transported back in time about a hundred years."

She had to agree. "It's old, but there's a lot of love radiating off these old walls." He looked at her kind of funny. "I'm a witch, remember?"

"Ah."

James returned with a tray carrying three tall glasses. "Please sit."

Without paying attention to which seat Jackson would choose, she dropped down on the hard sofa seat. He sat next to her, and instantly, pinpricks of lust stabbed at her.

Naliana, if you can hear me, please help.

She'd never asked any god or goddess for aid or guidance, but now seemed as good a time as any to ask. After hearing her love story, Ainsley felt as though she knew her quite well.

"What brings you here?" James asked, as he offered Ainsley her choice of drink.

Not wanting Jackson to misrepresent the issue, she went first. "I want to help find my friend's murderers." She didn't think it would be necessary to give the details. James probably already knew despite his question that implied he didn't.

"A real tragedy. I'm sorry for both of your losses."

"Do you know who killed Shamus?" Jackson asked.

James shook his head. "No, but I suggest you start by finding out where your cousin was killed. That might give you a clue."

Aha. James knew more than he was letting on. Ainsley nudged Jackson. It was what she'd wanted to do. "We can take a run tonight and look for where the fight occurred," she said.

Jackson shook his head. "It's too dangerous."

She was tired of him telling her how dangerous something was. "Trust me when I say I can handle myself in a fight."

He twisted toward her. "You're merely a wolf who—"

"She's right, Jackson. Don't underestimate her Wendayan capabilities."

They both froze, and their gazes locked. She wasn't ready to tell Jackson what she could do, and certainly not in front of James, though he seemed to know about her magic. That knowledge was kind of creepy. What else did he know? The future?

"What can you do?" Jackson asked her.

"I can sneak up on people without them knowing."

Jackson shot a glance at James who merely held up his hands. "Listen to your mate. She's telling the truth. In fact, you need to cut her some slack and trust her more."

Go, James. Coming here had been so worth it. Other than Shamus and Blair, Ainsley didn't have many supporters.

She picked up her glass, took a long draw, and groaned at the rich flavor. "This is wonderful." She returned her focus to James. "I want to help infiltrate the Changeling organization, but I don't want to make any fatal mistakes. I'll gladly take any suggestions."

"Just be careful," James said. "John Ernst is a powerful man in the organization."

Her muscles tensed. That was good to know. "I'll watch what I say around him."

Jackson stood. "I appreciate you seeing us."

She wasn't ready to leave and looked straight at James. "May I ask you one more thing?"

James nodded. "Of course."

She glanced over at Jackson. "I've been told that your wife is able to cleanse Changelings if they wish to be rid of their evil blood. What do I need to do for that to happen?"

He smiled. "In a few days, when the moon is white, have Jackson bring you to the lake. I'm sure Naliana would be happy to cleanse you."

Her breaths came out so fast she nearly hyperventilated. "I can't thank you enough."

James nodded as Jackson placed a hand on her back and led her out. Oh, my goddess. She was finally going to be rid of her defective genes! That would mean she'd be free to mate.

Ainsley suddenly sobered. The only thing stopping her was Jackson. He might decide she could never be pure, no matter what Naliana did. Well, damn.

JACKSON'S HEAD SPUN. Not only did James confirm they were mates, he didn't act as if that would be a problem. Jackson probably should have asked more questions about mating, such as once Ainsley was cleansed, would she be like every other shifter from his Clan? If that were true, then halleluiah.

From the positive way James acted toward Ainsley, she was what she professed to be—a Wendayan at heart who had the ability to shift.

"I take it you're still up for a late night run?" he asked, finally getting it through his thick skull there was no stopping this woman from doing what she wanted. The last thing he needed was for her to go on the hunt alone and be killed.

"Absolutely."

For the first time ever, she actually smiled at him, and boy, did that wake up his bear. Jackson quickly returned his focus to the road. "I figure we'll park where Shamus left his vehicle and head on in from there."

"Sounds like a plan."

"But first, I want to send the drone overhead to make sure there aren't any surprises that might waylay our plans."

"A drone?"

Pride filled him. He loved talking about work and how his team was good at using technology to stop the bad guys. He explained how the drone helped them find the location of the bunker in the first place.

"That's really cool."

He thought so too. "I was able to watch everything in real time. When the Changelings' reinforcements arrived, I sent our men in who were standing by. We won, but we weren't without injuries or casualties." Fortunately, Ainsley seemed content not to ask for details.

Less than ten minutes later, Jackson escorted her into his office. The place was dark, implying Connor had wisely decided to get some rest. Never in a million years did he think he'd be escorting a partial Changeling into his office, but after James's comments, he'd decided to trust her, and it felt good to bury his doubt.

He flicked on the lights and Ainsley looked around. "Nice place."

His company prided themselves on their upscale digs. "Thanks. Let me get the drone set up, and then I can show you some live feed regarding where we'll be going. Have a seat." He pointed to the comfy lounge chair near the entrance specially put there for clients. "Can I get you some water or something?"

She held up a hand. "I'm good."

Jackson rushed across the large room and unlocked his office. Against the back wall was a storage closet where they kept the drone. Once he retrieved it, along with his laptop, he returned.

"Come on over to the central command station," he said as he escorted her to the front of the main room. He pulled down a screen, set his computer on the table, and then turned on the overhead projector. "Once I send out the drone, you'll be able to see what's happening real time. I'll be up on the roof watching from a remote screen. It'll take about fifteen minutes for the drone to circle and return."

"Do you want me to stay here or join you?"

"Your choice, but it's cold on the roof." Having her sit next to him would be too distracting.

"I'll enjoy the warmth here then."

As quickly as he could, he rushed to the top of the building and set up the drone, making sure the infrared camera was loaded. He wanted to be able to see any animals or humans. By now, he was quite good at identifying landmarks in that area. Using Shamus's rental car as a starting point, he entered the coordinates. Figuring he'd be tracing the path at some point, he'd already calculated some of the longitude and latitude points on the trail, which he plugged in now.

"Ready, drone boy?"

Jackson set the company's new purchase on the top of the railing and then moved the lever. Up, up, and away it went. Now on autopilot, he could watch the drone do its job. The running trail had a switchback about a mile from the bunker, so he doubted Shamus would have been even close to that area, yet something told him it was near there where his cousin had died.

For the next few minutes, he watched the drone fly over mostly darkened land. Heat signatures from small animals flickered across the screen, but he didn't detect anything large.

Like a homing pigeon, the drone returned after one full sweep. Jackson gathered up his gear and returned it to his office. When he entered the main room, Ainsley was standing close to the screen. "I can't see the bunker," she said without turning around.

"I didn't fly the drone far enough. Where we're going, it should be safe."

She turned around, faced him, and ran her hands down her jeans. "Then let's go."

Chapter Ten

A INSLEY WAS SO excited to look for evidence that would help lead them to Shamus's murders that she jumped into the front seat of the truck, anxious to get on the trail. "What makes you think the Changelings don't have a drone that can detect us coming?" she asked as soon as Jackson slid into the front seat.

"It's possible they do have one, but they didn't when Kip, Connor, Kalan, and Elana's brother Sam went into the bunker."

"Let's hope they haven't figured out a way to keep their perimeters safe after that attack." Her brother had always tried to stop others from entering their compound, though he hadn't been astute like Jackson.

Ainsley wanted to ask him more questions about his past interactions with the Changelings and what they were capable of in the States, but decided to table that discussion until after the cleansing.

The drive up the mountain brought back bad memories, and she had to work hard to push them aside. Thankfully, Jackson turned off before they reached the spot where she'd found Shamus. Tomorrow, however, when she headed up to Mr. Ernst's home, she wouldn't be so lucky.

Ten minutes later, he parked on the side of the road. A small wooden stake in the ground marked the beginning of trail number 503.

"If you're not up to this, you can wait here," he said.

She laughed at that ridiculous comment. "I'm the Changeling, remember? If we're caught, I can always say some big bear was chasing me. I think they'll believe me."

Jackson chuckled and nodded. "Remind me not to cross you."

"Smart man." Fearing the necklace would break and scatter when she shifted, she unhooked it and placed it in the glove compartment.

Jackson kicked off his boots and unbuttoned his jacket. Oh, shit, she forgot about undressing in front of him. While she had no problem being naked in general, she hadn't been with her fellow wolves in such a long time that she'd actually developed some modesty. Plus, if she even caught sight of his cock, she couldn't be sure how her wolf would respond.

Yes, I do know. I'd be hotter than hot for him.

"I'll change outside."

Before he answered—or made fun of her for being shy—she pushed open the door and rushed down the path. A slight hint of bear lingered and might have been Shamus's scent, but she couldn't focus on that now. If she did, she might do something stupid, like run off on her own.

Ainsley stopped about fifty feet into the forest, ducked behind a tree, and disrobed. *Brr.* She neatly folded her clothes then stacked three stones in front of the tree to make sure she could find her gear when she returned.

Just as she let her wolf out, Jackson's lumbering bear came down the path. Oh, my. He was huge. While it was too dark to tell his exact coloring, his snout was lighter than the rest of his face and contrasted nicely with his body.

He spotted her and growled. She guessed that meant she should follow him. Because she could move so much faster than he could, he probably didn't want to be left behind, which why he led. Ainsley didn't mind. Actually, she didn't want to be the first one to find the spot where her dear Shamus had died.

Jackson took off down the trail. She expected him to be lumbering, but his bear was actually graceful and quite powerful. While it was chilly outside, the sky was clear, and the moon's rays shafting through the trees made this forest rather magical. Ainsley couldn't remember the last time she'd even gone for a run in her wolf form. Her legs were a little stiff, but the clean air helped invigorate her. As long as she could forget why she was here, she might be able to enjoy herself. She kept remembering James saying that he saw no reason why Naliana couldn't cleanse her. That would be a dream come true and open up so many opportunities for her.

For a good twenty minutes, they loped and darted until human voices sounded, forcing Jackson to slow. The bad part about being a shifter was that in order to discuss a plan, they needed to return to their human form in order to talk, and then shift back. Her big objection, besides having the sound travel, was being naked in front of him. Stupid, perhaps, but she didn't trust herself—or rather, she didn't trust her wolf. It didn't seem to matter they might be in a life and death situation, her animal knew what it wanted and was determined to taste him when the opportunity presented itself.

Stupid wolf.

Puffs of cigarette smoke floated their way and nearly made her cough. From the map, the Changeling territory wasn't for another mile, yet here they were. Why? Up to no good, most likely.

Jackson remained frozen as if he hoped to hear what they were saying, but she couldn't understand a word. He then held up a paw, she guessed to indicate she should stay there. He then patted his chest and motioned he'd circle behind them.

Ainsley nodded, though she had no intention of sitting idly by. As soon as Jackson's bear was out of sight, she drew on her inner cloaking device to become invisible and was thrilled when she succeeded. After all these years of keeping that talent hidden, she'd worried she might have forgotten how to do it.

Moving as quietly as possible, she edged closer to the men. So far, she only detected two voices, but that didn't mean there weren't more. The tips of their cigarettes glowed brightly, leading her right to them. *Dumb asses...* If they hadn't been laughing and talking so loudly, they might have recognized that one or two animal signatures were closing in on them.

If she could see them, Jackson would be able to locate them too. The question was what did he intend to do about the men? Unless they shifted and attacked, he might decide merely to scare them. It wasn't like he could question them. Even if he did, they wouldn't tell him squat, and they surely wouldn't admit to killing Shamus, even if they were standing next to a pool of blood with a piece of his clothing in one of their hands.

No, most likely, Jackson would wait until these men moved on before continuing their search.

"Brother Jacob said we have to find more sardonyx," the man with the low, gravelly voice announced. "Where the fuck are we supposed to get some? Even Brother Richard said he'd struck out in India."

What was up with all this *Brother* stuff? Her Clan back home never used that title. Her ears had perked up at the mention of the sardonyx however.

"I heard some was buried in a well under Donaldson's property. We should just dig up the place and see."

"That's a rumor," the first man replied. "Besides Brother Jacob wouldn't appreciate us going rogue."

Ainsley was close enough now to count four men. Shit. She didn't like the odds. Dropping down on her haunches, she waited to hear more.

"At least we won't be bothered by that fucking bear again," the tallest of the four said.

She stiffened, and her stomach twisted. *Fucking bear?* Were they referring to Shamus? Or had Jackson and Kalan been poking around? And what did *bothered by* really mean?

"What was that?" the first man said.

"What's what?" another one asked as he stomped out his cigarette.

"I heard something. We don't need anyone else snooping

around." As if they were readying for a fight, the other three stubbed out their smokes too.

"After the ranting we had to sit through, I'm in the mood for a scuffle. You up for finding our interloper and having some fun?"

"Fuck yeah."

"Hell yes."

"Let's do it."

Suddenly, all four men shifted into their wolf form, but Ainsley wasn't sure if that made things easier or harder. The gray wolf howled and all four of them charged into the woods—straight toward Jackson. Crap. She hoped he was ready for them. Four against one would test any bear. Hell, Shamus, who'd defeated many of her clansmen hadn't been able to handle a lot of them at once.

The hairs on her back stood up straight, and her heart beat too hard. Fear for Jackson tightened her gut. *Go!*

Because they had no idea she existed, she charged after them. Their growls and stomping seemed to prevent them from realizing she was closing in. With cigarette smoke on their skin, their senses wouldn't be as sharp either.

Suddenly, a roar sounded, along with too many howls. Branches cracked, and bear paws stomped. Oh, shit. She darted down the path and nearly stumbled when she spotted all of the wolves clinging and biting Jackson.

He swatted at them, hitting his mark once or twice, but missing at other times. Unfortunately, as soon as he threw off one, another would take his place, clawing and ripping Jackson's fur. Her heart nearly exploded at the quick devastation. Was this what had happened to Shamus?

Without thinking, she charged. The gray wolf at Jackson's neck had to be stopped first before he succeeded in ripping out Jackson's throat. She crawled up the side of Jackson's leg, but she doubted he even noticed given he was fighting for his life. With a swipe of her paw, she attempted to dislodge the wolf, but he wasn't ready to let go.

He'd be sorry. Mouth open, she lunged and clamped down hard on the weasel's neck. This time, he released his death grip on Jackson and tumbled to the ground, taking her with him. Because he couldn't see her, all he could do was swipe at the air. While she hated killing, she couldn't let these wolves live. Jackson's life would be forever in danger.

With a big inhale, she dug her teeth into the soft flesh and ripped out the wolf's throat. Blood spurted, and the coppery liquid filled her mouth and ran down her chest. Pulse racing, she jumped back and spit. Victory mixed with the horror of the kill, but she couldn't sit back and ponder what she'd done.

Jackson was now on his knees, wheezing. He'd killed one of the wolves and injured another, but the fourth was still attacking him, biting, growling, and clawing. She sprinted toward them then leapt up into the air, landing on Jackson's back. From there, she had a good vantage point to attack. The dumb wolf had no idea what was coming. She launched herself at him, and the two of them went flying. They landed on the hard packed earth a few feet from the wounded bear. Her attacker yelped and pawed, but only one of his swipes did any damage. The cut stung, but she'd heal.

Knowing she had to finish this one off, she dug her teeth into its neck and tore out his throat too. Ainsley then sat on her haunches and watched as the wolf wiggled and jerked until he returned to his dead human form.

Jackson keeled over, his eyes glassy. Oh, no. The final wolf that Jackson had injured was on the ground, barely alive. As much as she hated to do it, leaving any witnesses wouldn't be good. With a quick bite, she ended his life too.

With all of the attackers dead, she returned to her visible wolf form. She must look a mess with blood all over her, but right now, she wanted Jackson to see her, to know she was there to help.

His eyes flickered open, and his breathing was labored. It looked as if he'd lost a lot of blood. For a moment, she wondered if he was too dazed to recognize her as his mate, but when he didn't swat at her, she figured he knew. She thought about shifting into her human form and suggesting he do the same because she wanted to assess the damage, but he'd heal faster as a bear.

He was bleeding from his throat, arms, legs, and stomach. As much as he needed to rest, staying there might not be smart. No telling if more Changelings would come looking for their missing comrades.

She howled then trotted down the path, hoping Jackson would recognize the need to follow. With a grunt, he leveraged himself to his feet, took a few steps then stumbled once more. Her heart cracked, but given the size difference between them, she couldn't help carry him.

Ainsley thought about running back to the car, shifting, and then calling Kalan. She supposed he could rally the troops, but what could they do? Even if three bears arrived, they might not be able to carry Jackson back to the car if he passed out.

Shit. She returned to his side, sniffed, and then licked one of his wounds. The tang of her future mate's blood caused a rush of anger to fill her. She bayed once more before trotting down the path, needing him to leave this dangerous area.

Jackson must have recognized what he needed to do because he lumbered onto all fours and tried once more to follow. He passed the three other dead bodies, and then very slowly worked his way down the path behind her. Jackson must have thought he was crazy because he had to believe he was the only one fighting, and yet all four wolves were now dead. Those answers, however, would have to wait.

An hour later, after many starts, stops, and encouraging howls, they reached the car, and then shifted. This time she put her feelings of unease about being naked aside. Jackson needed her. "Crawl into the back. I'll drive."

"I don't understand what happened," he panted. Grasping onto the passenger's side handle, he jerked the door open then collapsed on the ground.

Crap. She shook him. "Jackson. Wake up and get in the car."

He groaned. Since she needed to dress in order to drive, she raced back to her clothes, and spotted the location of the three rocks she had piled up. As fast as she could, Ainsley threw on her clothes. Running back down the path, her mind spun. If she couldn't rouse him, Jackson would freeze if he had to spend the night outside in his human form.

When she returned, he was partially in the front passenger seat—naked with the door open with his legs hanging out. At least he'd moved.

He would be really pissed when he saw how much blood he was leaving on the upholstery, but the damage had already been done. No way could she dress him either. The best she could do was get him in the car, turn up the heat, and drive back to his house as fast as she could.

With care, she lifted his legs and stuffed them in front of him, but it was really hard because he was a big man who was dead weight right then. Using all of her effort to maneuver his butt on the seat, her feet slipped and she did a face plant right on top of his cock. Holy crap. Heat raced up her face. Had he been conscious, she might have turned around and run.

Her wolf, however, howled.

Stop it, right now. Stupid wolf. *There can't be any mating if he doesn't live, so back off.*

Once Jackson was completely inside the cab, she shut his door and raced over to the driver's side. Damn. Where was his key? Leaning over once more, she dug through his clothes and retrieved it. The moment the engine turned over, she let out a long held breath.

"I can drive," Jackson said, coming to life and pawing at her arm.

Was he kidding? "You're injured. Rest."

While she was warm from the exertion, she dialed up the heat, not wanting Jackson to be chilled. He'd already lost a lot of blood. Disregarding the speed limit, she zinged down the mountain. Her hands shook as she realized she'd killed three men tonight. In the process, Jackson had been injured. Pure rage bubbled inside her. What kind of man attacks an innocent bear?

Who else? Changelings, of course, but why? They didn't know she'd overheard them talking. If she hadn't had the talent to become invisible, she might be lying right beside those men. At that thought, shivers consumed her.

When she drew close to town, she slowed, not wanting to be pulled over. The last thing she needed was to explain to some cop why she had a bloodied naked man in the truck. The officer would insist she take Jackson to the hospital, and then the questions would begin. Nope. Not going to happen on her watch.

Duh. Kalan. He could help. She slowed and carefully fished out her phone only to remember she didn't have his number. She'd have to call on Jackson's phone once she returned to his house.

As soon as she spotted the shifter compound, she let out a long breath. "Getting closer, Jackson. Hang in there."

His response was a groan. He couldn't die now. She wouldn't allow it.

Her car came into view and then his cabin. Yes, they'd made it. She parked as close to the front door as possible, cut the engine, and then ran over to this side.

When she pulled open the door, an arm and a leg fell out as the top part of his body collapsed onto the driver's side seat.

"Oh, no you don't. You have to sit up so I can help you get inside. You can do this."

"Tired."

That was because he'd lost a lot of blood in the fight then walked a mile. Using all her strength, she tugged on his arm until he was in a seated position then gently dragged him to the edge of the seat. "Can you stand?"

As if he could tell he was close to home, he wrapped an arm around her shoulder, and leaned on her as he inched his way to the front porch. Thankfully, he was able to grab onto the porch handrail and haul himself up the steps. Not knowing if he locked his door, she tested the handle and found it open, thank goodness.

It would be best if he showered first to wash away the dirt from his opponents' claws ripping away the flesh before he shifted. He'd heal better that way. "Where's the bathroom?"

"Huh?"

The place wasn't that big. She'd find it. Not wanting to let go, she walked him down the hallway, testing each of the doors. Finally, she reached what was probably his room and flicked on the light next to the door. His bed took up most of the room. He had a shitload of pillows on the bed and the blue sheets were in swirls, like he was a restless sleeper.

When she spotted the en suite, she led him over to the bathroom. "You need to get clean."

"Can't stand…anymore."

"Then sit." She opened the shower door and helped him inside. Her inner wolf was going crazy in the small confines, but she had to ignore her. Jackson's life was on the line. With his back against the tiled shower wall, he slid down to the floor and passed out. Well, damn.

She turned on the water, but kept the flow away from him until it heated. When he showed no signs of waking, she shucked her shoes and stripped. Hopefully, he wouldn't remember a thing.

She stepped into the warm water and felt its soothing warmth. She was a mess too, and needed to wash, but she'd worry about herself later. Pouring a ton of body wash on him, she cleansed him the best she could. Jackson roused once or twice, but only when she hit a particularly deep gouge. If he didn't wake up when she finished, she wasn't sure how he would be able to shift.

Kalan! As soon as she finished cleaning Jackson, she'd call him.

If his brother didn't answer, Ainsley would have to appeal to Jackson's inner bear. What that entailed she wasn't sure, but what she did know was that it could be dangerous to their lives if it came too close to her.

Chapter Eleven

PAIN WRACKED JACKSON'S body as he swatted the air in front of him, but hit nothing. Daring to check out his surroundings now that he was able to breathe better, he opened his eyes, but it took a few seconds for him to figure out that he was in his bed at home in his bear form. What the fuck had happened?

Ainsley had her back to him, dressed in a pair of his boxers and his University of Tennessee sweatshirt, looking adorable. She was sleeping on top of the bedspread and had dragged a throw over her shoulders. Clearly, she didn't want to be tempted at intimacy.

He, however, wanted to throw caution to the wind. Jackson growled softly and was tempted to grab her, but he didn't because he feared he might hurt her. Being this close to his mate had his bear going crazy.

Jackson shifted into his human form. Ainsley must have been dead to the world as she barely roused. He slipped out from under the covers and moved as quietly as possible to the bathroom. Everything was a jumbled mess. The last thing he remembered was climbing in the shower in his human form. So how the hell had he shifted into his bear form?

Everything was a blur before that. One minute he was in the woods and the next he was back at his house. *Think*. He had been enjoying a pleasant run on the trail—with Ainsley. Their purpose for being there was to find the location of Shamus's murder, but Jackson had no idea what they'd found, if anything.

First things first, he glanced at the mirror to check his injuries and halted.

"Holy fuck." His body was laced with scrapes and gouges. An ugly welt that had recently closed ran across his throat. The possibly life-altering slice was still tender to the touch, despite his bear healing most of the wounds.

If he was so incapacitated, how the hell had he made it back to the house? Ainsley wasn't strong enough to carry him. The images of wolves charging at him flitted across his mind and helped jar his memory. He shouldn't have had a problem handling multiple wolves, but they all came at him at once, attacking strategic places.

He would bat one away, only to find three others attacking him in every vulnerable spot. There had been a lot of pain and mental fog. Then, as if they all decided to die on their own, the last two wolves jumped off his body and bled to death. *Sure they did.* Clearly, his injuries were still messing with his mind.

Jackson needed answers and returned to the bedroom. The clock read 3:18 am. Damn, it was too early to wake her. He edged closer to the bed, ready to crawl in when she sat up, leaned over, and flicked on the lamp on the night table. She must have forgotten about him and crawled under the sheet. His inner bear roared.

Mine, mate.

Her eyes widened. "Oh, my. You're awake. And very naked." She turned her head away. "How do you feel?"

Shit. Only now did he remember how shy she had been. Then again, she must recognize that being this close to one's mate wasn't a good idea—especially given her makeup as part Changeling.

"Battered, but alive. Listen, you go back to sleep. I'll dress and rest in the living room."

With the sheet wrapped around her, she placed her feet on the floor and stood. "No, you need to rest. I'll sleep out there."

In all honesty, he wanted answers more than rest. "How about I fix us something to eat and you can tell me what went down."

She looked off to the side. "You don't remember?"

"Only bits and pieces."

He grabbed some clean clothes and pulled them on. Feeling almost human, he followed her out to the galley style kitchen. Coffee was first on the agenda. She stepped next to him, and his internal sensors shot to high alert. *Bad bear.*

"How about I make us some eggs and you rest?" she asked.

Normally, he'd never let someone barge into his kitchen and take over, but right now, he wasn't up to speed. Besides, the two of them couldn't move around in there without touching. "Sure."

Jackson sat at the table in the corner of the small kitchen. "Tell me what happened, including how you got me to change into my bear."

She pulled the eggs and milk from the refrigerator. "You tell me what you remember and I'll fill in the gaps."

"Okay. I'll start with where it became fuzzy. I heard voices and motioned for you to stay back while I went to check out what the men were doing. I remember hearing some snippets of conversation, but it wasn't anything concrete. Seconds later, four wolves came at me. I'll be honest. I wasn't expecting that many so fast."

She nodded in sympathy. "When I arrived, you had all four of them attacking you. The one at your throat was about to take a fatal bite." She bent over and pulled open a few cabinet doors.

"Mixing bowls are above the stove."

"Thanks."

He didn't like that she hadn't followed his instructions, but if she had, he would be dead. "If you saw them attack me, then how did you stay alive? Hell, they nearly killed me."

She cracked the eggs into the found bowl. "Yeah, about that. Remember, I told you my father was a Wendayan?"

"Yes."

"Well, I can do this."

He looked down at his hands for a mere second before her words registered. He glanced up, and Ainsley was nowhere to be seen. One second she was there, and the next she wasn't.

"Whoa! What the hell?" Suddenly, she reappeared right in front of him, and he blinked then opened his eyes wide.

"I have a special talent."

"That's more than special. You freakin' disappeared!"

She leveled him with a stare. "Yes, I did."

This was too much to comprehend. "People can't just disappear."

"Some witches can."

She'd just blown his mind. "But you never left the kitchen."

"No, I didn't, which is how I was able to rip those wolves off your body, and they had no idea what was happening." A small smile lifted her lips. "Those fuckers just pawed at the air, and even lifted their little heads, willing me to rip out their throats."

"Holy shit. Then I wasn't dreaming." Jackson wasn't so sure he liked the idea of a woman saving his butt, but he had to admit that she had done a fine job. "Now, I can see why James said you could fight. Did he know of your talent?"

She shrugged. "I never told him."

That was odd, but then again Naliana was a goddess in charge of the Wendayans. Ainsley poured the eggs in the pan he kept on the stove.

"Thank you for saving my life," he said, but it sounded almost hollow.

A brief smile crossed her face. "No problem. I had an advantage you didn't have."

"That's the truth. I vaguely remember shifting when we got to my car, so how did I end up in my bear form?"

Heat colored her pretty face. "I seduced you."

If he'd had any coffee in his mouth, he would have spit it out in surprise. "I don't remember." Damn.

"I was hoping you wouldn't. Your bear responded to me touching you. I was about to call your brother to come help, but then your bear came out and greeted me. Once I rinsed you, you roused enough to crawl into bed. I have to say, you do hog the bed."

"I don't remember any of it, but yeah, the bed's not designed for large animals." Maybe she had other talents, like erasing his memory. "Once again, thank you. I wouldn't have healed so quickly had I not shifted."

"I know."

Ainsley was something else. Wanting to put that humiliating experience behind him, he focused on the case. "Would you mind leaving your pink blouse with me?"

From the stove, she looked over her shoulder. "I don't think it's a good color for you."

He cracked up, but then stopped as pain shot through him. "I thought perhaps Dr. Williams, the coroner, could collect some DNA off your shirt and compare it to any blood on Shamus. It's a long shot, but maybe one or more of the same wolves had attacked him too."

She spun around and clamped a hand over her mouth. "I never thought about blood samples. Tell your doctor to check the inside of my shirt. When I put it on after shifting, my arms and chest were covered in their blood. Your blood is probably on the outside."

Jackson nodded. "I bet he'll be able to tell the difference, but he might need a sample of your blood for comparison."

"Anything he needs. By the way, I did overhear a few things."

He sat up straighter. "What's that?"

She explained how one of the men had said that there was sardonyx buried at the bottom of some well, but then another guy said it was only a rumor.

"It might not be," Jackson said. He'd done a lot of research on that tale. "What else?"

"They said something about not being bothered by that bear again, but I didn't know if they were referring to Shamus."

"I can't think of another bear they might be thinking of, unless it was when Kalan attacked their men at the bunker."

"That's what I was thinking."

A minute later, she delivered the eggs then poured the coffee.

She sat across from him and he marveled how well she was holding up. "You're so calm. Have you killed before?" he asked.

"No."

Now he was even more impressed. "Are you okay with it?"

"No, but I was brought up to be tough."

"That you are." It was one of the many traits about her that he was beginning to appreciate.

ONCE AINSLEY WAS certain Jackson would be okay, she had to get out of there or chance giving into her urges to press up against him and feel his hot body against hers. Her damn wolf was too fascinated by the man. Any other guy might have ranted at her stupid move of trying to save him, but not Jackson. He appreciated what she'd done for him, and that made her want him all the more.

After retrieving her necklace from his glove compartment, she took off. By the time she returned home, it was almost five in the morning, and she needed to return to her wolf form for at least an hour to help heal some of her rather minor wounds. She worried that if there was any evidence of a fight, when she worked on Mr. Ernst's father, he might call her out on it.

Ainsley undressed then lifted Jackson's college sweatshirt to her nose and inhaled. It contained his yummy scent. To prevent her from obsessing over it though, she would launder it and then return it to him. She walked over to the small closet that contained her stackable washer-dryer and tossed his clothes in.

Jackson, Jackson. Throughout this whole ordeal, he'd been so nice, despite his initial dislike of her kind, but she could hardly blame him for that when she hated the Changelings just as much.

The image of jumping into the lake to be cleansed appeared in her head. Being free of her altered genes would be a dream come true. The big question now was what did she need to do next? As much as she wanted to locate where Shamus was killed, it didn't seem to matter now. Most likely, he'd run into those men, or ones like them, and had been attacked.

Her job at the moment was to eliminate all evidence of the fight, heal, and then dress to meet up with Mr. Ernst at eight that morning. She debated wearing her new necklace, but because the stones were sardonyx, she decided against it, as she didn't need Mr. Ernst eyeing it. She could almost hear Shamus tell her never to take it off, that it would protect her from many things, but she couldn't chance some Changeling stealing it.

"Sorry, Shamus."

After resting for an hour as her wolf, she shifted back, checked in the mirror, and concluded she looked fine. She then tossed on her uniform, packed up her portable table and loaded it into the back of her Jetta. Next to it, she placed her case that contained her needles, therapeutic magnets, herbal medicines, and other accessories.

Let's do this. With her stomach still upset, she jumped in the car and headed back up the mountain toward the Changeling compound.

This time, when she drove by the site where she'd spotted Shamus, she didn't look. "We'll make the men who did this to you pay, Shamus. I promise."

More determined than ever, she drove to her location. Mr. Ernst's directions were spot on, and she arrived with a few minutes to spare. A large black SUV sat in the drive in front of a sprawling one-story red brick home that had white shudders and white trim. Mr. Ernst must do quite well for himself if he could afford such a nice home. Because of his father's failing health, John Ernst had told her he'd moved his dad in with him. He'd never mentioned if there was a Mrs. Ernst, however.

The front door opened, and the large Changeling filled the frame. Her stomach tumbled. When invisible, Ainsley felt invincible. Now that she had to lie to his face, she wasn't so sure she could pull this off.

Do it for Shamus.
Do it for Jackson.

Ainsley eased out of her front seat. No sooner had she stood than Mr. Ernst was there to give her a helping hand.

"I see you found the house."

Way to state the obvious. "Your directions were good."

No surprise, his chest puffed up. "Come on in. Dad's waiting for you in the den. You can set up in there."

"Great." She put Mr. Ernst close to fifty, which meant his dad was probably in his late seventies. At least he wouldn't be any physical threat.

With her portable table in his hand, he led her into the den. Using a cane, the old man stood and then winced. Changeling or not, she didn't like to see anyone in pain. She introduced herself then set up the table.

"I'll leave you with my father. If you need my help moving him, I'll be around." John Ernst then rushed off.

She patted the table. "Can you get up here by yourself?" she asked the old man. She should have asked Mr. Ernst to stay. "Or do you need help?"

"I'm good." He wobbled over to the table. "You're a Changeling. That's good."

Either his son must have told him she was related to Owen or he could tell himself. "I am."

"Do I detect a slight accent?"

She saw no harm in telling him, though she was surprised his son hadn't filled him in. "I grew up in Scotland, though I have to admit your Changelings here seem to be more violent than the ones we have across the pond."

The old man beamed. "That's good, right?"

Being rotten would be a good trait to a Changeling. "I suppose as long as it doesn't draw too much attention from the humans. Actually, I was walking through the grocery store last night and heard two ladies talk about a visitor who'd been attacked by several animals the other day and killed."

He looked off to the side, his brows knitting together. "I hadn't heard."

She believed him. "Not that these ladies knew anything about shifters, but I was wondering if this kind of violence is common around these parts."

The old man looked toward the door. "Not usually, but I did hear some of our own were attacked last night and killed: a real shame. In the old days, it wasn't so violent in Silver Lake."

"That is bad." She actually meant it. This was, most likely, all she was going to get out of this guy. "Now tell me about your bad back."

By the time he filled her in, and after she'd worked on him, close to an hour had passed. "All right then. You can roll over," she told him.

The senior gentleman grunted and tried to lift up, but he was too weak. "I can't. Can you get John?"

"Sure. I'll be right back."

Ainsley stepped into the hallway and walked back to the living room but didn't see Mr. Ernst. Perhaps he was down the hall. She retraced her steps, and when she spotted an open door, she peered in. It was an office—and it was empty. Her pulse soared at the possibilities. The wall behind the desk contained bookshelves that were stacked with not only books, but with what looked like rather expensive souvenirs. He had everything from small sculptures to a box that looked to be made of ivory—illegally obtained no doubt. On the north wall was a louvered closet door and across from that was a large picture window with two dark blue chairs and a small table underneath. A large mahogany desk sat in the middle of the room facing the entrance. On top was a laptop. Bingo!

Because she was here to spy, she glanced back at the door then walked behind the desk.

Holy crap. What looked like a map of the town with red dots scattered at various locations filled the screen. Ainsley had no idea what it represented, but Jackson might have an idea. Whatever it was, it seemed important. Retrieving her phone, she snapped a picture of the screen then tucked her cell back in her pocket.

Heavy footsteps sounded coming down the hallway.

Oh, shit.

Chapter Twelve

*T*HINK. QUICK. AINSLEY couldn't come up with a reason for being in his office. He'd know something was up if he caught her.

Her only chance was to disappear.

She managed to become invisible just as he walked into the room, but now she needed to see which side of the desk he'd go around. He stepped to the left, so she exited on the right. If she hadn't been cautious, she'd have run into him, and that would have shocked him if he bumped into what looked like nothing.

Her pulse raced, and she was glad the invisibility shield extended to masking her scent. As quickly as possible, she dashed out of the office, hustled down the hallway then reappeared. Walking with more force than usual, she headed back toward the office. With as much calm as she could muster, Ainsley tapped on the doorjamb. "Mr. Ernst? Could you help me get your dad down from the table? He's a bit weak."

John Ernst grunted then nodded. "Of course."

BY NOON, JACKSON felt well enough to go into work. He'd debated calling Ainsley to see how the visit went with the Changeling, but he decided to let her finish out her day before he contacted her. He had the sense there were some things about this particular job she hadn't confided in him.

When he got to the office, the first thing he wanted to do was fly his drone over the area where they'd been attacked, though he wasn't sure what he expected to see. He doubted he'd be able to spot the dead men's bodies through the trees—assuming they hadn't been found—but he might be able to identify where the fight had occurred.

He was up on the roof maneuvering his drone when Kip came up the steps. "You have a visitor."

Jackson swiveled around. "Who?"

"Ainsley."

At the mere mention of her name, his damn heart jumped to warp speed. Why was she at the office? He hoped nothing bad had happened. "Tell her that as soon as I bring back the drone, I'll be down."

Kip nodded and headed downstairs. By the time the drone returned and Jackson put their new purchase in the cabinet in his office, Ainsley had been waiting about twenty minutes.

He entered the main room, and instantly, his libido went crazy. This wasn't good. "Ainsley?"

She twisted around then stood. "How are you feeling?"

She came all the way to the office to ask him that question? Her concern warmed him. A pure Changeling never would have asked. "Good. My bear finished healing me."

"I'm glad. I hope it was okay to come here. I found something you should see."

The anguish on her face cut through him. Her white shirt with the wellness center logo on it made her look a lot younger than twenty-seven. If she didn't have purple streaks in her hair along with the tiny nose ring—two things that made her a bit edgier—he would have guessed she was closer to twenty.

"You want something to drink first? Coffee or tea?" he asked.

She huffed out a breath. "I could use a coffee."

"Come sit over here." Jackson hustled over to the machine in the corner and poured two cups. "Cream or sugar?"

She shook her head. "Black, thank you."

He carried the drinks over to the seating area, handed her the steaming mug, and then sat across from her. "Does this have something to do with your visit to John Ernst's dad?"

"Yes." She told him about the layout of the house and how, after she treated his elderly father, she needed Mr. Ernst to help her move his dad. "I'd wandered down one of the hallways looking for him, when I spotted an office door open. I couldn't help but look inside."

His grip tightened on his cup. "What did you do?" Damn. He hadn't meant to be so accusatory, but he didn't want the wrath of the entire Changeling organization to come after her.

"I didn't get caught, if that's what is worrying you."

"I'm glad of that." More than glad; he was relieved.

"So, once I entered the small room, I checked out his laptop." She pulled her cell phone from her pocket and located the picture. "I snapped this of his screen. I don't know what it means, but it looks important."

"Didn't you worry Ernst might catch you? You were snooping in his office."

Her face turned a bright shade of red. "Yes, I had some concern, and if you must know, he almost did catch me."

Anger raced up his spine, but then dissipated as soon as he caught the sly smile on her face. "You did that disappearing trick, didn't you?"

She held up one hand as if to stop him from chastising her. "I had to. If he'd caught me snooping, I'd lose all chance of learning anything in the future."

She was brash and rash, but oh so brave. "May I see what was on his screen?"

"Oh, sure. Sorry." She handed him her phone.

He studied the image. "I'm not sure what the red dots mean, but one of them is where Donaldson's warehouse used to be."

She shook her head. "That name sounds familiar. Why is that important?"

Jackson didn't want to jump to any conclusions, but his gut told him this might have something to do with the location of the hidden treasure, or treasures. What concerned him was the number of other dots besides the one on the Donaldson property. "Hold on. Let me get something out of my office and show you."

Jackson returned her phone and then trotted to his office where he retrieved the ancient looking map. He returned to Ainsley and placed it on one of the tables that sat against the wall. "Come over here and check this out."

She stepped next to him. It had been a big mistake asking her to join him. His libido flooded his brain with a need so strong that he had to dig his now sharpened nails into his palms to keep from touching her.

Ainsley studied his map and then opened up her picture. "I can see they're both of Silver Lake, but it would be easier to compare them if my picture were larger."

"Email it to me at jackson@McKinnonAssociates.com."

"Perfect." She tapped her phone. "Done."

"Follow me into my office." All he could think about was her heavenly scent, and that in a few days, Naliana would cleanse her, finally enabling him to let loose his bear. Right now, however, he had a treasure to find. Damn, but it was hard to keep his animal contained. Jackson pulled up a chair. "Have a seat."

"What are you going to do?"

"I'm going to upload this into Photoshop. That way I can super-impose the two images; I'll place one on top of each other to see if the location of the treasure on my map aligns with one of the red dots on yours."

"Sounds good."

She leaned forward and watched as he opened her email then imported it into his program. He'd already scanned his map. After he resized her picture to match his, and then placed them on top of each other, he had to improve the transparency by decreasing the opacity of his map in order for hers to show through. He tapped the screen.

"Yes, we have a match! See here? The well that had been on the Donaldson property overlaps one of the red dots on John Ernst's picture."

Ainsley scooted her chair closer, and he had to force his bear to behave. "What does that mean?"

He told her about the history of the treasure.

"Are you saying this new map proves there's something down there? For all we know, these red dots represent potential properties for sale."

His excitement dampened at bit. "The Ernst map alone might imply that, but when compared to this ancient map, I tend to think along the line of treasure." He faced her. "What I do know is that without your help, I might not have searched further."

He pushed back his chair, stood, and without thinking, drew her to her feet, and then hugged her.

Kiss her, his bear urged. *She's going to be yours soon anyway.*

Heat soaked into his body, and every cell exploded with need. What was one kiss? Ainsley leaned her head back, probably to look him in the eye, and Jackson pounced. He drew her close and kissed her.

Bam! Wow! His cock nearly burst through the zipper. She clasped his shoulders, and her sharpened nails dug into him. Her equal need ignited him. He increased the pressure of the kiss, and her eyeteeth slightly protruded. What looked like blue sparks shot off her body. What the hell? Jackson stepped back. "Sorry."

"Why? I'm not. It was nice. But I agree, we can't. Not until—"

"I know, but that's not why I stopped. I saw something. It looked like you were glowing blue."

She looked off to the side. "My mom briefly mentioned something about my Wendayan father emitting a blue light when he was…um…excited."

He'd never heard of that. Talk about embarrassing. Just then his cell rang, giving him a much-needed distraction. One look at the screen caused him to let out an audible groan. It was Tawny. Damn.

Her call couldn't have come at a worse time.

"Aren't you going to answer it?" Ainsley asked with one brow cocked.

He was staring at his phone, trying to figure out his next move. If he didn't pick up, it would look like he didn't want to speak with his *girlfriend* in front of Ainsley. "Sure." He answered. "Hey, Tawny."

"Is this a bad time?"

"Yes." Damn, his lack of enthusiasm must have shone through. That sucked for her. She was a great gal, but he wasn't interested anymore. Out of instinct, he turned his back, not wanting Ainsley to overhear what Tawny might say.

"I just called to tell you that one of the two bids I told you about on the Donaldson property went through."

"It sold?"

"Yes."

His gut soured, and he dropped down onto his chair. "I thought Donaldson wasn't interested in selling."

"That's what he told me. The offer must have been something he couldn't refuse.

Everyone had a price. "Who did he sell it to?"

"That's the strange part. It's a corporation. I didn't broker the deal, so I can't find a name."

It didn't matter. He'd never be able to dig there now. On a positive note, neither could John Ernst—not unless he was the corporation. The man was an account, with ties to many lawers, so anything was possible. Shit. "Thanks for letting me know."

"Let me know if you want to grab a drink."

Jackson refused to string her along anymore. "I'm sorry, but I'm seeing someone else."

"You are?" The pain in her voice tore at him.

"It's a friend of the family. I'm sorry."

"Sure." She disconnected.

Ainsley slipped a hip on the desk. "A family friend?"

He shrugged. "I had to tell her something. If you must know, I was dating Tawny before I met you."

Ainsley stepped closer, and his inner bear took notice. When she placed a hand on his chest, heat seared him. His teeth lengthened, and the hair on his face thickened.

"Are you saying you're attracted to *me* now?" she asked.

He clasped her hand and lowered it to her side. "We're mates— or rather we might become mates if you behave yourself. And only after the ceremony."

She laughed. "Well, then, we're doomed, because I never *behave* myself."

Damn. He stepped away from her. "Let's go back to the war room."

She chuckled, and the sound resonated deep within him. "Can't handle being so close to me, can you?"

Why did she have to be so damn perceptive? "Are you saying your inner wolf is totally calm right now?"

Two could play at this game, or so he hoped. Steeling himself against her allure, he stepped closer and lifted her chin with his thumb. As expected, she lowered her gaze. From the way her breaths were coming out faster and faster, she was affected.

"No, I'm not immune to your scent or your bear. Far from it."

Good, but they had other things to discuss beside their intense need for one another. "Come on then." He placed a hand on her lower back to prove that he was in control. Hopefully, she didn't see through his sham.

They returned to the seating area in the back of the large room. Something about her being invited to John Ernst's house didn't sit well with him. Was Ernst looking to recruit her? "How did you meet John Ernst?"

She drank her coffee that by now had probably turned warm at best. "He came to the clinic."

That didn't sound good. "Why?"

"He was in pain from a birth defect. He limped."

His senses shot to high alert. "Kalan mentioned that the third man involved in his mate's parents' murders had a limp. If that's true, John Ernst witnessed two people being killed or even participation in their deaths, so I'd be careful around him."

She set her mug back on the table. "That's good to know, but just so you know, I never took him for being a good soul."

"As much as this information was really helpful, I'd prefer if you didn't go back to his house again."

She stared at him. "Are you always this bossy?"

"Only when it comes to your safety."

Ainsley looked off to the side, probably trying to decide if she could handle an over-protective bear. "I appreciate you looking out for me, but I think I've proven that I can handle myself. I always have."

Arguing would get him nowhere. "Understood."

She leaned back and watched him. The casual way she dragged her gaze up and down his body caused more inner turmoil. Damn, woman.

"Now that your treasure hunting didn't pan out, what do you think the other dots on Mr. Ernst's map represent?"

"I don't know, but I sure as hell would like to find out."

Chapter Thirteen

ONCE AINSLEY LEFT Jackson, she rushed back to work. Before her next client arrived, she straightened up her workroom, trying to take her mind off Jackson's allure. The more time she spent with him, the more her inner wolf wanted to say *fuck it*, and just jump his bones.

Stupid wolf.

She had more important things to do at the moment than pine over what wasn't going to happen in the next few hours—like count the days until Naliana would perform her magic and cleanse her.

Two days. That was all she had to wait.

Oh, crap, she should have asked Jackson exactly what she needed to do to set up this cleansing. She could call him now, but she didn't want to bother him. James said that she should wait by the lake. While that was all well and good, didn't she have to tell them when she'd be there? And *where* by the lake?

Tomorrow she'd deal with the logistics. Ainsley's three o'clock appointment was about to arrive. She inhaled a few times to help center herself.

I will function. No, I must function.

It would be hard to concentrate though, since her head still spun from that kiss. Holy hell on a stick… Jackson's scent had invaded her body so deeply she feared she'd never survive if she didn't have her Changeling blood altered. If he decided he didn't want to be with her after all that, she wasn't sure what she'd do. Not that she would blame him if he decided not to mate. After all, she was stubborn to the core—and fiercely independent. Furthermore, she didn't need a psychic to tell her that she and Jackson would butt heads constantly if they ever ended up together.

Stop getting sidetracked.

Ainsley had a job to do. She refocused. According to her next client's chart, Mrs. Claire was a human with back pain, an issue that often drew many customers to her.

Right on time, Mrs. Claire arrived. To her delight, once Ainsley asked her a few questions, she managed to focus—despite having her mind a million miles away. After the successful treatment, the next two hours went by quickly.

When it was time to leave, Ainsley hurried out, anxious to shower, eat, and then delve into the mystery of the red dots. She couldn't help wondering what Jackson thought was buried under that well. One of the shifters on the path mentioned sardonyx. Maybe that's what was down there.

Just for fun, she would do a little research on her own. It didn't matter that even if she did learn what kind of treasure might be buried, Jackson would never be able to dig it up now that someone had purchased the property. Why he thought Mr. Donaldson would let him in the first place, she didn't know.

She arrived home and dashed into the bathroom. No sooner had she stepped out of her shower than her doorbell rang. The vibrations coursing through her body told her who was there.

With a towel around her body, she stepped into the small living room and pressed her face against the closed door. "Give me a few minutes, Jackson, okay?"

"Sure."

It wasn't like he had a choice. Greeting him dressed in almost nothing would be asking for trouble. Quickly, she dashed to her bedroom and threw on jeans and a thick, baggy sweatshirt so she wouldn't have to wear a bra. She looked a mess, but that was probably for the best.

Seconds later, she threw open the door. It didn't matter she'd seen him this afternoon; her body went wild. He'd changed his shirt to a soft green colored pullover that brought out the streaks of gold and green in his eyes. Whoa. Her nails sharpened and her bones cracked. That wasn't good.

She didn't dare lower her gaze. Dangerous thoughts would crumble her resolve. "What's up?"

"Can I come in? I have a few things I need to discuss with you."

"Sure." Ainsley stepped to the side, pleased she sounded in control, when she was anything but. "Can I get you something to drink?"

He held up a hand. "No, thanks. I need to keep my wits about me."

She managed not to smile, totally understanding what he was going through. To make sure they didn't accidently sit next to each other, she dropped down on the green leather chair while he took the sofa.

Jackson leaned forward, his elbows on his knees and his fingers dangling. He looked sexy as hell. "Shamus will be cremated tomorrow, and his father has asked that either you or I fly his ashes home."

Her heart jammed in her chest. Shamus. With all that had gone on in the last few days, she hadn't thought about him often enough. "I want to take him to Scotland."

Jackson nodded. "And I will come with you."

She leaned back, her ire flaring. "I can do this alone. I don't need a babysitter."

His eyes narrowed. "Shamus was *my* cousin. He's *my* family. I'm sure Uncle Gordon would appreciate it if a family member came over. That doesn't mean you shouldn't come too." Thankfully, his voice had softened with the last few sentences.

Pushing aside the slight, her thoughts jumped toward the erotic. A shared hotel room, maybe? Hot sex? Heat swamped her, and her bones cracked.

Just as she was about to squash those ideas, she remembered she would be cleansed in two days and might not be able to go if he insisted on leaving tomorrow. "When would you go over?"

"I thought after the cleansing."

She blew out a breath. He seemed to care about eradicating the Changeling part of her as much as she did. "That works for me."

"So should I buy tickets for us then?"

She mentally went through her list of clients, checking to see if any of them had to see her. "How long would we be gone?"

He shrugged. "Maybe two days? Fly over on one day, give the ashes to my uncle, and fly home the next day. It'll be hell on the body, but I don't want to be away from work for long."

Jetlag would be a bitch, but this was for Shamus. "I can go if we leave on a Friday afternoon. We'd arrive Saturday morning. If we leave early Monday morning, we'll by home by noon."

"It needs to be done. I'll see what I can find ticket wise." Jackson sat up. "The other piece of news doesn't really affect you, but I thought you might like to know. I learned who purchased the Donaldson property."

From the way his voice almost shook with excitement, this was good news. "Who?"

"My father and Connor and Rye's dad."

That didn't make any sense, especially in light of the fact that a corporation bought it. "I don't understand."

He explained that his dad and Connor's father used to own McKinnon and Associates. "When they retired, Connor took over. They now miss the action, but said that our place is too small for them to join the team again."

His voice had risen with excitement. "That sounds amazing, but are you sure they don't want the property for the *treasure*?" It was the only thing that made sense.

"No, they didn't know anything about my map when they purchased the place. They claimed that they want us to have a bigger, better office—one with more room. Now that they understand what it takes to be successful, they want everything to be state-of-the-art. Part of the building might even be built as a safe house. Besides, if they unearthed the sardonyx they would just turn it over to the Clan anyway."

She sank back against the chair. "That's remarkable that they would do this for you. I can tell you my parents would never have done anything so wonderful. You're lucky."

"I am, but my folks aren't Changelings; no offense. They plan to travel for a portion of the year, but when they're home, they'd like to help out."

"Will you tell them about the treasure?" This seemed important to Jackson.

He nodded. "I just told them, but I didn't have the map with me at the time. I could tell they didn't believe me."

"But they'll let you look first, right?"

He chuckled. "You are something else."

She hoped that was a good thing, but she didn't want to ask despite the smile on his face. "Blair told me stories about your life growing up, and while your folks were strict, they were really loving. They sure proved it today."

Jackson stretched out his legs and looked good enough to eat.

Snatch one kiss, her wolf demanded.

"They are the best."

Wanting to take her mind off her desires, she changed the subject. "Before you go, let me ask you. Is there something I need to do to let James and Naliana know that I want to be cleansed?"

"I'm not sure, but I'll ask Rye. He'll know."

"I appreciate it." Jackson was such a nice man.

He stood. "When I buy the tickets, I'll let you know, but I'll need your passport number and other information."

Ainsley shot to her feet. "I can pay for my own."

He waved a hand. "It's our family."

She was about to say Shamus wasn't just her friend, he was like family to her too, but she had the sense Jackson needed to do this.

"Thank you. Let me give you the information now." She ducked into her room and retrieved her passport then handed it to him. She trusted Jackson.

Ainsley then walked him to the door, her body jittery and needy. Just as she reached for the knob to pull it open, Jackson focused his gaze on her. Her mouth turned dry and wetness pooled between her legs. Her pulse sped up, and her bones began to crack.

Stay away, she pleaded to her inner wolf.

Jackson leaned over. "It won't be long, Ainsley. Then watch out."

Her heart racing, he pulled open the door and left. His footsteps pounded down the stairs, but his scent lingered. Holy hell. What had she gotten herself into?

AS SOON AS Jackson reached the outside, he plastered his back against the door. Being around Ainsley had been pure torture. He wanted to rip off those baggy clothes and sink his cock deep inside her, but he understood that he couldn't—at least, not yet.

He had to work to convince his bear that all he had to do was wait two more days. The bear agreed to be patient. Jackson didn't want to rush her, but the yearning was growing stronger by the hour. His bear would only wait so long.

Ainsley already seemed skittish around him, but he couldn't blame her. He hadn't exactly been welcoming. Knowing full well what Changelings could do, he'd fought against them for years. Having one in his presence had messed with his mind, so it was understandable that his first reaction had been rather negative. Hopefully of late, he'd shown her that he could treat her with respect and even love.

Pushing off from the building, he headed to his truck. Needing to take his mind off his enchanting witch, he went into work, antsy to find out more about the supposed treasure. Jackson was thrilled that his dad and uncle wanted to build a better office for them, but he was happy where he was. However, if Kip's brother-in-law, Sam, came on board in a few months, he'd have to take over Devon's old office. If they needed Connor's brother's help again, they'd be short on space. With the new building, if they needed to add more personnel, they'd be able to.

On the way to town, Jackson stopped at a fast food joint and ordered a chicken sandwich and fries. He figured fueling his grumbling stomach would help him think better.

When he arrived at the office, a light was on. It had to be Connor, though Kip had been known to work late too. Ever since he'd mated with Teagan Pompley, Kip's extra hours had been cut short. Jackson understood why. Kip's own brother had his powers stolen by the fucking Changelings, and then they'd tried to steal Teagan's magic twice. If she were his mate, Jackson wouldn't leave her side either.

As soon as he entered the building, Connor stepped from his office with a cup in his hand and headed for the coffee maker. "I thought you were going to talk with Ainsley."

"I did."

"And?"

He shrugged. "She wants to deliver the ashes with me."

Connor's brows rose. "Being so close to her won't be a problem?"

"We won't go until after the cleansing."

"Won't that be a fun trip?"

"It will be a sad trip," Jackson said. "Remember, I'm delivering my cousin's ashes to his father."

Jackson didn't want to talk about the details. It was the mating process that concerned him. How could he be certain her cleansing had worked? And if it did, would it change her personality? To be honest, he didn't want her to change. Ainsley was bold and aggressive. If anyone had asked him what he wanted in a mate even six months ago, he probably would have said someone who was a bit shy and demure but who had an edgy appearance. He inwardly chuckled. Boy, had he been wrong. Who knew he enjoyed a good challenge?

Connor dropped his gaze. "You're right. I'm sorry. Why are you back here?"

"I'm going to do some more research on that treasure. First though, I'd like your opinion."

"On the map Ainsley found?"

"Yes."

He motioned for Connor to follow him into the office. When they were at Connor's parents' house, Jackson had explained that Ainsley had taken a picture of the map from one of the Changeling's laptops.

Jackson slipped behind his desk, booted up his computer, and then brought up the two overlapping maps.

Connor studied the images. "I see the one red dot on Ainsley's map aligns with yours. What do you think the other dots mean?"

"I have no idea. Our only hope of finding out is to identify the exact location of the well and dig from there."

Connor straightened. "Our dads won't close on the property for another two weeks, so you can't excavate until then."

"I know. I'm here merely trying to take my mind off Ainsley's cleansing and what comes after that."

Connor smiled. "When do I get to meet her?"

"How about joining us at the cleansing?"

"I can't wait."

Chapter Fourteen

AINSLEY WAS NERVOUS. Jackson had explained that she could invite any shifters she wanted to her cleansing ceremony, and naturally, she asked all of Jackson's family. Having Blair there helped, though being in Naliana's presence had her in awe. The goddess might have lived on earth until she was sixty, but she looked beautiful with her long, white flowing hair. Wearing only a yellow gauzy dress, she didn't seem to be affected by the weather at all. Ainsley, however, was freaking cold standing near the lake at night with the cold wind blowing across it.

Because Rye's mate, Izzy, was needed to part the waters, she and Rye were there. Jackson had asked if his two coworkers could also watch, and she'd said yes.

It's time.

Ainsley was going to be cleansed, though the whole concept was still surreal.

She studied the cold looking shimmering lake. Just the thought of jumping into the water made her visibly shiver. It didn't matter that Jackson had explained how at the last cleansing, a witch by the name of Ophelia had somehow heated the lake. How that was even possible, she had no idea. Then again, she didn't understand how she could become invisible either. Some things might always remain a mystery.

James clapped his hands, and Ainsley returned her focus to what was about to happen. Even though it was evening, between her shifter vision and the white moon illuminating the lake, she could see rather well. Everyone looked almost as eager as she was.

"Ophelia," Naliana called. "Please join us."

A very old woman with slumped shoulders appeared out of nowhere. Wearing a long, black dress, she walked up to the lake, not even glancing toward Ainsley. The witch raised her arms then lowered them, pointing toward the water. If Ainsley hadn't been standing there and seen it for herself, she would have never believed steam could rise from the cold lake.

Naliana moved next to Ainsley. "Please remove your clothes then walk in to your waist. Once in position, dive down. When you reach the solid stone bottom, lower your head to the ground and wish away your Changeling ways."

Was she kidding? Hell, if that's all it took, she could have done that herself. *Don't question her.*

While Jackson had told her she'd need to undress, being naked in front of him made her a bit self-conscious. With so many people watching though, she believed her wolf would remain hidden.

Ainsley slipped off her clothes and placed them in a neat pile next to the lake. The only thing she refused to remove was the red-stoned necklace that Shamus had given her. She wouldn't be required to shift, so it would be safe.

"Go on," Naliana prompted.

How hard could this be? Walk in. Dive down. Think cleansing thoughts.

Then why was she so scared? She knew. What if this didn't work? Perhaps she was too damaged to succeed.

Jackson placed a hand on her shoulder. "Go."

Oh, my goddess. She'd been frozen in place. Ainsley nodded and stepped into the lake. Warmth surrounded her, and suddenly, she felt lighter. Trudging through the lake water, she walked about fifteen feet until the water reached her waist.

Here goes.

Holding her breath, she dove in. Only it wasn't like being in an ordinary lake. The water suddenly changed color from blue to a shimmering pink. Her vision sharpened, and it was almost as if she could breathe underwater. Ainsley didn't even struggle for air.

She reached out, and when her fingers touched bottom, it was as if the stone rose to greet her. White light surrounded her and love poured into her. Waves of healing seeped deeply into her soul, and Ainsley never wanted to leave. The beauty of the blues, pinks, yellows, and oranges of the water mesmerized her.

A figure, who looked like Naliana, seemed to appear before her, but the glowing light was so bright that Ainsley couldn't make out her face. Arms reached out toward her. Wanting to be embraced by this wonderful being, she too stretched out her arms.

Then, as if someone had turned off this magical event, the water surrounding her disappeared, and the lack of buoyancy caused her knees to press hard against the surface. She wanted to cry out and shout that she wanted to stay cocooned in this love forever, but she bit back her response. Izzy must have parted the water. Ainsley wished she'd waited a little longer before performing her magic.

"Come on, Ainsley." Strong hands clasped her shoulders and helped her up.

Reality came crashing down on her. Jackson was right in front of her. A second later, he swept her up in his arms and carried her to shore. As soon as he set her down, James handed him a towel.

"Lift your arms, Ainsley," Jackson commanded, as he stepped to the side, blocking the crowd's view of her.

As if someone had tossed a bucket of ice water on her, her senses returned. She did as he asked, and as Jackson wrapped the towel around her, his fingers burned a scorching path of lust on her skin.

He leaned closer then lifted her necklace away from her chest. "It's different."

"Oh, no." She unwrapped her towel and glanced down at the belly ring that had changed too. While she didn't care as much about that, the necklace was precious. Shamus had given it to her. She couldn't be sure, but the red stones appeared lighter. It had to be her imagination though. The lake water was ordinary.

Naliana approached. "How do you feel?"

It took a moment to put the experience into words. "It was amazing. I think I went someplace."

She smiled. "That means it worked." Naliana nodded to her necklace. "If you're wondering, the stones on your necklace and belly ring changed from onyx to pink quartz."

"Why?" She didn't want Shamus's gift altered in any way.

"After you dress, how about you and Jackson join me and James in the cabin? We'll answer your questions then."

All she could do was nod. The cold seeped into her body, and chills raced through her. As quickly as possible she dressed, and then Jackson rubbed her arms to heat her up.

"So you feel different?" he asked.

She inhaled the cold and clear air. "I think so." She explained what happened once she dove down. "I've never felt such unconditional love in my life."

Jackson smiled. "I'm glad."

Kalan came over with Elana, and they exchanged hugs.

"I'm so happy for you," Elana said. "To celebrate, a group of us—Izzy, Teagan, Missy, Rye's sister Chelsea, and I—would like to invite you and Blair to a girl's night out tomorrow evening."

Ainsley looked over at Jackson. "Did you figure out our flight to Scotland?"

"Yes, we leave Friday, just as you suggested."

That was perfect timing. Ainsley didn't have a lot of friends. Now that she was free of her Changeling ways, she wanted to remedy that situation too. "I'd love to."

"Great." Elana placed a hand on Jackson's arm. "I think your brother has something planned for you too."

He grinned. "I'm game."

The others came over to congratulate her, and Jackson introduced her to Kip and Teagan, as well as Izzy and Rye.

"That was some trick with the water," she said to Izzy.

The tall, beautiful redhead smiled. "I couldn't let you stay down there too long."

Would she have drowned? "I appreciate the help."

Jackson wrapped a possessive arm around her waist. "Ainsley and I need to meet with Naliana and James. So if you'll excuse us."

The group said they understood and then dispersed. Jackson had picked her up from her apartment and driven her to the lake. He would be taking them to Naliana and James's house.

He glanced over at her, put his truck in gear, and drove back the way they came. "What are you thinking about?" he asked. "I imagine your mind is going wild right now."

Should she tell him? Because she didn't want to be like her former Changeling family, Ainsley had long ago adopted the view that lying was never good. "You. Us."

He flashed her a smile then quickly sobered. "It's complicated, isn't it?"

Hope flared that he understood. Her wolf was doing the happy dance, but she didn't want to rush into anything. "Totally."

Jackson returned his gaze to the road. After what seemed like a three-minute drive, they arrived at James's home. She wasn't sure if Naliana and James were back at the cabin yet since the inside appeared rather dark.

Jackson opened her door. Crap, she hadn't even noticed he'd gotten out of his side. "Ready?" he asked.

Not really. "I guess. What do you think they want to talk to me about?"

"I'm sure it's good." He reached in and snagged the towel. It belonged to James.

When Jackson knocked on the door, James answered. Those two sure were fast.

"Come in!" James smiled brightly.

JACKSON HOPED THIS conversation with Naliana and James didn't take long. His bear wanted to start their mating process. He'd explained to his wild beast that he wouldn't bite her, that Ainsley needed time. Who was he kidding? So did he.

For the moment, his animal agreed to stand down.

Naliana appeared from the hallway, carrying a plate of cookies. "I baked these for you both."

Really? Naliana only saw James for twenty-four hours every month, yet she spent her time cooking? Or did she possess the talent to nod and have the food just appear? That would be sweet if she had that ability.

Kalan had once told him how Izzy had baked cookies for him that had been laced with some calming spice. Maybe these would do the same for him. He sure as hell needed something to keep his bear at bay.

Jackson placed a hand on Ainsley's back and led her to the settee. Too bad that little maneuver woke up his inner animal again. Damn.

James knelt in front of the fire and tossed in two more logs then looked over at Ainsley. "I bet you're a little chilled from your swim."

"I am, thank you."

She ran a hand over her wet hair, and Jackson itched to use the towel he was carrying to dry it for her. He settled for reaching an arm across her shoulder and rubbing it, trying to give her some of his heat.

Naliana placed the tray of sweets on an ottoman then sat down next to the fire. "I'm sure you have a lot of questions for us."

Ainsley fingered her necklace and seemed off in space, so he asked a question. "I have one. How did the water change the onyx?" It was now pink.

Naliana smiled. "It wasn't the water. I put a spell on it. The necklace, given to Ainsley by her dear friend Shamus, is designed to protect her. Now that she is no longer a Changeling, but rather a member of the bear and wolf Clan, she'll need pink quartz instead."

"That makes sense." The thought had never occurred to him. Ainsley was still staring off into space as if she was trying to come to grips with some kind of loss—perhaps that of the original necklace.

Jackson had one more concern. "Ainsley stated that several of the Changelings could tell that she was one of them. What will happen when they see her again? Will they know she isn't one of them and turn on her?"

He honestly wasn't sure what he wanted the answer to be. If the Council knew she wasn't one of them, it was possible they might leave her alone. On the other hand, they might feel betrayed and try to kill her.

"No," James said. "I asked Naliana to put an extra spell on Ainsley that shields the established Changelings from seeing her new identity."

Ainsley leaned forward. "You're saying that if I meet one of these Changelings, he'll believe I'm still one of them?"

Naliana nodded. "However, I should mention that the mark on the back of your shoulder has now changed. Instead of a circle outlined in black, your new identity has a wolf paw on the left to signify your wolf status and a vine on the right that comes from your Wendayan half."

She sucked in a breath. "That's amazing. In other words, keep it covered when in the presence of a Changeling."

Naliana smiled. "Yes, dear."

These two had thought of everything. They chatted a bit more until Jackson felt they might be intruding on Naliana's time with James. He stood. "Thanks for the towel."

Ainsley stepped over to the couple and hugged them both. Jackson held his breath waiting to see their reaction. He'd never heard of anyone touching either one. When they both smiled and hugged her back, he relaxed.

Once they said their farewells, they left.

Mate, mate!

Jackson tried to ignore him, but it was damn hard. When the time was right, he'd know.

Now, now.

Chapter Fifteen

AINSLEY JUST MIGHT be an even bigger mess now than before the ceremony. Thankfully, any evil thoughts and urges that had once lived inside her were now gone. The whole concept that she might give into the dark side had always loomed over her. Now, she was free—free to meet people and free to love.

Which brought her to Jackson. Her body was vibrating with need, and she had to work hard to keep the blue sparks from randomly escaping. She wished now that she'd questioned her mother more about this sparkly stuff escaping her skin. Sure, in the past when she was excited, there might have been an occasional flare, but she'd never experienced anything like what happened when she kissed Jackson. Hell, she almost glowed blue.

Before she had the chance to calm down emotionally or sexually, they arrived at her apartment. He parked in back of her building then escorted her upstairs.

This is it!

Was she even ready for him to bite her? No. She barely knew him. Her wolf wanted it all, that much she knew—the sex, the mating, the emotional connection—but the human part of her? She wasn't sure. She was scared.

Ainsley unlocked her front door and Jackson followed her in. "You want a drink?" she asked, not knowing the protocol on how to start the seduction. Should she undress and motion him to follow her into the bedroom? Or should she let Jackson take the lead? In the past, she'd been the aggressor because she had to be ready to put a halt to things if the man wanted to take it too fast.

"I could use something to drink," he said. "I have to admit all this cleansing stuff has me a bit off-kilter."

She whipped around and stared at him. "You? Why? I was the one who had to dive into the water."

He chuckled. "We're mates, or rather we're destined to be mates, and I don't want to mess this up."

Relief poured through her, and she almost smiled at the worry skating across his face. "Me too. I have so many questions about what will happen that I need some time to think."

"That's what I'm saying."

Thank goddess they got that worry out of the way. She now could relax a bit. "I'm glad we're in agreement. Let me pour us a drink."

Ainsley headed into the kitchen and was reaching for the glasses when Jackson placed his hands on her waist. Anticipation shot through her.

Take him; fuck him hard, her damn wolf demanded.

"I changed my mind. I can't wait," he said, as he twisted her around to face him, his eyes shimmering an amber-gold. He reached behind her, and when he unclasped her necklace, the heavy metal and stone pendant dropped into his hands. He glanced down and fingered the large stone. "I can't believe these changed. It truly is magic."

He was truly magic. "I know."

After placing Shamus's gift on the counter, he drew her close and leaned over. "It's been so hard to keep my hands off of you. Seeing you naked at the lake, I was so close to shifting." He placed his thumb and forefinger a quarter of an inch apart.

His need to be with her matched her own desires. Before she could tell him, he cupped the back of her head and kissed her. Sparks flew, and her pulse soared. Without the fear of harming anyone, she could finally let loose and just feel. And boy did she feel. Pinpricks of lust darted up and down her body, throwing off blue light every-where. The random sparks kind of freaked her out, and she wondered if she just might combust.

Ainsley wrapped her hands around his waist then slipped her fingers under his flannel shirt. She dragged her palms up his corded back, and the flexing of his muscles sent her hormones into a state of chaos. As amazing as that was, she needed more. Slightly opening her mouth, she ran her tongue along the seam of his lips and demanded entrance. His earthy scent swirled inside her and created havoc with her thoughts. All she could think about was devouring him. All of him. Totally. Fully. Divinely.

Jackson opened his mouth, and the moment their tongues touched, her need exploded. Bones cracked, and she couldn't tell whether the noise was coming from her or from Jackson. His eyes lightened, his teeth sharpened, and his hair sprouted.

He broke the kiss, stepped back, and bumped into the small center island. Fur spun and suddenly a huge bear loomed before her. Ainsley's wolf went crazy. She wanted this bear. Now. Uncontrolla-ble lust swamped every cell, and her vision sharpened as her body transformed into her wolf.

Holy hell. Now what? She looked up at the giant animal. Jack-son's bear lowered his cute snout and sniffed. Her wolf looked up at him and licked his face. He growled, but she wasn't certain what that meant.

Needing some fur-to-fur contact, she walked in between his legs, rubbing up against him. Pinpricks of erotic lust skittered up and down her body. Wanting more room to maneuver, she darted around him and rushed into the living room. He followed.

It might have been out of fear that things had already become out of control, but she cloaked her body with invisibility. Seconds later, Jackson returned to his human form—make that his gloriously naked human form.

Ainsley shifted back too, but remained invisible.

"Where did you go, magic girl?"

Oh, this could be fun. As much as she wanted to make love with him right now, she had to calm down a bit. Rushing into mating with him wouldn't be smart. It didn't matter that she wanted him more than life itself.

As he stepped farther into the living room, presumably to locate her, his huge cock bounced, and Ainsley couldn't take her eyes off it. Jackson was a thick man, packed with muscles. His long legs bulged with thigh and calf muscles, and when he moved, they flexed with power. His upper chest was thick with hair, but his flat belly was spared, save for a sprinkling of hair that led to where she was looking.

She might have been cleansed of her Changeling ways, but that didn't mean Naliana had taken away her challenging spirit. Still invisible, Ainsley moved toward him. Inches from him, she leaned over and swiped a tongue up the length of his cock. Jackson jumped.

"What the hell?"

Ainsley materialized and giggled. At his look of fake outrage, she bent over laughing.

A second later, she was in his arms. "You better not be laughing at my cock."

"Never."

He marched them into her bedroom and tossed her on the bed. Jackson seemed to be trying hard to play the macho man. What she didn't expect was for him to sit on the bed and then drag her across his lap.

The spanking he gave her was thankfully light. "You are not to disappear like that again."

Really? Was he scared? She was about to act all defensive and say he didn't own her, but if they mated, he would be her partner for life. She rolled over so she could watch his face. "Why?"

"I want to know where you are at all times."

His protective nature was showing, and she liked it. She sat up and grinned. "Worried about me?"

"Don't sass me." He tapped her nose.

Now he was being silly. "Whatcha gonna do? Huff and puff and blow my house down?"

One corner of his lips quirked up. "I'm not a wolf."

"Oh, that's right. You're a big bad bear. Are you going to eat me then?"

Now the full grin appeared. "That I'll guarantee." Leaning onto his back, he scooted them onto her unmade bed. "Now, stop stalling," he commanded.

She was procrastinating. Scared how her body was reacting to him, Ainsley had been delaying the inevitable, but she couldn't wait any longer. "You mean you'd rather do this?"

Clutching his head, she brought his lips down to hers. This time, he opened his mouth first, and she welcomed him in. Tasting him had her reeling. Blue sparks shot off her with wild abandon, and it was as if he'd plugged her in. Her lower half was vibrating with an intense need, and if she didn't have his cock soon, she might shift again.

As their tongues delved, plunged, and explored, their teeth sharpened, and she almost cut her tongue on one of her incisors. It was time to change positions. She broke the kiss. "I want more. Would you roll onto your side?"

Jackson had been on top of her, and once he rolled off, she flipped around so that her mouth was directly over his glorious erection. Jackson grabbed her hips, and positioned her opening over his mouth. Before she had the chance to take one lick, he took a hard and fast swipe of her wet slit.

Her bones cracked, and the hair on her head tingled. No, no, no! *Stand down.*

Shifting would ruin everything. Her wolf seemed to understand the consequences and thankfully pulled back, but Ainsley was left with a trail of passion that could only be quenched with his cock. She grabbed his hard shaft and marveled at his size and girth, but because she was slight, she feared it wouldn't fit. Wouldn't that be horrible?

Normally, she'd have been content just to have his dick in her hands, but when Jackson nibbled on her clit, a jolt of pleasure electrified her. Her eyes rolled upward, and she sucked in a lung-filling breath. His earthy scent stimulated every cell in her body, and her inner walls contracted.

He's mine!

Lowering her hand, she drew his hard shaft into her mouth—salty, tangy, and totally yummy. When Jackson slipped two fingers into her slickness, she nearly swallowed him whole.

He grunted. "Be careful."

Ainsley let up on the pressure and gently swirled her tongue around his thickness. He grabbed her ass and squeezed. The faster he flicked his tongue across her opening, the quicker she pumped her fist. Just as his cum tinged her tongue, she found herself on all fours.

"Fuck, condom's in the other room."

This was the man she would be with, hopefully, forever. "I'm on the pill."

She had to be. Ainsley had never had sex without protection, but now things had changed. The first time she made love with Jackson needed to be extra special, and she wanted to ride him bareback.

"Praise every goddess whoever existed."

Jackson leaned over her back, his cock between her legs. Shudders of lust swept over her as he palmed her tits. She had feared he'd find them too small, but from the way he was stroking her nipples and groaning, that thought hadn't even entered his mind.

"What are you waiting for?" she whispered more to herself.

"I don't want this to end."

She never thought Jackson would be that sentimental. Having him stroke her breasts brought unsurpassed joy, but it was her wolf who wanted more—a wolf, who by the way, was demanding satisfaction right now.

Jackson's distracting pinches and rubbings ratcheted her desire to the point where she might have to flip him over and ride him.

Dragging his lips across the back of her neck, the tip of his cock found her entrance. Pulse soaring, she gently pressed back, giving him the *go* signal.

"My bear is screaming for me to take you, but I don't want to hurt you."

She was so wet she honestly believed she could handle him. "You won't."

With his hands on her breasts, he slid into her, but then stopped halfway. Those few inches already had her climax knocking, but they weren't enough. She lowered her head and dropped down onto her elbows. The change of angle allowed him to slide in farther.

"You feel so fucking good. I don't know how long I can last," he panted. "Your scent, your delectable body, and those amazing tits are making my bear want to claw right through me."

She understood. Her wolf was doing the same thing. "Take me then."

Ainsley hadn't meant for her words to come out strangled, but her vision was blurring, and even though they hadn't turned on the light in her bedroom, the colors had intensified. She had to be hallucinating.

He slid his hands to her hips and plunged in. She inwardly howled. Having skin-to-skin contact was better than she could ever imagine. Her inner walls stretched, and the slight pain ignited her even more. Clutching the sheets to help keep her from climaxing too soon, she pressed her hips back, only to be met with a huge thrust. His cock filled her to the hilt, and she could no longer hold that looming climax back. Blue stars shot out from every part of her body and nearly lit up the room.

Jackson grunted with each push, and her moans grew louder and louder, right up to the point where he drove into her one last time and held still. Gulping in mouthfuls of air, her orgasm swept in just as his hot seed filled her. Her nails grew and her incisors lengthened. The euphoria encasing her was even better than what she'd experienced at the bottom of the lake. Filled with total bliss, she was satisfied beyond her wildest dreams.

Even after her climax, her body continued to explode, and her heart was filled with a sensation she couldn't even begin to name.

Elation perhaps? It certainly couldn't be love, though someday it might be.

Jackson lowered his cheek onto her back and wrapped his arms around her waist. "That undoubtedly was the hottest sex I've ever had," he said, taking several breaths to say those words.

All she could do was nod. Still inside her, he rolled them to his side and held her tight. Minutes later, he withdrew and jogged into the bathroom. When he returned with a warm wet towel, he cleaned her up. "I bet you want to shower after being in the lake."

Cleaning up hadn't even crossed her mind. She'd been too preoccupied with needing to make love with him. "Sounds good. My shower stall is small, but would you like to join me?"

"I thought you'd never ask."

This was going to be some adventure. Her shower was tiny, but it would be fun to rub up against him while she tried to scrub him clean. When they stepped into her bathroom, she realized asking him might have been a mistake. He was just too damned big.

"I hope you fit."

He tapped a nipple. "I'll try." She turned on the water and waited for it to warm. "Go ahead and soap up," he said. "Then I'll join you."

She appreciated his thoughtfulness. Her hair was probably spiked every which way from her dunk in the lake. Believing he'd only wait so long, she dipped her head under the warm stream and lathered her hair. Just as she started to rinse, he stepped in. His back was pressed against the far wall and his chest was almost touching her back. Ainsley laughed. "I think I underestimated the space." She spun around to face him.

"It's perfect."

He snatched the bar of soap from the tray and dragged it across one nipple, sending her urges upward once more. How was that possible? She'd just been satisfied more now than she had in her entire life. "That tickles."

"So? I need to wash you, remember?"

"You don't look so clean either." Two could play at this game. She slipped the bar from his fingers, soaped up her hands, and then grabbed his erect dick. "Definitely need to clean this."

When she lowered her head, the water hitting her back sprayed him, so Jackson reached around her and shut off the water. "How about we soap each other up and then rinse?"

She'd do anything to get in more touches. Ainsley would have thought that after the mind-blowing sex, her libido and her wolf would be satisfied—but no! It seemed to be worse. Good goddess, she'd never gone a second round before, but tonight she wanted to.

When Jackson snatched the soap from her hands once more and swiped it between her legs, her need exploded. Suggesting they shower together had been a mistake. His large size and presence was messing with her rational thought.

"I need to finish rinsing my hair." She turned on the shower and leaned her head back.

Another mistake.

He leaned over, and when he drew a nipple into his mouth, pulses of need stimulated every nerve ending. How was this intense reaction possible? Jackson looked up at her and grinned. His eyes shimmered an amber-gold color, flecked with green, and then his teeth sharpened.

"You clean yet?" He lifted her chin and touched his forehead to hers.

"Yes." Ainsley had no idea if she was, but his words held a kind of power over her that she had to say yes.

Once more, he turned off the shower and pushed the door open. As soon as they slipped out of the confining space, he snatched a towel and rubbed her body with the soft terrycloth. At times he was rough, and at other times, he slowly dragged the material over her body until she pulsed blue. Her dripping hair made it difficult for him to keep her dry.

She slipped the second towel off the rack and rubbed her hair. "You need to dry off too," she said as she pulled the towel from her head. Then she twisted him around to face the small sink and mirror.

With his back to her, she took a moment to study his body in detail. And what a fine body it was. She patted his back dry then dropped to her knees. His ass was biteable—so she bit him—lightly of course.

"Hey," he complained. She laughed at his attempt to sound hurt.

Just as she was about to dry his calves, he turned around. "Well, well. Somebody's excited," she said, glancing up at him and grinning.

"It's all your fault."

A second later, she was over his shoulder, being carried back to the bedroom. Blue sparks shot off her body in every direction. If she'd known this was what it was going to be like to find her mate, she might have searched for him sooner.

Chapter Sixteen

THE NIGHT AFTER the most amazing sex he'd ever experienced, Jackson pulled into Rye's driveway. He hadn't expected to see so many cars. In truth, he wasn't sure what the get together was even about, other than to let Elana host a celebration for Ainsley at her house, which required Kalan to relocate.

His future mate had implied that other than Blair, she didn't have many friends, so Jackson was thrilled that the women wanted to welcome her into the Clan.

The whole concept of having a mate still scared him, yet at the same time, it was a balm to his wandering spirit; strange, but true. Ainsley was funny, smart, talented, and beyond tempting.

A few questions remained about this whole mating process, and he hoped Kip, who was also a Wendayan, could answer them. Then again, all that blue stuff might be a Changeling thing. Even Ainsley didn't seem to know much about it.

Jackson slipped from his truck, rapped once on Rye's door then opened it. Laughter sounded as he entered.

Rye looked up and raised his beer bottle. "Here's the guest of honor." He motioned to the cooler next to the coffee table. "Help yourself."

Because of tomorrow's flight to Scotland, Jackson needed to limit his intake. Once he grabbed a drink and opened it, he dropped down onto the lounger next to Kalan and Connor. Rye and Kip sat across from him.

"So?" Connor asked, waving his bottle.

Jackson wasn't sure what he was asking. "So what?"

Connor chugged half of his beer. "How was it?"

It? They'd seen him drive Ainsley home after the cleansing, and knowing shifters, Jackson assumed they were asking if he'd consummated their relationship. Did they really think he would talk about it? "It was fine."

Rye laughed. "Fine? If that's the case, then Ainsley is not your fated mate."

Jackson could see where this was headed. "All right. I give. It was amazing, but kind of scary at the same time."

He swore every one of them leaned forward, their eyes bright. "Did you mate with her?" Kalan asked.

Geez, what were they? A bunch of high school girls? He had to chuckle to himself; the guys were a nosey bunch. Even if he lied, the physical manifestation of their markings would have combined if they'd mated, and these four just might insist on checking out the marking on his shoulder. Then they'd know he wasn't telling the truth. "Not yet."

Kalan sobered. "Did she turn you down, bro?"

"Hell, no." Surely, his brother didn't think that little of him. "We decided it was better to wait. "Did *you* bite Elana the first time you were with her?" He knew the answer to that question was no. He then glanced to Rye and Kip. "How about you two?" They shook their heads, and the tension between his shoulder blades released.

Kip leaned back and sipped his beer. "Did her blue aura envelope you though?"

Jackson sat up straighter. This was one of the things he wanted to learn about. "I'm not sure, but I can tell you there was a shitstorm of blue sparks flying off her. Hell, I thought she might be allergic to me or something." They all laughed. "If you're laughing, you must know what it means, so tell me."

Kip set down his bottle. "Ainsley is part Wendayan." He went on to explain how the blue sparks meant she was excited, and that eventually, there would be so many sparks that it would appear as a blue glow. "When Teagan and I mated, it was incredible. Mind you, we are both pure Wendayan, so it will be different for you, but our blue auras encompassed each other, and a white light connected us. That was when we passed our talents to each other."

Jackson stilled. He'd completely forgotten about their abilities being transferred—albeit to a lesser degree. "Are you saying that if, or rather when, Ainsley and I mate, that I might inherit her talent of invisibility?"

"Invisibility?" they said in unison.

Oh, shit. She'd had no reason to tell anyone. He had to think back to the last time he'd spoken with Connor. After those Changelings had attacked him—and Ainsley had saved his ass—he'd returned to the office the next day, but Connor hadn't been there. The next time he saw his boss was at his parents' house, and his and Connor's fathers had dropped the bomb that they'd purchased the Donaldson property. Ainsley having the ability to disappear at will had slipped his mind. *Be honest.* He was still embarrassed at having a woman come to his rescue.

"I need to start from the beginning." Jackson told them about visiting James and how he'd said if they wanted to find out who killed Shamus, they should find where he was killed. "So we went on a run that night."

"You took Ainsley with you?" Kalan asked, sounding as if he would never have asked Elana to join him on a potentially dangerous mission.

Jackson held up his hand. "Just wait. I thought that too, but James said not to underestimate her talents. At the time, I didn't know what that meant."

He described how he was attacked, and then, all of a sudden, two wolves flew off his body.

"Ainsley did that?" Kip asked.

"Yes. Being invisible has its advantages, but the girl can fight. She tore out their throats once she took them to the ground."

Pride swelled at their wide eyes. "Holy shit," Connor said. "If she is ever open to doing some consulting work, I'd hire her in a heartbeat. We could use someone with her talent."

Jackson bristled, his protective side flaring. If she couldn't be seen, how much danger could she really be in? Regardless, he wasn't sure he wanted her to take the risk. "I'm not sure how long she can remain invisible." That was the truth. He'd never asked her.

Connor nodded. "I'm still interested."

He wasn't ready to talk about it. Besides, it would be up to Ainsley to make that call. Knowing her, however, she'd jump at the chance. The woman seemed to have this inner need to prove herself.

"Back to my story: after the Changelings attacked me, I was disoriented and really weak. I can't even tell you how I made it back to the truck. All I remember is collapsing onto the front seat. I do know I was in human form at that point. I then woke up in my bed in my bear form."

Rye pointed the tip of his bottle at him. "I say mate with her as fast as you can." The whole group smiled and held up their bottles in a show of unity.

When the time was right, he would. Kip had partially explained about her blue glow, but perhaps Rye could add something. After all, he was a shifter and Izzy was a Wendayan. "Rye, when you and Izzy mated, did you bite her and she just glowed blue to indicate the mating process was complete?"

He nodded. "Kind of. Her aura totally encompassed both of us. That was her signal that she was accepting my bite."

"Do you think Ainsley has to both encompass me and bite me? After all, she is part wolf, and part Wendayan."

Rye glanced away. "Let's just say, Izzy now does both."

From the way his Alpha's voice had trailed off, Jackson didn't need to be asking any more questions. That was okay. He now understood what to expect.

Kalan propped his feet onto the coffee table that sat between them all. "Do you know where you'll be staying in Scotland?"

"With Ainsley."

IT WAS AROUND eight p.m. when Ainsley picked Blair up to drive over to the shifter compound to meet with some of the Clan women. Ainsley still couldn't believe that her life had made a one hundred and eighty degree turn in such a short period of time.

"Have you packed for the trip?" Blair asked, interrupting her thoughts.

"Yes, as we leave tomorrow. I only have to pack for two days, but since it might be much colder there than here, I have to wear a lot of layers."

"I'm chilled just thinking about it." Blair pointed to the next street. "Elana lives down that road."

The homes, most of them brick, sat on large lots. Personally, she liked Jackson's log cabin better, but she'd keep that opinion to herself.

Four cars took up the driveway, so Ainsley parked on the street. Excited, she exited the car. Before she could raise her hand to knock on the front door, Elana pulled it open. "Hey, come on in."

There wasn't a reason to be nervous, but she was. Her whole life, Ainsley had stayed away from groups, fearing she'd let something slip. For the first time ever, she had no secrets. After all, beside Blair, Elana, Teagan, and Izzy had been at her cleansing ceremony.

Four women were seated on both of the leather sofas. The two women she hadn't met had to be Missy, Izzy's sister, and Chelsea, Rye's sister. Ainsley could definitely see the family resemblance between Missy and Izzy—both had auburn hair and a creamy complexion. Chelsea was a pretty brunette with bright blue eyes and a turned up nose.

"Have a seat," Elana said.

As soon as she and Blair were seated, Izzy began asking Blair what she did for a living and when she'd returned to Silver Lake. While Blair told them a little about what she'd been up to since high school, Elana stepped into the kitchen then returned with two wine glasses. Several bottles were already on the coffee table. "Help yourselves," she said.

Izzy picked up a tray of oatmeal raisin cookies. "I made these. They're delish, if I do say so myself."

They looked divine, and the first bite of sweetness managed to lower Ainsley's anxiety level. "These are amazing. I'd love your recipe. I bet Jackson could eat the whole batch in one sitting." Not that she'd been with him often enough to know that fact, but she had a feeling he liked his sweets.

"I can guarantee you Kalan can." Elana sat down. "So you and Jackson seemed rather cozy at the lake." Her eyes sparkled with mischief.

He'd carried her from the water and then never left her side. As much as Ainsley didn't want to share the intimate details, she did have questions—questions that only another Wendayan could answer. "We're taking it slow."

She poured a glass of white wine while Blair went with the red.

"Slow is good," Teagan said.

The women snatched more of the cookies. Aw, what the hell. Ainsley just needed to ask about her blue sparks. "Can I pick your brains?"

As if their cookies no longer held any appeal, they all turned toward her. Surprisingly, she was most embarrassed talking in front of Blair. After all, Jackson was her brother. "When, um, Jackson and I *made love*, I had this really strange reaction."

"Did you glow blue?" Izzy asked with a glint in her eyes.

"Yes! And sparks kept shooting off my skin. Is that normal? I mean, when I've had sex before I'd see some random blue sparks, but nothing this intense."

"Totally." Izzy laughed, and then explained that anything blue was a good thing. "Have you mated?"

"No." That comment came out so fast they might not think she intended to. "But soon."

Izzy smiled. "If it's the right time, your blue aura will totally encompass Jackson. Because you are a wolf—like me now—you will also have this intense desire to bite him."

It was a relief to know the details, even though the idea of biting anyone didn't sit well with her. Bites were for killing. "I appreciate the info."

"Any other questions?" Izzy asked.

Three of the women were mated, so one of them should be able to help. "Any pointers for when Jackson and I do mate?"

The three of them looked at each other, probably trying to decide who should talk.

"Since I'm mated to a bear, I'll start," Elana said. "Mind you, I didn't even know bear shifters existed when I first met Kalan; I just thought he was über hot."

Learning about what Jackson's brother was like in bed might be too much information. "I agree he's good looking," but not as attractive as Jackson.

"Thanks. Even before we mated, Kalan had to work hard not to shift whenever he was around me. He was so clumsy that I thought he didn't like me."

"Jackson's not clumsy."

Izzy waved a hand. "No, he's not, but what Elana is trying to say is that if you think the attraction is bad now, wait until you mate. It's ten times worse. You won't be able to last even a few hours without ripping off each other's clothes." Izzy stopped and glanced around. "Too much information, right?"

Everyone nodded. Holy hell. Ainsley was already in need of him, and they hadn't mated. It would be best to divert the conversation away from sex, now that she'd learned the facts of mating. "As you might know, tomorrow Jackson and I are headed to Scotland to return his cousin's ashes. While it will be sad, I'm looking forward to seeing Shamus's father again and showing Jackson a town I know quite well. Any suggestions on how I should handle this kind of situation? I'm not really good with death."

Missy smiled. "That's totally understandable. Just be yourself. Show Jackson that you're there for him. Help him heal, but make sure you take time for yourself too. I imagine it will hit you harder when you're in Scotland. That's where your relationship with Shamus began, so don't be afraid to express what you're feeling. Grieving is a natural and necessary process to healing."

"That's good advice. Thank you." This was going to be harder than she thought.

Teagan lifted her hand. "I agree with Missy, but may I suggest you do something crazy and fun to boost both of your spirits. Keep in mind that the most important thing is being honest about what you are feeling and what you want. If you're unsure or don't want to do something, tell Jackson. If I had been truthful with Kip, our relationship would have been a lot smoother."

Ainsley felt immeasurably better. "I can do crazy and fun. I really appreciate all the advice."

Blair reached out and clasped her hand. "Jackson can be a fun-loving guy, but he's also driven to be the best. When he gets something in his head, he doesn't want to let it go—like that treasure map of his. So just be flexible if his needs become single-minded but don't hesitate to try and redirect him."

His dedication and ambition were two of the things she found most appealing about him. *Okay,* his cute smile, sense of humor, and protective nature, all made for a complete package. She was pretty sure both their needs became single-minded as soon as they were together. Ainsley needed to quit thinking about Jackson because her thoughts were waking up her wolf, and she was yearning to find him for a repeat of last night.

For the next hour, as she sipped her wine, she learned more about these brave, wonderful women. Ainsley even surprised herself at enjoying her time with them—and what a delight that was.

Once she and Jackson returned from Scotland, she was determined to work hard at keeping her new friends close.

Chapter Seventeen

THE FLIGHT OVER to Scotland was long and tiring, but Jackson enjoyed getting to know Ainsley better. Thank goodness their shifter bodies could handle jetlag better than their human counterparts.

There were a ton of topics they couldn't discuss surrounded by a plane full of people, but it was fun to learn everyday things about her—like what she liked to do for fun, what her favorite desserts were, and did her family do anything special on her birthday?

Sadly, the answer to that last question was no. Because both of their birthdays were a week apart in May, he promised they'd do something special next year. When he told her his intention, joy sprang to her eyes.

After they landed and went through customs, they headed to the rental car agency. Unfortunately, he couldn't stop yawning, despite his better physiology. Ainsley on the other hand, looked perky and alert. Jackson hadn't slept a wink on the plane, and losing additional hours due to the time difference made it even worse. As much as he wanted to rest, he had too much to do.

Suck it up, his bear said.

When they finally received the keys, the service representative directed them to their car. Ainsley held out her hand. "I can drive."

"I'm good." The fresh air had suddenly revived him. Unfortunately, as soon as he slipped into the driver's side and started the engine, the weight of the world bore down on him. He was in

Scotland for a daunting task, and not for a vacation or to meet the rest of his family. Delivering a loved-ones remains ranked up there with being attacked by four Changelings at once. Right now, he'd take the attack.

"Do you know the way to my uncle's house?" he asked as he pulled out of the lot.

"Of course. That's assuming none of the roads have changed in the last eight years."

The car had a GPS system, but since he hadn't plugged in the address before getting underway, it wouldn't do him much good now. "How far is it to the town?"

"It's less than an hour to North Dunwick. This is more reason why I should be driving."

Ainsley was probably right, but he needed to feel in control. "It's just past eight a.m. Because it's kind of early to be visiting, do you mind if we get something to eat before we head to Uncle Gordon's?" he asked. "I'm starving."

She smiled, and much of his tiredness evaporated. "Are you hungry as a bear?"

He groaned. "I'm hungry as any healthy male would be after not eating for twelve hours."

"Fine. There's a cute breakfast place in Dunwick that serves really good food. Shamus and I would often meet there after school, and because I lived two towns over, I felt safe from the prying eyes of my family." Her voice trailed off, and he reached over and squeezed her hand. She was clearly in pain.

He hadn't brought up the topic of whether she wanted to let her family know she was nearby, because he wasn't sure of her reaction, but he had to ask. "Do you want to visit your family while you're here?"

Her chin jutted out. "Remember, I told you they never even celebrated my birthday. I didn't grow up with a lot of support or love. So, no, I prefer not to see them. Ever."

He couldn't imagine growing up without love. "How did you

end up so nice?"

She chuckled. "From my dad." She told him some stories about growing up and how he always played with her. "He taught me how to throw a baseball, though I never could hit the damn thing. We played croquet every summer, but then he died when I was eight. I miss him even now."

The strong ache in her voice hurt him deeply. "I'm sorry."

She shrugged. "Thank you. When my mom married Owen's father a few years later, it went downhill from there. Changelings only want sons to help them rule, so I was kind of shoved to the side. It was partially why I spent a lot of time with Shamus."

"Didn't they object? I mean I would have thought they'd believe that Changelings shouldn't mix with us regular shifters."

Ainsley waved a finger. "You're assuming they knew. I was very circumspect and highly resourceful."

He had a feeling there was a lot more to Ainsley Chancellor than she'd let on. "Do you possess other Wendayan powers besides being able to disappear?"

She planted a hand on her chest. "I'm not telling."

He glanced over at her. He would have tried to stare her down, but Jackson didn't want to take his eyes off the road. Between the roundabouts and driving on the opposite side of the road, he needed to stay focused. "We shouldn't have any secrets between us if we're to become mates."

Her shoulders sagged as if that was one of her hot buttons: honesty.

"Fine. I do have another talent that I think I inherited probably from some grandparent on my mom's side."

"What talent is that?'

"I know what kind of shifter a person is."

"Seriously?" He wished he could do that. Hell, maybe he ought to suggest she come to work for McKinnon and Associates. "While I've never met a panther shifter, assuming that kind exists, you could tell if someone was?"

"Yup."

"I'm impressed. That could really come in handy someday."

Ainsley shrugged then pointed to the next street. "Take a left and park wherever you find a space. It comes in really handy if you're a wolf and a bear shifter comes your way."

"True. Not knowing could result in someone's untimely death."

The small town of North Dunwick sat on the North Sea and was incredibly quaint. How cool to think his family came from here. On what he thought could be the main street, the buildings were arranged in one long row, all touching. They varied in height from two to three stories. Given the location of the windows, he guessed apartments took up the top floors. Most of the upper level facades were brick, while the bottom half of the buildings were painted bright colors—many of which were different shades of green. "I love all the dormer windows."

"Wait until you see the homes on the sea. They're so freaking cute."

He loved her enthusiasm. Jackson found a spot and parked. When he stepped out, the air was cold and damp, but after being cooped up on the plane, he welcomed the fresh air. Before he could step over to Ainsley's side and help her out, she exited and moved to the sidewalk.

When he reached her, to his delight, she threaded her arm through his. "Come this way."

She led him to an adorable restaurant called The Bloomin' Bistro. The red awning and ornate molding bordered a large picture window that had the name painted in gold leaf. He held open the door for her and immediately smelled the rich aroma of coffee. His stomach grumbled, and Ainsley smiled. The inside held about ten tables, three of which were occupied, and was cozy as hell. The golfing memorabilia on the walls added an interesting touch. "So this is where you came with Shamus?"

"Yes, but the awning used to be a dark green and the inside held a few booths." From the wistful way she said his name, talking about his cousin might renew her grief.

The waitress who seated them handed them menus. "Can I get you two something to drink?" she asked with a thick Scottish accent that he found wonderful.

Jackson glanced over at Ainsley. "Ladies first."

She shot him a look that said *really?* "Coffee, black."

"Make that two." As soon as their server left, he studied Ainsley. "I know you've been gone a long time, but do you recognize anyone?"

She reached out and took his hand. "No, but don't worry about me. I'll be fine."

"Look, I might have been trying to take your mind off our mission, but I'm not really patronizing you. I want to get to know you better."

She released her grip and looked away. "Sorry. I've been raised to expect people to think the worst of me."

Poor Ainsley. She'd had it rough, but he'd make it a goal to put joy into her life. He picked up the menu and was instantly confused by some of the items. "What's Weetabix?"

She chuckled. "It looks like a granola bar, but it's really just shredded wheat packed together. Let's say it's not my favorite Scottish breakfast item."

"Thanks for the warning."

He was surprised they served baked beans for breakfast, but since he was in Scotland, he wanted to try it all. In the end, he went with the broiled tomato and cheese on top, a rasher of bacon, some kind of potato scone called a *tattie*, and an egg. Did the Scots really think a large man would be happy with only one egg?

As he waited for his meal to arrive, he studied the patrons around him. He loved how many of the men wore beards. Most had hair color that ranged from bright red to dark auburn. "How come no one is wearing a kilt?"

"It's cold out." She was probably making that up.

"Was your dad fair haired?" he asked.

She giggled. "Didn't ya look between me legs?" Ainsley poured on a thick Scottish accent that he found charming.

"Ah, yes. Dark brown it is." Her skin was light like the Scots, however. "So tell me what my uncle is like."

"You've never met him? Didn't you say Shamus came to the States for a visit?"

"When I was eight, yes, but I really didn't pay much attention to him at the time."

"I see. Well, Gordon MacLeod is a highly principled man."

"I know he works at a University." Jackson should have taken the time to find out more about his overseas relatives, but when he'd approached his mom about them this week, she'd just cried.

"Unless he's changed careers, he's a math professor at the University of Edinburgh."

That was impressive. "I can't imagine what he's going through now. First he loses his mate and now his son."

"It's very sad, but he won't show his grief around you. He's that kind of man."

Now Jackson wished they'd had the time to stay longer so he could get to know more of his family members. Maybe someday.

Their coffees arrived, followed by their food, and they both dug in. "This tastes amazing." He probably should have tempered his surprise.

She smiled. "It is good to be eating Scottish food again. I didn't realize how much I missed it."

For the next few minutes, they ate in silence. Because Ainsley knew Uncle Gordon quite well, she had volunteered to contact him and let him know they would be bringing his son's ashes. "What time does Uncle Gordon expect us?" Jackson asked.

"He said to come anytime. He knows when our plane arrived. We can't check into the hotel until the afternoon, so we should head on over there once we finish eating."

Jackson wiped his lips with his napkin, finally feeling full. "Sounds like a plan."

Once he paid the bill, he escorted Ainsley out. Despite breakfast being delicious, his gut was churning. Most likely it was because he wasn't looking forward to handing a man his son's remains and seeing the pain of losing his only child on his uncle's face. Jackson wasn't one to handle a lot of emotion very well.

She held out her palm. "I'll drive. The way can be a bit tricky."

Digging his hand in his pocket, he located the key and handed it to her, happy to give up the harrowing chore of navigating these streets. "Be careful."

She winked. "Always."

The trip to Uncle Gordon's house took less than ten minutes. He lived in one of the row houses that faced the water. Ainsley was right. They were damned cute.

While having a beach in the front yard was peaceful to look at, Jackson couldn't imagine the water ever being warm enough to swim in—unless he was in his bear form.

Once she parked, he reached for the box that contained Shamus's ashes. They discussed buying an urn, but she thought his dad might like to pick one out himself—one that spoke to him. She faced Jackson. "Ready?"

"As I'll ever be."

AINSLEY WAS TORN. As wonderful as it had been to reconnect with Shamus's father—the man who provided so much guidance to her growing up, it was also very sad. Much of their three hours together involved Jackson's uncle talking about his son and how much Shamus wanted to start his own investment firm. The man's love for his son was heartwarming, and it made Ainsley want to kill every Changeling in Silver Lake.

I'm not one of them anymore. I can't think like that.

After meeting Jackson and being cleansed, Ainsley wanted to live in peace and pretend Changelings didn't exist.

Good luck with that.

Once Gordon finished reminiscing, he caught up on his nephew's life. Jackson filled him in on McKinnon and Associates and then on what Kalan and Blair were doing.

About the only thing that had made Shamus's dad smile was when she explained that Naliana had shown up and cleansed Ainsley of her Changeling ways. Gordon hugged her and told her Shamus would have been so pleased. She nearly cried.

As much as she wanted to stay and rehash all of Shamus's antics growing up, Gordon MacLeod needed time to grieve too.

"When are you flying out?" Gordon asked. The desperation in his tone was hard to swallow.

"Early Monday morning. I just started my job and couldn't take off much time, and Jackson has cases to solve."

"I understand."

With watery eyes, Ainsley hugged him goodbye—as did Jackson. After they left his uncle's house, he was rather quiet. "What did you think of your uncle?" she asked. It was possible, his mom had told him stories about her sister's mate and had built up the man in the young boy's head.

"You were right. He's a wonderful and honorable man. It tears me up to see him suffer like that."

"Me too. Me too." She had to look away or fear breaking down. Being depressed when Jackson was trying to cope wouldn't help anyone, so she decided to take the advice of the girls and do something kind of wacky and out of character to cheer him up—and cheer herself up too. "I know of something that might boost your spirits."

He wrapped an arm around her waist. "What's that?"

"I'm not telling. You'll just have to trust me." They hopped in their rental, and Ainsley returned to High Point Road where most of the businesses were located. She wasn't sure he'd go along with her crazy scheme, but she had to try. When she reached Studio IV on the north end of town, she parked in front of the entrance.

Jackson studied the storefront window. "Wait a minute. I'm *not* getting a tattoo. The one on my upper back is enough."

"That's not a tattoo. You were born with the circle with the bear paw print inside." He looked off to the side. "Besides, I wasn't going to suggest you get one."

He returned his gaze to her with raised brows. "You're getting one instead? Is that why we're here?" He smiled. "How about having the artist ink my name right below your belly button?"

She just shook her head. "I was going to suggest you get a gold stud earring. It'll give you that bad boy look."

He furrowed his brows and pressed his lips together. He then lifted his chin and struck what he probably considered was a Hollywood pose. "You don't like my look?"

Ainsley laughed and lightly punched him. "You know better than to ask, but you do seem a bit uptight. I thought you could use some loosening up."

"Really? You think I'm straight-laced?" He waved a hand. "When I'm on a case, I admit I'm focused, but not when I'm home or out having a good time."

"I'll have to take your word for it." However, it wouldn't do any harm to let him think he needed to be more carefree. "I bet there are times when you work too much and don't relax."

He focused his gaze on her. "You're right. What the hell. I say, let's do it!"

She hadn't expected him to give in so easily, but she was stoked. Ainsley could envision Shamus looking down at her and smiling.

They entered the tattoo and piercing parlor where she immediately spotted some really cool drawings of dragons. She'd love to have one of them tattooed on her arm, or maybe her back, but she didn't want to do anything that would create a tender spot. She had some hard loving to do tonight.

Jackson followed her over to the cabinet that contained earrings, and together they picked out a small gold stud. Ainsley had to admit he was being a good sport. Most men would have balked by now, but Jackson seemed to want to do this for her.

Once he chose the earring, Emily, the piercing artist, led him over to a chair. With precision, she cleaned and marked the area, and then pierced it. "All done," she announced.

"Let me see." Ainsley was excited to see his new look. When Jackson turned his head, the added touch of gold suited him. "Definitely more macho."

He wagged a finger at her. "I don't need an earring to look macho."

"I couldn't agree more."

"Then why suggest the new addition?" he asked.

She told him the truth. "Because it was something fun to do."

Jackson lowered his chin and seemed to think about her comment. "You're right. This might be the first thing we've done together that didn't involve… shall we say research."

He must be implying learning about who'd killed his cousin.

Emily explained how to clean the stud, and how long he needed to keep it in before moving onto a bigger earring.

"I'm good with this for now," he said.

Ainsley insisted on paying since she'd pressured him into getting the adornment. When they exited the shop, the cold winds had died down, and the sun was out. "You up for a walk?"

"Absolutely. Gotta show the Scots what a real man looks like."

She cracked up. "What have I created? I thought about getting you a leather jacket to complete the look, but I'm not sure I could handle your ego."

He winked. "Careful what you wish for."

"Ain't that the truth?" She pointed to the northeast, toward the town's icon, though the buildings blocked the view. "On the other side of the buildings are some castle ruins that I thought you might enjoy exploring. They overlook the water and are a huge part of our history."

"Fantastic." Several blocks later, they passed the last of the shops and the castle came into view.

"Wow, is that it?" Jackson asked.

"Yup. That's Panillor Castle. It was built in the mid 14th-century as a fortress and was one of the last curtain wall castles to be constructed. You can see how the cliffs protect the other three sides, making it the perfect spot to defend Scotland."

"If I lived back then, I'd feel safe here if enemy ships came in by the sea. Who owns it now?"

"The Historic Society of Scotland. Supposedly, the castle was handed down from one generation to the next, but when it was severely damaged in the late 1600s, it was sold to the Marquis of Perth. When he died, it became the property of Scotland."

"It makes me realize just how young America is. We have our forts, but nothing as grand as this structure."

As they neared the North Sea, the wind picked up, forcing Ainsley to pull her coat tighter. It didn't bother her as much as it had in the past because doing something with Jackson made any discomfort worthwhile.

A long stairway led to the entrance of the castle. Because the stone had crumbled in many places, a state-of-the-art metal railing had been installed to reinforce the sides. From the outside, the castle looked rather intact, but once they stepped inside, the extensive decay became evident. The ceiling had long since fallen, and most of the parapets on top of the walls had been destroyed.

Jackson walked over to a roped off area and looked down the several stories. "It's too big to be a well. What was this used for?"

"I'm not sure. I always figured the floors were missing."

"Is there a way down there?"

"Seriously? It's got to be crawling with rodents."

"I don't believe for one second that Ainsley Chancellor is afraid of a few rats."

"Make that sharp-toothed, disease ridden rats."

Jackson laughed, a sound that warmed her heart. Wrapping an arm around her waist, he led her away from the precipice and guided her over to one of the openings that were used to shoot arrows from and later, cannonballs.

"The view is fantastic. I can see for miles," he said with true awe in his voice. "I can see why they'd build a fort here. My enemies wouldn't stand a chance."

"It's quite marvelous." She had visited a few times with Shamus. Perhaps right now, he was looking down at her from above. Hell, knowing him, he'd found Naliana and had charmed her into giving him a front row seat. If Ainsley ever saw her again, maybe she'd ask.

"What are you thinking about?" Jackson asked.

Tell him. They shouldn't have any secrets. "I was thinking about Shamus and where his soul is right now."

Jackson glanced upward. "I'd like to think he's right here with us."

Those few words were just what she needed to hear. Without thinking, she faced Jackson and wrapped her arms around his neck. "I like being with you, Jackson Murdoch."

As if they were the only two people in the whole world, she blocked out the sound of the wind whipping across the sea and the seagulls squawking overhead, and kissed him. His response was so immediate that the instant connection and passion transported her back in time, to a place where Changelings didn't exist and the only worry was where to find food.

As their tongues entwined, several school children giggled on the landing area below. While the contact escalated her need, she didn't want to make a scene. The last thing she wanted was for her presence to somehow reach her family, so she broke the kiss. "I feel exposed out here."

"Oh, yeah? I know of a more secluded space," he said, his mouth an inch from hers.

She grinned. "Why Mr. Murdoch. Are you suggesting we head to the hotel?" *Please say yes.*

She was about to ask if all he thought about was sex, but then realized she wanted him just as much. The timing was right for them to mate. She and Jackson belonged together forever.

"I most certainly am."

Chapter Eighteen

ONCE THEY CHECKED into the quaint Dunwick Hotel, they took the tiniest elevator known to mankind up to the third floor. Their room didn't have a swipe card, but rather was an old fashioned skeleton key.

"Is most of Scotland still in the Middle Ages?" Jackson asked. From the way he was trying to hide his smile, he was pulling her leg, but she'd go along.

"Absolutely. We'll have to ask the porter to bring up buckets of hot water if we want to wash." The sheer horror on his face had her cracking up. "You are the most gullible man I know."

"Me? This place is old. Hell, the elevator shook so much, I feared we'd plummet to our death. Even you have to admit that not having key cards is a little backward."

"True." She pushed open the door to their room and was surprised by its spacious size. The fact it had a king-sized bed instead of one queen was a real plus.

Jackson followed her in, carrying both suitcases. "A flat screen TV? I didn't expect that."

"Me either." She hoped he wanted to do other things than spend the evening watching the tube. "I'm a little grungy from the flight. Mind if I shower first?"

He stepped closer. "Can two fit?"

"Let's check it out," she said. He placed their suitcases next to the bed then followed her into the bathroom. "The shower's tiny."

"You're right. It's definitely built for one."

While the sink was pedestal style and the toilet appeared to be modern, the shower stall was even smaller than what she had at home. "We should be thankful we have a private shower," she said.

"Really?"

"The sad truth is that in many small town hotels or B&Bs in Great Britain, guests often have to share a bathroom."

"Then I'll be thankful for what we have." Jackson stepped closer. "Do you need help undressing?" He dragged a finger down the front of her jacket.

If she said yes, she might never get to wash. "You can help if you're good."

He grinned. "I'm always good."

Ainsley didn't believe him. After kicking off her boots, she unzipped her jacket and placed it on the closed toilet seat. She then lifted her sweater off while Jackson worked on removing her pants. Between the two of them, she was naked in no time. "Thank you. Now if you'll excuse me."

He shook his head. "Not going to happen. My bear is ready to be released."

Her jaw dropped. "Under no circumstance are you to shift. Scotland isn't ready for that." It didn't matter they were in the privacy of their room.

As if he hadn't heard a word she said, he kicked off his boots then stepped out of his pants. "Don't worry about me. I'm just getting ready. Turn on the water."

She didn't believe he'd be noble and merely watch. Jackson didn't appear able to keep his distance, especially since both of them were naked in the small space. In case he could control his urges, she did as he suggested.

Once she scooped up the hotel's liquid soap container, she opened the glass shower door and stepped in, half expecting Jackson to pull her into a hug and kiss her silly. But he didn't. Instead, he leaned against the sink with his arms crossed over his chest and kept his gaze on her.

She might have considered objecting to his controlled behavior, but she hadn't slept in forever and was struggling to stay on her feet. Hopefully, the hot water would revive her.

Keeping an eye on him, she let the warmth soak into her skin while she readied to wash. Because her hair was clean, she made short work of the chore.

Jackson remained still, watching her. Where was the man who couldn't keep his hands off her? She hoped he wasn't having second thoughts about them mating. Or did he want to wait until they returned home? That would suck. She wanted him now, and she saw no reason not to mate with him.

As soon as she stepped from the shower, it was as if his bear came out of hibernation. His lids lowered, and he pushed off from the sink. When he ran a finger over her wet nipple, waves of lust shot straight to her core, and her body pulsed blue. "You're wet," he announced.

"I am." Ainsley grabbed a towel from the rack and handed it to him. "Want to help dry me?"

"Careful what you ask for. I might do more than dry you."

That would be fine by her. With care, he rubbed her tits with the soft towel, and each swipe had her pulsating with need. Navy sparks rippled up and down her body, surprising her in their brightness. "You can go faster," she pleaded.

That way they'd make it to the bed sooner. Inhaling his fresh scent had totally messed with her libido. Ainsley had no doubts that she was out of her comfort zone here. Sex never held that much appeal, but the moment she'd met Jackson, she couldn't help dwelling on being with him in the most intimate way—all the time.

"I'm in charge here, so I'll go as fast or as slow as I please, missy."

"If you're trying to turn me on, don't waste your time. I'm ready."

He stopped drying her and leaned closer. "This isn't a race; it's a slow seduction—assuming I can wait that long. Rest assured I want you right now, but this is a special night, and I want us to enjoy it to the fullest. Who knows when we'll return here?"

"I like romance as much as the next, but I suck at expressing my feelings. You're so good at it."

He smiled. "You're pulling the Changeling card on me?" He held up a hand. "Don't answer. That's all the more reason why I need to take my time. Someone needs to show you what loving is all about."

She inwardly groaned, and as hard as it was to say nothing and not move, she remained still. Finally, he finished drying her breasts and stomach. If he'd been content to finish the job by drying her back, she might have lasted, but when he dragged the towel between her legs, she lost it. Her bones cracked and her teeth sharpened.

Don't shift.

Needing some control, Ainsley grabbed his hard shaft and directed him out of the bathroom. How she thought that would help reduce her desires, she didn't know. She stared at the dark floral pattern on the floor to help stop her shift from happening.

"What are you doing?" he asked. Jackson didn't sound too concerned, nor did he swat away her hand.

"Clearly, someone who wants to get laid needs to be in charge."

"Is that so?" As if she'd lit his fire, he lifted her up and tossed her onto the bed then shook a finger at her. "Don't ever think I don't want to be with you. I'm working hard just to stay in human form."

"So am I." She grabbed his cock again, needing the connection. "Stay right here while I tempt you."

"Merely looking at you tempts me. Your smell tempts me. Your luscious—"

"Okay, okay." He wasn't making this any easier.

She sat on the edge of the bed, leaned over, and dragged her tongue up the length of his cock. He groaned and grabbed her shoulder. When she glanced upward, his brows rose as if he couldn't believe she'd just done that. Hell, after a few swipes, he'd be so close to the edge that he'd have to impale her.

The mere thought of him driving his cock into her and then biting her, made her body heat and her inner walls spasm with intense need. Returning to his glorious length, she flicked her tongue across the tip of his cock, and his hard shaft twitched. This was fun, but it was also testing her resolve. If only she could pretend to be indifferent, she could really make him squirm. Too bad, every part of her was radiating blue.

She grabbed the base of his cock and pumped her fist. He sucked in a breath, and his sharpened nails dug into her skin. When she looked up once more, his eyes were closed. As she lifted her hand once more, he grunted. Victory was near!

Wanting to taste him, she sucked on his cock hard. Two seconds later, a huge blast of cum shot out of him. Holy crap! She could barely swallow fast enough to keep up with the flow. When he finished exploding, she leaned back on her elbows. "I can't believe you came."

His hands straddling her on the bed, he leaned close. "What did you expect? I've been with you for close to a full day, touching, rubbing, and smelling your delicious scent. I've seen your kindness and your considerate actions, despite you trying to play tough with me. Well, news flash. I might be a shifter, but I'm also a man. I couldn't take the temptation any longer."

She glanced down at his dick and was delighted that it hadn't deflated at all. "I trust you are up for more?" She wanted him so badly.

"I can go all night long, my invisible witch." He slid a hand under her legs and lifted her more fully onto the bed. Like an animal hunting its prey, he crawled on top of her. "I want to see how long you last."

"I'll admit I'm weak around you. I give myself maybe fifteen seconds, so if you want to go straight to the final episode, I'm good with that."

He grinned and then nabbed her earlobe. "That so? Well, I'm not. Now that I'm partially defused, I can last a lot longer."

Oh, shit.

His mere touch made her want to do all sorts of nasty things with him, but first, she wanted to sink her teeth into his neck and be transported to paradise.

Wait a minute. Did I really think that?

Clearly, Jackson had robbed her of all thought. His nibbling on her ear, coupled with his palm caressing her breast, was almost too much to handle. She spread her legs wide, hoping he'd get the hint, but he seemed content to kiss her and then drag kisses down her neck.

"I can't get enough of your scent," he said.

Even better to drive him to the brink with. Too bad there wasn't a pump attached to her body like on a spray can of perfume that would send her scent straight into him.

Nabbing his earlobe, she then wrapped her arms around his waist and drew him close. When his hard chest pressed against her breasts, she nearly combusted, and she had to force herself to stay strong. How was it possible that she was seconds from climaxing, yet they'd barely begun?

As if he could read her mind—or else he could tell how excited she was from her blue glow—Jackson lowered his lips and kissed her with such urgency that she couldn't take it any longer. Ainsley wrapped her legs around his waist and lifted her hips, begging for his cock.

With their tongues plunging to some imaginary beat, her aura grew and grew. "Please, Jackson."

"Please what?"

He knew. "I want you."

His grin exposed his sharp teeth, and her body nearly detonated. "Then you shall have me."

Her heart pounded at this monumental step. Her whole life, she'd adjusted to the idea that she'd be alone. Then Shamus came to town, and she'd met Jackson. Now, they would join and become mates for life.

Tears welled on her eyes. As if he understood what she was experiencing, he swiped away the brimming tears. "Let me love you," he said in the softest, sweetest tone.

"Please."

Cupping her face, he kissed her gently at first, and then with more urgency. When she lowered her feet to the mattress, he aimed his cock at her entrance and plunged in.

Holy Hades. Fire scorched her insides and a feral urge to mate encompassed her. The room glowed blue as he stretched her wide. Ainsley grabbed his shoulders and hung on for dear life, her nails growing and her teeth sharpening.

Not only did her body seem to be altering from the inside, her emotions were running out of control. It might have been from the lack of sleep, being in a town that held wonder as well as disappointment, or perhaps, it was the process of mating, but she was totally overwhelmed with passion.

Love, love, mate, mate.

Where had that thought come from?

Jackson broke the kiss and lowered his face to her neck. Her pulse soared. Surrounded by the most intense sexual haze ever, she pressed on her heels and lifted her hips to meet each thrust.

He drove into her, and Ainsley could almost feel the union form between them. Desire flowed. Nails sharp, she dragged them down his back, scraping his skin. She opened her mouth to draw in more air.

"I need you, Ainsley."

He needed her? No one had ever said that to her before. On the next thrust, it was as if some kind of a magnet drew her to his neck. As she bit him, her blue aura encased both of them, and when his incisors sank into her neck, emotion swamped her completely. Her climax claimed her so hard that she visibly shook—or else it was because Jackson's cock had exploded again.

Her vision swam, and her senses heightened. Seconds passed before she remembered to breathe.

"Are you okay?" he asked.

Her lips wobbled, but she managed to smile. "I'm more than okay."

Jackson smiled at her as they lay there letting their heart rates return to normal. Leaning over, he ran his finger down her cheek and then kissed her sweetly before slipping out of bed and heading to the bathroom. Something about the marking on the back of his shoulder seemed different. When he returned with a cloth to clean her up, she motioned for him to turn around.

When he did, joy spread through her. "Well, I'll be damned."

"What?" he asked then turned back to face her.

"The marking on your back changed. You now have a Wendayan vine underneath your bear paw print." She was thrilled at the physical manifestation of their mating. "It really happened!"

"For real?" He grinned. "Let me see yours."

She twisted around. "Holy crap. Instead of the wolf print on one side and the vine on the other, yours have combined. The vine is under the wolf paw too."

Ainsley rolled onto her back and raised her arms. "I think that calls for another celebration."

"You, my mate, may be the death of me. But trust me, I'll love every minute of it."

Chapter Nineteen

FLYING BACK TO the States had been pure torture. If Jackson thought delivering ashes to Uncle Gordon had been hard, sitting next to his mate and not touching her had taken every ounce of his control.

To keep his mind off his need, he focused on what came next—getting Ainsley to move in with him. No way would he agree to live in her insanely small apartment. Not only was the location unsecure, the shower alone would have been enough to dissuade him. The shifter compound could better protect her from any Changeling attack. As much as he wanted to discuss a lot of things with her on the plane, he had to be content to wait until they landed.

Making the trip over one weekend had been crazy, but Ainsley was dedicated to her job. She'd explained that a few patients were in serious need of her treatments, so he couldn't fault her for wanting to be there for them. He also wanted to return to his work.

When they finally stepped foot on US soil, he was exhausted but happy to be home. It was early afternoon, and Jackson was eager to convince Ainsley to move in with him. If she balked, he'd have to use some persuasive tactics. At least, he'd look forward to that.

Once they settled into his car, he maneuvered out of the airport. "Do you feel any different after mating?" he asked.

"I'm not sure, but I can say I'm hornier that I was before." She reached over and squeezed his leg. That was the last thing he needed—intimate touches from her.

"That makes two of us, which brings up my next topic. Now that we're mated, I'd like you to move in with me." Her shoulders stiffened, and he could physically feel her angst. *What is it?* he telepathed.

She whipped around toward him and smiled. *I heard you!*

When her voice came in loud and clear, his damn pulse soared. "We're mates, but I'm sensing a resistance to the idea of you moving in with me. Why is that?"

She looked out the car's side window. "Are we ready for that?"

"I am." Hell, even if he wasn't, he didn't want to spend another minute away from her. "But we can take it slow if you want."

Please say no, that you can't live without me.

She smiled. "I heard that."

"Good."

He hoped that once she thought about it, Ainsley would see the wisdom of his suggestion.

"I just need a few days," she said, her voice soft and rather distant. She twisted toward him. "Don't get me wrong. My body is climbing the walls right now to be with you. Hell, my hair is tingling, my teeth are about to show, and my wolf is crying for me to say yes."

"Then why don't you?" He honestly didn't understand.

"I don't want to get my hopes up."

He glanced over at her. "Do you think I'd leave you? I won't, I promise."

"I know. I can't explain it."

Pushing her wouldn't serve either of them. Poor Ainsley had gone through so much already. Not only did she move to a new town and start a new job, she'd finally reconnected with her old friend only for him to be murdered. Add in finding a mate and being cleansed on top of that, and he was surprised she hadn't had a break down.

When they arrived at her place, he seemed to have developed amnesia about all the stress she'd recently experienced since he wasn't ready to be apart. With the engine in neutral, he twisted toward her. "How about you spending the night with me? Or maybe a few days to see if I drive you crazy?"

Her brows rose. "How do you know I won't drive *you* crazy."

"Never. Come on. What do you say? I'll be at work much of the time, and you have your job, but it'll be easier to learn about each other if we're sharing the same space. You tell me about your day, and I'll tell you about mine."

Jackson was at a loss about what else to add. He'd never asked a woman to move in with him before.

She blew out a breath then grabbed her stomach. "I want to so much, but I'm scared. I can tell you if I say no, my wolf will claw me to death from the inside. So yes!" She grinned. "How about I shower, pack for a few days, and then drive over to your place? We can take it day by day."

He liked that she was willing to find a win-win solution. "Sounds like a plan."

After turning off the ignition, he slipped out the driver's side and retrieved her luggage from the back.

She reached out to take it from him. "I got it," she said.

From the determined way she said it, Ainsley was still waffling about giving up some of her independence. Deciding it was best to give in this time, he handed her the light case. "See you soon?"

She nodded and headed toward the door.

Follow her, his bear demanded.

Dammit, no. As much as he wanted to run after her, Jackson needed to give Ainsley some space. She would come.

Once the light in her apartment clicked on, he headed home. When he entered his front door, he glanced around to make sure he'd picked up before he left. She had mentioned she liked all the wood in the house, but he had to admit the furniture was a bit masculine. Giving up the brown leather sofa and chairs would be hard, but if she wanted her yellow sofa and lime green chairs, he could compromise.

Because Ainsley would be there soon, he straightened up then headed into the shower. Just as he finished drying off, his cell rang. Wrapping a towel around his waist, he rushed down the hall to answer it, having left his phone on the dining room table. He hoped it wasn't Ainsley saying she'd changed her mind.

It was Connor. "Hey," he answered.

"Wanted to see if you landed safely."

"We did." He gave him the quick rundown of delivering the remains to his uncle and then how awesome it had been to tour the castle ruins. Because Connor would find out soon enough, he told him that he and Ainsley had mated.

"Hey, that's fantastic. Are you with her now?"

If she had been, Jackson would be making love with her, not talking on the phone. "She's cleaning up and will be over shortly."

"Great. I won't keep you, but I wanted to let you know that our fathers convinced Mr. Donaldson to let them start work on the property before the closing date."

He whistled. "Holy crap. When our folks want something, they sure go after it."

"You got that right. Once an Alpha, always an Alpha," Connor added.

How true. His dad still tried to tell Kalan how to do things with regard to the Clan. "Knowing them, they offered Donaldson an added incentive."

Connor chuckled. "My thoughts exactly. Are you coming into work tomorrow?"

Why wouldn't he? "Absolutely. I can't wait to get started."

"Good. We can go over your plan to find the treasure."

"That would be great."

As soon as he disconnected, his senses heightened. Ainsley was here. She must have rushed over! Jackson debated dashing back into the bedroom and changing, but he was curious what she'd do when she saw him in a towel. Knowing her, she'd pulse blue. That worked for him. It would save him the hassle of undressing.

Before she had the chance to knock, he opened the door and winter air rushed in. He was so riveted on seeing her rush up the driveway that the cold didn't even register at first.

As soon as she was close, he reached for her suitcase. "Come in."

"Do you meet all your guests in a towel?" she asked, fighting a smile. The second her gaze dropped to his erection, his willpower shattered.

Mate, mate.

Goddess help him. His need truly was more intense after mating. The lust, the demanding need, and the powerful throbbing in his groin forced him to focus on one thing—Ainsley.

She asked me a question.

"No. Never. I showered, and just as I was about to dress, Connor called."

"Everything okay?" she asked. Stepping past him, blue sparks jumped off her.

"Yes. He was just checking to see if we'd arrived home safely."

"That's nice of him. Mind if I get a glass of water? I meant to when I was home, but forgot."

Forgot, hell. Ten bucks said her wolf's yearnings had taken over her brain. "I'll get you one. Have a seat." He set her case by the door, and as he turned around to head to the kitchen, she yanked off his towel. "What the—"

Her laughter stopped him short. "Gotcha!"

What a feisty woman. If she was going to play that game, he would indulge in her luscious body right now. The moment he turned around and drank her in, his teeth and nails instantly sharpened. Controlling his bear now that they'd mated seemed to take a lot more work.

"You're asking for it," he said as he came near. Just as he reached out to draw her near, she disappeared. "Oh, no you don't."

Ainsley was still there. He just couldn't see her. Slowly, he waved his hands in the air, not wanting to hurt her if she hadn't moved.

"I'm behind you," she telepathed.

He swung around and there she was. Not giving any thought to his next move, he rushed her. When she remained visible, he snatched her up before she pulled that stunt on him again. Three steps later, her butt hit the kitchen counter.

"You aren't getting away from me this time," he said.

"I don't want to." She threaded her arms around his neck.

"Smart ass." An hour ago, she was tentative, but now she was a little minx. Would it always be like this? He hoped so.

Kiss her.

And kiss her he did. The moment their lips touched, his bear scraped and clawed at his insides. Devouring her mouth, he fumbled to unbutton and then unzip her jeans. With her wearing boots, he'd never get her undressed fast enough. With each passing second, his desperation grew—as did his need to shift.

He stepped back. "Help me get you naked."

"I thought you'd never ask."

Once she kicked off her footwear, she worked to remove the several layers above her waist while he divested her of her jeans and then her panties. With two quick flicks of her hands, she tossed off her socks.

Now naked, he returned her to the counter and then shoved aside the toaster and coffee maker. "Lean back," he demanded, his breathing way too ragged.

Not able to wait any longer before tasting her, he lifted her legs over his shoulders and prepared for a feast. The first swipe of his tongue brought him some relief, but it was like a drug—one that made him want more. A few additional licks gave him his reward— her glorious blue glow pulsing and shimmering. He loved the Wendayan expression of excitement.

Even without the telltale signs, he'd have known. Her fingers were clenched, and her teeth had sharpened. When he nabbed her little pearl and flicked his tongue across her sensitive nub, she wiggled and sucked in an audible breath.

"Damn you. Take me before I shift," she growled.

"You don't have to ask twice." Jackson slipped her to the edge of the counter. "Wrap your legs around my waist and hold on."

As she positioned herself, he placed his hard dick at her entrance. When she hugged his neck and leaned forward, his cock slipped into her wetness and his teeth extended. If he thought he was excited in Scotland, he was more so now. Her blue pulses jacked up his hormones to a new height.

Between her lavender scent, her bare breasts, and those divine lips that could kiss like a goddess, he lost it. With one arm around her back and the other supporting her butt, he withdrew then plunged into her again.

"I can't get enough of you," he telepathed. If he'd had enough oxygen in his brain, he might have been able to say the words out loud.

Ainsley kissed him, plunging her tongue into his mouth. The sweeping motion made his bear roar. Squeezing her legs tightly around him, she lifted up and dropped down, all the while encasing him in her blue cocoon.

Take her completely demanded his pushy bear.

Breaking the kiss, he slid his lips to her neck and drove his cock into her hard over and over again. His mate met him thrust for thrust. When Ainsley's sharp canines touched his neck, he couldn't control his climax any longer. Just as he dug his teeth into her, his hot seed exploded. Ainsley bit down on his neck at the same time, and his body shuddered with the full force of a tsunami.

Her orgasmic scream followed and was coupled with her inner walls clamping down on him, holding him tight. Both of their hearts beat with the fury of a wild storm, and he never wanted to let her go.

Sweet goddess. If every time they made love was like this, he might not survive.

WHEN AINSLEY WOKE up the next morning, she was delighted to find herself snuggled against Jackson. She smiled at the amazing turn her life had taken. How had she even considered not living with him?

You were a fool, her wolf said.

True. To think her mate was her best friend's brother. The whole concept that she was mated to a non-Changeling still blew her mind, but delighted her at the same time.

Ainsley wasn't sure Naliana had made the best pairing as far as Jackson was concerned. Blair had commented a few times that Ainsley wasn't the easiest person to live with. Poor Jackson. What if she got on his nerves? She could try to remain non-confrontational, but as a reformed Changeling, she could only bend so far. If he expected a woman who would give into his every wish, he'd be sorely disappointed—that is unless he was naked and touching her all over. Then she'd probably say yes to anything.

With her thoughts on sex, she remembered her shock when Jackson opened the front door last night wearing nothing but a towel. Man, did he look like a god, or what? Her body had gone crazy, what with navy sparks zooming off her everywhere. Sure the girls had warned her that she'd experience an increased level in her need, but she never thought it would be this bad. Izzy had claimed she needed to be with Rye several times a day in the beginning, and Ainsley had the sense it might be even worse for her.

She rolled over, needing another hour of shuteye, but as soon as she spotted the time on the clock, she stilled. Crap. It was Tuesday morning, and she had to be at work in less than forty-five minutes. Why hadn't she set the alarm? Oh, yeah, she was enjoying Jackson too much to remember.

She gently shook his sleeping form, suspecting he would want to get into work soon too. The snoring ceased and was followed by a grunt. "We need to get up," she urged.

Jackson had explained that Mr. Donaldson had given his dad and uncle permission to clear the property, and that Jackson needed to come up with a plan on how to find that treasure—fast. For his sake, she hoped something existed. If it did, she prayed it wasn't worthless.

She slipped from the bed and headed to the bathroom for her morning shower while Jackson roused. Staying in bed when the bear came out of hibernation was asking for trouble.

Because his shower was large, it was a good guess that Jackson would want to join her, but if he did, she'd definitely be late to work.

Come on. How late would you be if you kissed him a little with the water rushing over your naked bodies? her wolf asked, sounding so innocent.

I'd be very late. Now behave. Do I want to spend the day making love to him? Hell yeah, but no matter what we do or how often, I don't think I can be satisfied. My need for him can't be fulfilled. He's part of me now. Forever.

Her wolf harrumphed.

Once the water warmed, she stepped under the flow and realized that she wasn't nervous anymore about living with him. When she was in Jackson's arms, she felt safe, cherished, and exactly where she needed to be.

Just as she finished rinsing out the shampoo, the bathroom door opened.

"Well, well," Jackson said in all his naked splendor.

Her wolf growled and urged her to indulge in another sexual exploit. She was tempted. Her rational side insisted she shut off the water, dry, and get the hell out of there before she gave into her desires.

Slam him against the wall and ride him hard, her wolf demanded. *It won't take but five minutes.*

Shut up. I have clients to see.

Ainsley cut the water and stepped out. Before Jackson could grab the towel and do wickedly wonderful things to her, she snatched one from the rack and wiped herself dry. He winked then picked up his electric toothbrush. As much as she tried to look away from the intimate act of him brushing his teeth, she couldn't.

"I don't know if me living here is a good idea," she said as she slid her hands up his back.

He shut off the power, spit out the toothpaste then whipped around, acting as if he believed she was serious. "Why?"

"Because I have a one-track mind." She dragged a finger down his chest.

His eyes lightened and his gaze drew her in. "I hope it's on the same track as mine." He grabbed his cock and waved it.

That one ridiculous action made her laugh. "As much as I want to do you right here, right now, I don't want to be late for work. Can I have a rain check for tonight?"

He gave her his best frown. "Absolutely, but if you get horny, you know where to find me. We have a bed in the back of the office."

She grinned. "I'll keep that in mind."

Chapter Twenty

JACKSON COULDN'T BELIEVE how hard it had been to watch Ainsley leave this morning, but he couldn't let his weakness for her get in the way of either of their jobs. He had a treasure to locate. His dad and uncle would only wait so long before starting to build on the site. Today, they were removing the remains of the burned down warehouse, which would give Jackson a small window of opportunity to figure out the precise location of the well.

If he believed the old treasure map, he roughly knew its location, but he wanted something more precise—like a surveyor's map. For that he'd have to go to the County Courthouse and do research. One benefit of traveling to Andersonville, the County seat for Hope County, was that it would put more distance between him and Ainsley. He hoped being farther away from her would lessen his feral urges.

Dream on, his bear announced.

He needed his wits about him, and always thinking with his dick would only distract him. His wonderful shifter-witch had already messed with his head, and his body, and his bear today.

Andersonville was a thirty-minute drive from Silver Lake. Because Jackson had made a big stink about wanting to search in the well for the treasure, he'd look like a fool if he stopped now. Too many times he thought he should have his head examined. Treasure indeed. All kids believed in digging a hole and finding something special, only he wasn't a kid anymore.

What could possibly be down there—besides water and dirt? Was it sardonyx? If John Ernst had it marked on his laptop, it might be. His luck, the treasure would be a stack of useless Confederate notes. Unfortunately, he wouldn't know unless he dug it up.

When he arrived at the courthouse, he found a nice older lady named Agnes who worked in the records department and seemed anxious to help him find any land plots and surveys associated with the Donaldson property. He felt a little silly showing her the old treasure map, but when her eyes sparkled, he could tell she was all in.

Two hours later, after pouring through plat map after plat map, he was satisfied that he had all of the information he needed to locate the well. He then had Agnes make copies of the survey plats. After he handed her a nice tip, and accepted her gratitude, he left.

All through the searching process, Jackson had this nagging thought. John Ernst wanted the land. Why? Sure, it was close to the hills where the Changelings lived, but it wasn't like he'd build an office on the land. He worked for an accounting firm downtown. It had to be because he believed sardonyx was buried there.

Once Jackson returned to Silver Lake, he drove past Ainsley's workplace, and the temptation to stop by was intense. Knowing how his randy bear was right now, Jackson feared he'd do something stupid like kiss her in front of everyone and then shift. All hell would break loose. No, he had to stay away from her whenever he was near humans. With time, he might learn to control this new mating lust.

Since it was around lunchtime, he stopped by his favorite chicken drive thru for a few sandwiches, fries, and a soda. He was so hungry he managed to scarf down his meal in the few minutes it took him to drive to his office.

Both Connor and Kip were there and they rushed up to slap him on the back. "Congrats man, on finding your mate," Kip said. "There's nothing like it."

Jackson chuckled. "You can say that again. My bear won't shut the fuck up when I'm trying to concentrate. I swear he has a one-track mind." They both laughed. "Because I don't want to get home late to Ainsley on her first full night at the house, I'm going to dig into my treasure hunt." He waved a stack of papers. "These, my friends, tell me exactly where to dig."

After they briefly discussed Jackson's plan, he headed to his office. If he could figure out what the treasure was rumored to be, he might have a better idea how to retrieve it.

As he leaned back in his chair, the image of Ainsley came into his head—again. Only this time she was in her wolf form surrounded by trees, which triggered the events of that terrible night in the forest. Unfortunately, much of it was a blurry, bloody mess.

The first semi-coherent thoughts were of him standing in the kitchen while Ainsley told him what she'd overheard the Changelings say. When she'd mentioned that one of the men had said that sardonyx was buried at the bottom of the well, and a second man claimed it was pure rumor, that was more proof it was sardonyx down there. One thing for sure, he couldn't let the Changelings get their hands on it.

Knowing the lazy bastards, they'd try to steal it once it was un-earthed. Jackson pushed back his chair and marched into Connor's office.

His boss looked up. "You figured it out already?"

He explained what Ainsley had overheard the Changelings say. "We can't take any chances in case their precious stone is down there. We'll need to protect it."

Connor looked off to the side. "Hire a few men from the Clan to watch over the excavation site during the evening when we're not digging."

"If we're digging a hole that big, I'm thinking we might only want to dig at night. It'll attract less attention."

"You might be right," Connor said. "Is there any way we can make sure sardonyx is down there?"

"Not without digging."

Connor scrubbed a hand down his jaw. "What do you think about sending your mate back to Ernst's house and checking out his laptop again? There has to be some key that tells what those reds dots represent on his drawing."

"No fucking way. If she's caught, Ernst would kill her." It didn't matter that he wouldn't be able to tell she was no longer a Changeling.

Connor's brows rose. "He can't catch her if she's invisible."

His heart nearly stopped. Every objection that came to mind evaporated. "True."

Connor leaned forward, his eyes bright. "She might find nothing, but it's worth a try. Ask her."

Ainsley was a risk taker. She'd say yes. "I'll think about it." If he let his mind wander to what might happen, he'd go nuts. "Ainsley aside, I need to find someone to dig up the well."

"Try Wayne Forehand. My dad has used him quite a few times. He's fast and accurate."

Wayne lived about a mile from his parents. "I'll give him a call."

Not wanting to have another discussion about Ainsley, he left Connor's office. The rest of the afternoon was spent scheduling Wayne and then asking around to see if a few shifters could watch over the site.

Jackson hadn't spoken with Kalan since his return from Scotland, and he wanted to not only catch him up, but also to ask his opinion on what would happen if they did find sardonyx. It wasn't like he could sell it. He couldn't chance it landing back in the hands of the Changelings. The question was where to store it.

"Let's see what you find before we decide on a plan," Kalan said. "I agree that if Ernst tried to get involved in purchasing the property, there's a good chance the stone is down there."

"Do you have a few minutes to stop over at the office? There are a few things I want to fill you in on—in private."

"Sure. Give me hour and I'll be there."

AINSLEY STAYED A little later at work than she had planned because she wanted to make sure one of her clients understood all the options available to her for healing. Taking the time to explain each of the supplements, as well as how the magnets worked, caused Ainsley to be late getting back to the cabin.

By the time she reached the shifter compound, it was close to six, and she pressed down on the accelerator to get there sooner. When she spotted Jackson's truck in the drive, the tension left her body. All she wanted to do was hug him, collapse on the sofa with a glass of wine, and prop up her feet.

No, she didn't. She wanted to rip off his clothes and do him again, but she had to put some limit on making love until she caught up on her sleep. While she was looking forward to living with him, at some point, they'd have to discuss moving the rest of her stuff into his house. Her retro style furniture didn't match his more masculine leather sofas and chairs, but she wanted something of herself in the cabin.

Personally, her living room set would look better with the wooden beamed ceilings and hardwood floors. The yellow and red hues in the open concept granite kitchen countertop would also blend beautifully with her yellow sofa and green chairs. Getting into an argument over possessions was the last thing she wanted though. There'd be time later to discuss what they should do.

The moment she stepped inside the cabin, the rich aroma of tomato sauce assaulted her senses. Her stomach responded with a grumble. "Something smells good."

Jackson was in the small open kitchen with his back to her. "I'm making you dinner."

That sounded wonderful. "You are such a suck up," she teased as she set down her purse and keys and then took off her jacket.

He spun around. "What? A man can't make his mate dinner?"

"Why yes you can." She walked into the kitchen, wrapped her arms around his waist, and inhaled his scent. Her wolf went wild. Ainsley stepped back. "I need a glass of wine and to sit for a bit. I'm beat."

"I'm one step ahead of you. A bottle of Chardonnay and two glasses are on the coffee table."

He sure knew how to seduce a woman. "I've already decided to move in here permanently, so you don't need to sway me."

He turned around, a wooden spoon dripping with tomato sauce in his hand. "I'm offended."

She laughed and a few blue sparks shot off her hands. "Why's that?" She moved closer and inhaled his rich scent.

"I'd assumed after last night that you'd already agreed. My cooking is not a bribe."

She laughed. "I know that. It's fun to tease you."

From the sparkle in his eye, he enjoyed the banter. Before she had a repeat of their sexual exploits in the kitchen, Ainsley moved into the living room and kicked off her shoes. Relief at last!

She poured them both glasses of wine and took a sip of the soothing liquid. "That hits the spot. Thank you."

Jackson set down the spoon next to the stove and sauntered in after her. "I had an interesting day."

Hers was hectic and rather routine. "Do tell."

Dropping down next to her on the sofa, he explained about finding the location of the well. "As I was sitting in my office chair dreaming about you, I remembered what you told me about overhearing one of the Changelings say something about finding sardonyx,"

"The second man said it was a rumor. I wasn't sure what to believe. Changelings wouldn't bury something as valuable as sardonyx. It would have to have been a non-Changeling shifter who put it down there."

His eyes widened. "I never even questioned who buried the treasure—mostly because I didn't know what the treasure was. If it is sardonyx then I agree with you."

"Thank you."

Jackson sniffed his wine then tossed back half of the glass. "I can see burying it down the well for safe keeping, but that doesn't explain all of the red dots on Ernst's map."

Her mind spun, trying to think about what Owen would have done. "Maybe Silver Lake had a sardonyx mine way back when, and someone unearthed a ton of it. If that were the case, they'd want to spread out their prize. If someone located one spot and stole it, they would still have more. We had a sardonyx mine in Scotland, but it ran out about fifty years ago—or so my family claimed. It's how they got their money."

Jackson leaned back. "I'll check to see if anyone registered a mine back then."

"Did you check to see what is now in the location of those dots?" she asked.

"Yes. They're random buildings from banks to bookstores to supermarkets."

"Do you know what year the well was dug? I'm not sure why that's important, but perhaps you could cross reference which building existed at that time."

He smiled. "You are truly amazing!"

Joy spread upward. "Little ole me?"

"Yes. Just today I found out that the Donaldson property was surveyed in 1889. I haven't had a chance to note which buildings were in the town at that time, but it brings me to my request."

Jackson looked off to the side and her stomach tumbled. "What is it?"

"Connor suggested that if we could get access to Ernst's laptop again, we might be able to see if he had other maps—anything that will clue us in as to what the red dots might mean."

Ainsley could connect the dots, pun intended. "And you want me to go in."

He hissed in a breath. "Only if you're invisible."

He didn't seem to understand what that entailed. "I can't walk through walls, you know. When I'm invisible, if I open a desk drawer, someone watching will see the drawer move."

"Then forget it. I don't want you to do anything that's dangerous."

Now he was being silly. "Do you have a choice? I'm the only one who can get in and out without Ernst finding out."

Jackson stood and paced. "Connor was the one who came up with that brain child of an idea, but I don't like it. Something could go wrong."

She appreciated that he wanted to protect her, but it wasn't necessary. "I can defend myself. Or did you forget what happened in the woods?"

He spun toward her. "That's low, and you know it."

So he was embarrassed that a woman saved him. Tough. "You're rather pigheaded, you know, which is why I have to resort to those kind of tactics."

Jackson returned to his seat. "You win, but are you sure you want to do this? I'll bring a ton of backup and wait outside. I can't chance anything happening to you. If you tell me you're in trouble, we'll charge in."

"You better not. It would ruin everything."

Jackson gathered her in his arms. "I can't lose you."

He was the sweetest man. "Nothing will happen."

He lifted her chin. "Okay, but we do things my way."

"Deal." Once she was inside Ernst's house, he'd never know if she followed his rules or not.

Chapter Twenty-One

THREE A.M. WAS too early to be out and about, but the job required that John Ernst be asleep when Ainsley snuck in. She had to admit that she was nervous about breaking in and then searching through his laptop, but Jackson had a good plan. She just hoped it worked.

As promised, he'd brought backup. Kalan and his partner, Dalton Garner, were in the car behind them, and Kip and Connor were in the backseat of Jackson's four-seater truck.

Jackson had gone over the drill a hundred times, focusing mainly on how she needed to telepath her every move. Her biggest worry was being able to stay invisible for a long enough period of time. She hadn't practiced in years, and she feared she might be rusty. It was the one thing she hadn't confessed to Jackson.

He stopped about a quarter of a mile from Ernst's house and cut his lights. "Let me know if you have any trouble, okay?"

He'd only drilled it into her a hundred times. Unless Ernst could sense her presence and then attacked, she didn't see any reason for this to end badly. The worst thing would be if they went to all this trouble and she didn't find anything.

"Yes, I'm ready," she said, fingering her good luck necklace from Shamus. Surely, nothing would happen to her if she wore this. She didn't expect to shift, so the necklace would be safe.

Ainsley slipped out of the front seat and Kip emerged from the back. His job was to use his electrical skills to disrupt power to the house. She'd suggested they merely cut the wire—assuming they had access to it—but Jackson said Ernst would know someone had sabotaged the place if they did. They didn't need him knowing someone had broken in. He'd alter his plans for stealing the sardonyx for sure if he suspected someone was onto him.

Jackson rolled down the passenger side window and leaned across the seat. "Good luck."

She nodded and headed off with Kip Landon. Not only could he disrupt the power using his magic, he could pick a lock. Both of those traits would come in rather handy. While the moon provided some light, as did the rather dim lamp next to the door, Ainsley was lucky she had excellent vision. Maybe that was why Kip followed closely behind her.

When they reached the front of the house, Kip motioned she step back. Having no idea what to expect, she did as he asked.

With anticipation, she watched as he raised his arm. Out of nowhere, a huge bolt of electricity shot from his palm and she jumped. Holy hell. That was the coolest thing she'd ever seen. Instantly, the door light extinguished. He did it! She held her breath, half expecting John Ernst to come running down the stairs to see what happened to his power. No electricity meant no heat. Eventually, when he became chilled, he'd investigate. Time was ticking.

Now came for the picking of the lock. She whipped out the flashlight with the red filter on it that Jackson had given her. It would hopefully allow Kip to see. He took out his lock picks and went to work. Seconds later, the tumblers clicked.

"All yours," he said. "And good luck."

She hoped Ernst didn't have one of those chains across the inside of his door. While she could have had Kip bust it open, it would make way too much noise. Inhaling the cold winter air, she depressed the lever and pushed the door inward. It moved.

Yes! Step one complete. *"I'm in."*

Kip tapped her on the shoulder then motioned he was taking off.

She nodded. Jackson had suggested that as soon as she was inside she become invisible in case Ernst snuck up on her. While she believed she could hear him coming, especially with his limp, she didn't want to take any chances. *Invisibility, here I come.*

Not wasting any time, she stepped toward his office. Being invisible didn't mean she was silent, which was why she'd worn rubber-soled shoes. The office door sat open. Darn. Not wanting Ernst to suspect something was going on in there, she would have to leave things exactly as she found them.

Even though the power was off, and the laptop was plugged in, it could still work on battery power. She lifted the lid and smiled as the screen shot to life, displaying his home screen. Thank goodness, he hadn't shut down completely or else she would have had to get past his password.

As she sat in his chair, she was disappointed that her heart was racing. She'd always prided herself on keeping cool. Maybe the cleansing had messed with her more than she'd realized.

Calm down. I can do this.

Unfortunately, Ainsley had no idea what she was looking for, so she studied his computer, searching for anything that would clue her into what his red-dot map might mean. She was the one who suggested the map might indicate the location of sardonyx buried in the town long before the buildings had been built, so she put the word *map* in the search function.

As she waited for the computer to locate anything with that word, she glanced up at the entrance, fearing Ernst would hear her fingers hit the keys and wake up. Hell, he might wake up anyway when the heater didn't click on, notice his clock was off, and come downstairs. His father, however, didn't pose a threat at all.

Bingo. Two documents with the word *map* showed up. The first one was the one she'd already copied. Crap. The second one was titled, "Silver Lake 1905."

Not taking the time to study it, she pulled out her cell phone and snapped a picture. As she closed the computer window, footsteps sounded on the stairs. Shit. Shit. Shit.

Just as she lowered the lid, her arm reappeared. What the hell? She looked down at her lap. Oh, no, she was no longer invisible.

Her heartbeat increased as she fought to stay invisible. Footsteps neared.

"He's coming!" she telepathed.

Ainsley had to get out of there or else hide.

"Get out of there now," Jackson commanded.

Ten feet away. Now five. She didn't have time to explain why she couldn't just walk out. Ainsley pushed back the chair and made a dash toward the closet on the far wall. The damn louvered door squeaked when she pulled it open. Crap. Just as she ducked inside and closed it, Ernst entered the office.

Flick, flick.

He tried to turn on the lights, but without electricity, nothing worked. Heavy steps moved toward the desk. "What the fuck?"

Had she left the laptop in a different position? Or hadn't she pushed back his chair? Blood pounded in her ears. Even with her excellent vision, she couldn't tell if she'd been able to disappear again. Why hadn't she practiced more?

Because I'm arrogant and think I'm invincible.

It was her stupid Changeling mentality showing up again. Damn. *Think about Jackson.* His face came to mind and her blood pressure dropped. The closet door opened and her heart nearly stopped.

"AINSLEY'S IN TROUBLE," Jackson said to the other men. "Her fear is attacking my body."

"Ainsley, are you okay?"

When she didn't answer, a piece of him died. He'd never been so upset in his life. Jackson's own heart was beating in unison with hers, and his gut was churning wildly. It was almost as if he was in that house and Ernst was about to find *him.*

Kalan and Dalton both had their hands on their weapons. "Give us the word and we'll go in with you."

"Talk to me, baby."

Kip was huddled next to them, ready to charge too. While he couldn't shift, Kip could take down Ernst with one blast. The problem would be with the cleanup. Jackson knew first hand how hard it was to make a Changeling disappear. If Ernst was as powerful as James implied, there would be an out and out war if any harm came to him. Council members were revered.

"I'm good. I'll be right out."

Jackson let out a breath. "She's coming out." The men nodded. "In case Ernst figures out she's there, let's move closer."

The four of them jumped back into their cars. Wanting to time his arrival to when Ainsley exited the front of the house, he drove slowly. *"Where are you?"*

"In the living room. I can see your lights moving up the road. Okay, I'm opening the front door."

He wouldn't relax until she was in the car. Jackson stopped about fifty feet from Ernst's house and cut the lights, but kept the engine running. *"I'm parked to the left of the drive."*

He strained to catch sight of some movement, but saw nothing. It was only when the passenger door opened and the overhead light clicked on that he knew Ainsley was there. A second after she slammed the door shut, she materialized.

"That was close," she said. Trembling, she sent off mixed vibes of elation and fear. "Can we leave now, please?"

Damn. He'd been too focused on checking her out instead of taking off. "You don't have to ask twice."

"Wait," Kip said. "Let me turn his lights back on. Ernst will think it's the power company's fault for the blackout if his service is restored. He won't think it's sabotage."

"Good thinking, but hurry."

They didn't need Ernst to look out the window and see both of their cars, so he motioned for his brother to back up. Once out of sight of the house, Kip slipped out of the truck and rushed up the front yard. A bright light flashed a few seconds later, followed by faint rays of light skipping across the lawn. Kip came barreling around the corner and jumped in. "Go."

With his headlights off, Jackson sped away. Not until he was out of sight did he flip them on. When he was half way down the mountain and was certain they hadn't been followed, he glanced over at Ainsley. Her anxiety level had tapered off, but she was definitely rattled. "Are you sure Ernst didn't see you?"

"I'm sure."

He believed her. "Good. I know it's late or rather still very early, but would you mind if we stopped at the office? It'll be easier for you to debrief us when everything's fresh in your mind. I've got some good coffee I can brew."

She glanced over at him. "You sure know how to sweet talk a girl."

Jackson chuckled, totally relieved that his mate was safe.

It was after four a.m. before everyone was seated in the conference room with coffee all around. "Tell us what happened," Jackson said, thankful Connor didn't seem intent on leading the discussion.

She gave them a brief rundown of what occurred at the house and then fished out her cell phone. "I took a picture of another map I think you might find interesting. I didn't have time to study it though." She told them how she'd started to materialize.

Jackson grabbed her hand. "What do you mean, you started to materialize?"

"Just what it sounds like. My ability to remain invisible kind of failed me." Ainsley let her voice trail off, but he had no doubt everyone heard. "To be honest, I have never tried to remain in that state for any length of time before tonight. I'll need to practice if I have to do something like this again."

There wouldn't be a next time, but they'd have that discussion in private. He knew he'd get some push back. "Go on."

"Something must have alerted Mr. Ernst—whether it was the

lack of electricity, the fact the heater had stopped working, or perhaps my tapping of the keys. Who knows? But he came downstairs. I was closing the computer top when I noticed my arm appeared visible, and then the rest of me showed up. All I could do was hide in the closet."

Ainsley had come within seconds of being caught. He had to make sure she understood how dangerous these assignments could be. His protective nature took over, and his intention of delaying the discussion flew out the proverbial window. "This needs to be your last assignment."

"She did fine," Connor tossed in. "With a little practice, she'll be good to go."

All Jackson could do was glare at him. He refused to argue with his boss now. They were all tired, and he might say something he'd regret later. Jackson then returned his attention to Ainsley. "How did you get away if he could see you?"

"When Ernst opened the closet doors and looked in, I'd managed to cloak myself again. I think I just needed to recharge. With the door open, I stepped out. I guess he was satisfied no one had broken into his house because he then returned to his computer. I thought he'd search more because I didn't have time to push his chair in or return the computer to its original position. As soon as I could, I slipped out of the office and out the front door. I'm hoping he didn't hear me open and then close the latch." She fingered her necklace, acting as if it had protected her.

"Hopefully." Ainsley had kept a cool head under dire circumstances, and Jackson was proud of her, but that didn't mean he'd let her take on something like this again. He swiped her cell phone, and when he spotted the map, excitement charged through him. "This looks exactly like what we need. How about we head out to the overhead projector? It'll be easier if I put it on the big screen."

With coffee cups in hand, the six of them moved to the front of the large room. In no time, Jackson had both maps displayed on the screen side by side. He stepped up to the front to get a better view.

"What are we looking at?" Dalton asked.

"Sorry." Kalan's partner, Detective Dalton Garner, probably hadn't been brought up to speed. Jackson walked back to his computer and opened another tab to display the original treasure map. "While I can't be certain, I believe that something important is buried right about here." He swirled his mouse where the well was supposed to be located. "Trust me, I've done a lot of research."

"What do you think is down there? Gold?"

"Something more precious—at least to the Changelings: sardonyx." Dalton hadn't been in Silver Lake very long, but he and Kalan had dealt with the bastards enough to know what they were capable of, especially after they got ahold of the stone the last time.

"We can't let them get their mitts on any of that," Kip chimed in.

It was his twin who'd had his magic stolen by those mutated freaks. Jackson's anger subsided when he remembered not all Changelings were bad—at least those who were only part Changeling.

"I can see why you're so interested," Dalton said as he studied both images.

"Give me a sec." Jackson superimposed Ernst's original map with the red dots on top of the new map of the town that dated back to 1905. "I'll be damned."

Chapter Twenty-Two

JACKSON WAS REALLY excited as he pointed to the red dots. "Back in the olden days, no buildings existed where these dots are currently located."

"Meaning?" Dalton asked.

"It's possible Silver Lake once had a sardonyx mine, which might be why the Changelings settled in this town. I'm thinking—or rather Ainsley suggested—that some non-Changeling shifters mined the stone, and when the Changelings tried to steal it, they had to hide it. The local shifters might have been aware back then that the Changelings used the sardonyx to rob Wendayans of their powers." He waved a hand. "That's all speculation. Bottom line is the miners could have buried their findings all over town. These red dots might represent the other locations. As I've said, it's just a theory."

Connor whistled. "From here on out, we need to operate on the assumption the Changelings want whatever is down there. On the way back here, I got to thinking that we should make it look like we're digging a small retention pond where the well is located instead of just drilling in one spot. It will attract less attention."

"Sounds good. I contacted Wayne, and he's starting tomorrow," Jackson said. "I don't think he'll have a problem digging in a larger area."

Connor slapped his thighs and stood. "It's almost daylight, so let's all get some shuteye. Thanks everyone for your help." He looked over at Ainsley. "Especially you, Miss Invisibility. You were very impressive."

"Thank you."

Jackson shut down his computer as the rest stood. Kalan, Kip, and Dalton shook her hand, telling her what a great job she did. Ainsley smiled, and even blushed once, but he could sense she was running on fumes. It was time to go home.

BECAUSE IT WAS almost five in the morning when they returned, Jackson suggested that Ainsley sleep in, but his little overachiever said she was going to work at her regular hour. His mate reminded him of himself in so many ways; she was as dedicated and ambitious as he was.

Right now, she seemed to be in some kind of fugue state. She barely spoke on the way home, and when he asked if she wanted a coffee, she shook her head and went straight to bed. He needed a shower, but by the time he finished washing up, his mate was sound asleep.

Her exhaustive state might be why he wasn't sure he could believe her when she'd told him that Dalton Garner was a tiger shifter. That was crazy. The only shifters he'd ever run into were either bears or wolves, though he admitted tigers existed—just not in Tennessee. Sure, she said one of her talents was being able to tell what kind of shifter someone was, but he figured she'd missed the boat with this one. Perhaps Kalan could shed some light on it since they were partners.

Jackson set his alarm for eight so he could get up early and fix Ainsley a nice breakfast before work. Food perked up any shifter. After a quick two-hour snooze, he rose and made her a meal. He then went in to wake her. To his surprise, Ainsley didn't grumble at being roused. Still in a zombie-like state, she dressed and came out to the table. He thought she'd want to discuss what happened at the Ernst residence, but she remained silent, eating her food as if on automatic pilot. He understood she was still processing the near disaster earlier this morning.

"How about tonight we watch a movie? Your choice," he said.

Finally, a smile appeared. "I'd love that. Thank you."

Jackson kissed her goodbye. "Text me when you arrive at the clinic." In her state, she might become distracted and run off the road, and he wanted to make sure she arrived safely. *Or send me a message with your mind*, he telepathed.

"I'm fine." She ran a hand down his chest, and his body exploded with need. Fortunately, he succeeded in talking down his randy bear.

"I know you are, but send a message anyway." He kissed her forehead because he didn't trust himself to do more. "Have a good day."

He debated following her, but that would only lead to an argument about him being overly protective.

Once Ainsley left, he cleaned up, dressed, and then headed to the Donaldson property to make sure Wayne understood exactly where he was to dig. At least Jackson didn't have to hide what might be hidden below. Being a shifter, Wayne would understand.

When Jackson arrived, to his surprise Connor and Kalan were at the site. "Hey, what are you two doing here?"

"I don't trust Ernst," his brother said. "If one of his Clan spots you digging, he might report back to the Council. Ernst is probably just biding his time before he tries to steal it."

Jackson wasn't worried. "Bring it on. We'll have five men here at all times once Wayne digs down far enough. By the way, he said he'll have it dug by tonight."

"Great," Connor said. He looked up and nodded. "Speaking of which, here's Wayne now."

Just as Jackson turned to meet the man who would excavate the well area, he sensed two other shifters besides his brother, Connor, and Wayne. He searched the woods across from the property but didn't see anyone. "I'm sensing company," he said.

"So do I," Connor said, his mouth pinched and his gaze focused.

"Let them watch," Jackson said. "With what we have planned for Wayne, I don't think our work will raise any red flags—that is, until we unearth the sardonyx."

"I bet the Changelings will feel the power emanating from the source before it's exposed. Then they'll wait for the right moment to grab it," Kalan said.

"Let them try. We'll be prepared."

Wayne came over. With survey in hand, Jackson explained where he needed to dig. "Just be careful. We don't need to be left with a pile of dirt sprinkled with sardonyx."

Wayne smiled. "I can grab a one carat diamond with my scoop."

Jackson laughed. "See that you do."

For the rest of the morning, Jackson stood watch. Kalan left around noon, but Dalton stayed until two. Jackson had scheduled members of his Clan to show up in three-hour shifts starting at three. By six, Jackson was beat and called it a day. Until the treasure was actually found, he figured things would remain calm.

Suddenly, Wayne's tractor scoop hit something hard, and Jackson rushed over, his heart running in overdrive. Together, they checked it out.

"It's the well!" Jackson said. "I'll be damned. We're getting close."

"I'll go slowly around this area, but I'll continue to dig the larger pond to throw those bastards off. You look like shit. Why don't you head home and rest. I'll call you if I find anything."

"Perfect." In a few hours, Jackson would either be a hero or look like a fool. "Keep in touch. Connor should be back soon."

Of the five clansmen who'd volunteered to stand watch, three would station themselves around the area while the other two would do a larger perimeter search. That should be enough to dissuade the Changelings from charging in.

When Jackson returned home, Ainsley's car was in the driveway, and despite being exhausted and cold from standing outside all day, his bear wanted her.

"She needs to rest," he tried telling the animal inside him. Too bad his bear never listened. He'd promised her a movie, and that's what she'd get.

Tomorrow, after they found the treasure, they could celebrate in style. Not that he had any use for the red stone, but it would be one less source for the Changelings. Unfortunately, even if they kept this stash of sardonyx from the Changelings, it wouldn't stop Council members from buying up one of the buildings that was on top of the other burial sites, ripping up the floors, and digging down. Crimeny, their reign of terror would never stop.

Right now, Jackson hoped he was wrong about what was down there—that there were only useless Confederate notes. It sure would save the Wendayans a lot of grief.

He unlocked the front door and entered. Now that Ainsley was living with him, he had to make sure she was safe. "Ainsley?" he called out as he tossed his keys on the kitchen counter and took off his gloves and jacket.

When she didn't answer, he headed into the bedroom. Aw. His sweet mate was still dressed in her uniform, faced down on the bed. He smiled. On the drive home, he'd thought about treating her to a massage, but it would be better not to wake her. If she did rouse and was in the mood, he'd make sure he provided all sorts of fun.

AINSLEY AWOKE AT ten p.m. after having crashed on the bed. She couldn't remember the last time she'd been that tired. When she realized she hadn't even taken off her uniform, she groaned then rolled over, only to find Jackson sitting next to her reading.

"Hey, you're home. Sorry, I must have passed out. I think not having used my invisibility for such a long time, exhausted me." She brushed the bangs from her face and wet her lips.

He smiled and looked so damn hot. "I can only imagine. The stress alone of breaking into someone's house and not getting caught would tucker anyone out." He closed his book and placed it on the nightstand next to the bed. "If you get naked, I'll give you a back rub."

Ainsley snickered at his comment. "Hmm, naked? Really? Is that a prerequisite for this back rub?" If she hadn't already decided that he was the most amazing man in the world, he'd win that award now. "Do I get to rub you down naked afterwards too?"

A burst of energy surfaced at that thought.

"Oh yes, Miss sassy. It is definitely a requirement for this back rub, but I don't think after touching every inch of your body that my bear will be willing to wait, especially if you are planning to do naughty things to my body."

"That's probably true." She'd never be content just to rub him down. Her mouth and tongue would have to join in the pleasure too. "While I undress, how about grabbing the bottle of lotion from the bathroom. You can rub it all over me."

"How about I watch you get naked and then I'll get the lotion?"

His eyes had already turned that yummy golden hue, implying she might never receive that back rub. "Deal."

Her wolf was going crazy. Because of the delay caused by last night's adventure up in the hills, it had been too long since they had made love. *Love*. Not only did Jackson's eyes shine with it, his actions showed her how much he cared for her. Ever since they'd mated, she'd promised herself that she'd allow herself to fully feel. For the first time in her life, she was ready to be in love and be loved.

As slowly as her wolf would allow, she unbuttoned her work shirt and tossed it behind her on the carpeted floor.

Jackson whistled. "I love white lace."

"Admit it. If I had on a plain cotton bra, you'd say the same thing."

He shrugged. "I can't help that no matter what you wear, watching you undress turns me on."

Everything turned him on, but she wouldn't play that game. She had some serious loving to do. "I'm glad."

Next came her pants and then her bra. When she flung them

behind her, Jackson's incisors extended, and hair sprouted on his face. Next thing she knew, he had her flung back onto the bed and pinned under him. "I can't wait."

"What about my massage?" Ainsley pouted and gave him some sad puppy dog eyes.

"How about I rub you until you come?" Jackson waggled his eyebrows at her seductively.

Ainsley giggled at his antics. She could imagine what that would entail. Somehow, her back and shoulders wouldn't receive the attention they deserved. That was okay. She didn't think she could last very long if he dragged his rough hands all over her body. "I'm waiting for the rubbing to begin."

"Geezus, I love that sassy mouth."

"Is that all you love?" *Me and my big mouth.* Damn, Jackson might not be ready to discuss something like the concept of love.

"Clearly, I've done a poor job showing you that I love everything about you. Your hair, your tits, your pussy…"

She cracked up. "You are all man. Now show me with your mouth and your hands exactly what you love the most."

He growled. The next thing she knew, he was all over her. Ainsley's blue aura shot to life as his lips found hers. His scent and taste spread through her body like wildfire, and her wolf demanded more.

She ran her fingers over his short hair, loving the bristled texture. His facial hair was a little rough on her lips, but she adored that he was as needy as she was. As she ground her pelvis against his hard cock, their tongues dueled for position.

Jackson broke the kiss. "Panties have to go."

With amazing dexterity, he slipped them down over her butt and dragged them to her knees. She had to intervene and take them off the rest of the way since his arms weren't long enough.

He slipped a hand around her back, and when he lifted her up enough to suckle on her tits, waves of ecstasy washed over her. He drew one nipple taut while he palmed the other breast. Streaks of pure bliss shot straight to her core, causing Ainsley to moan her pleasure out loud. If he continued for much longer, she'd come, and that wouldn't do. She was determined to have one huge climax timed precisely with his release. Tonight was about loving Jackson the way he deserved.

"Get on your back," she commanded.

Without a word, he did as she asked. Before he could take back control, she straddled his legs, leaned over, and then scooted backward until her mouth was close to his cock. Not able to wait any longer, she drew him deep into her mouth. Her blue glow intensified.

"Sweet goddess of love," Jackson whispered. "Your mouth is pure velvet."

Not wanting to break the seal, Ainsley worked hard not to smile. Her love for him bloomed. Each flick of her tongue and stroke of her palm heightened her desires. She wasn't sure how much longer she could last since her need for him surpassed everything she'd ever experienced.

Enough, her wolf demanded. *Ride him hard.*

Her aura expanding, she lifted up, drew his cock to her entrance, and plunged downward. *Whoa*. While she was wetter than the rose quartz at the bottom of Silver Lake, he stretched her wide. Ainsley had to stop in mid ride to allow the slight pain to subside. Once her muscles relaxed, she dropped down the rest of the way. Blue sparks burst everywhere. She was so close to coming.

"Need you," Jackson mouthed.

He clasped her shoulders, and when he drew her near, the change in angle hit more erotic spots than she knew existed. Dropping down to her elbows, she cupped his face and kissed him with all of her passion. He'd given her a new lease on life in so many ways, and she planned to thank him for the rest of her life.

In need of air, she lifted up. As if they both were overcome at the same time, he dragged his sharp teeth across the soft part of her neck just as she lightly touched his skin with her needle sharp canines.

Poised to bite, Jackson withdrew his cock partway and then

drove right back in. The second he hit her back wall, all hell broke lose. She sunk her teeth into his neck and rode him hard, her blue glow completely encompassing him. As he bit down, her climax came so hard and fast that she saw stars on the back of her lids.

Jackson lifted his head just as his cock exploded, sending his hot seed into her. Her mind blanked, and her body collapsed. She'd never been happier in her life.

AINSLEY MUST HAVE fallen asleep because the next thing she remembered was Jackson shaking her. "Ainsley, I gotta go."

She sat up. It was dark out. "What? Why? It's late."

"Connor called. Wayne found the sardonyx."

Suddenly, she wasn't sleepy anymore and sat up. "That's fantastic."

"It would be if Connor hadn't sensed a butt load of shifters near the property. I'm calling Kalan and Rye to see if they can rally the troops." He leaned over and kissed her. "I'll be back soon."

She scooted off the bed. "I'm coming with you."

"No, you aren't. I don't want to be distracted, and if you're there, I will be."

"Okay. Then go." She didn't want anyone to suffer because she'd delayed him.

He gave her one final kiss then ran down the hall. Her mouth kicked up at the corner as she shook her head. Did he really think she'd let him go alone? And here she'd thought he understood just how stubborn she could be.

Ainsley would give him a three-minute head start. If she parked down the road, shifted, and then cloaked herself, he'd never know she was there. Or so she hoped.

Chapter Twenty-Three

THE SECOND THE front door closed, Ainsley quickly dressed. As much as she wanted to wear Shamus's necklace, if she shifted, it would splinter apart, which meant she had to leave it at home. When Jackson had nudged her this morning, anxiety along with excitement had radiated off Jackson's body. No doubt, he anticipated a fight. Sure, he'd mentioned that Rye and Kalan would have men ready, but could he be certain it would be enough? John Ernst seemed like a resourceful man. After what had gone down when Kip, Kalan, and Connor stormed the Changeling bunker, the Changelings had probably found a ton of trained men to replace the ones they had lost in that battle.

Ainsley jumped in her Jetta and headed to the Donaldson property. Fortunately, Jackson had pointed it out when they'd driven by, so finding it should be easy. She was happy Jackson had found his treasure, but given what it was, it might cause more issues for everyone.

Damn Changelings. Thank goddess she wasn't one of them anymore.

As she neared, her senses shot to high alert. Just then, a strong pain raced along her arm, and then another one shot across her chest. Oh, shit. Jackson was being attacked. At least this time, he'd anticipated the assault.

The anger radiating from him nearly made her miss her turn. Pressing hard on her brakes she rounded the corner. Ainsley parked and estimated she was about a half mile away. While she undressed in the car, the hardest part was being outside naked for those first few seconds before she shifted. Brrr. Once she closed the car door, she shifted and raced toward the fray.

Howls, screeches, and loud growls sounded everywhere. She envisioned being invisible and suddenly disappeared. Three bears and about fifteen wolves were battling, but she couldn't tell anyone apart, except for Jackson and his light colored snout.

When she moved closer, the Changeling signatures became apparent. Thank goddess for that talent. Unfortunately, she was able to identify many more Changelings than non-Changelings. Three naked men were sprawled next to a pile of dirt, and she could only hope they were Changelings who'd lost their fight.

Jackson let out a roar when three wolves attacked him, two in front and one behind. *Time to move.*

Ainsley charged.

"What are you doing here?" Jackson telepathed in between swipes.

Damn. She'd forgotten that as his mate, he could sense her, and didn't need to see her. Just then a wolf bit his leg. Crap, she hadn't meant to distract him.

"I wanted to help." Now wasn't the time to debate anything. *"And I'm not leaving."*

Crouching low to gain some momentum, she sprang forward, aiming for one of the Changeling's neck. Her bite hit the mark, and the attacker rolled to the ground. Victory!

As she ripped out that wolf's throat, another snarling Changeling wolf ran into her, knocking her over. His paws scraped her neck and shoulder. Fire burned inside her.

"Ainsley!"

"I'm good," she telepathed, but Jackson could probably sense that wasn't true.

Just as she pushed aside the pain, two wolves charged each other and she was caught in the middle of their gnashing teeth. One of the wolves pawed her back while the other bit down on her spine. They pulled back as if they couldn't understand why they hadn't reached the other animal.

Just then, huge bear arms smacked the Changelings aside. *"Let me see you,"* Jackson demanded.

With so much pain consuming her, Ainsley was unable to hold her invisibility shield much longer anyway. As soon as her arms and legs appeared, Jackson scooped her up and carried her to the side of the fray.

"You need to stay and fight," she managed to communicate as her vision blurred, and a huge ache stole her breath.

"They're running for the hills. They spotted our clansmen coming. Cowards."

"I just need to rest…"

JACKSON WAS BESIDE himself. "I told Ainsley not to come to the property."

He strode over to the refrigerator, grabbed two beers, and handed one to his brother.

"Did you really expect her to listen?" Kalan asked. "She's your mate. When she felt your pain, she didn't want to sit home idly."

He spun toward his brother. "Whose side are you on anyway?"

"No one's side. We're shifters. We fight. We get injured, but she'll heal."

"Why couldn't she have learned her lesson after going into John Ernst's home? She almost got caught then. At the battle, she nearly died." Okay, that was an exaggeration, but she might have. Jackson had only himself to blame. He never should have agreed to let her help the first time.

"Calm down. Missy is doing everything she can to help her. Ainsley will be fine."

"She's strong, but I should have been the one who was injured. I can heal faster."

Kalan chugged his beer. "You should be lucky she showed up.

When I looked over at you, wolves were crawling all over your ass. She took out one that was about to rip out your throat. I will say it was spooky that the wolf suddenly dropped to the ground and was dead a minute later."

Maybe he was being too harsh. "She's saved my butt a few times now."

Missy came out from the bedroom carrying a flowered bag over her shoulder. "Ainsley is resting comfortably. When she wakes, she'll want to shift into her human form. If her cuts are healed, encourage it."

"I appreciate you coming here and helping out," Jackson said. Missy was a Wendayan healer who'd helped many of his shifter friends—including Rye and Kalan.

She smiled. "I'm happy to help."

Kalan set his beer on the counter. He'd driven Missy. "Let me know how Ainsley is tomorrow."

"Will do," Jackson said.

As soon as Kalan and Missy left, Jackson rushed into the bedroom. When he saw Ainsley in her beautiful wolf form, his heart ached for her. She had a white patch of fur on her face while the rest of her body was a combination of tans, blacks, and grays. She was so lovely.

He sat on the bed and examined her. Jackson had to admit that Missy was a miracle worker. While Ainsley's fur was matted with blood in places, the deep cuts had almost healed. Stroking her face, he hummed, hoping the soothing tone would aid her in getting better.

"I love you, Ainsley Chancellor," he murmured. Her eyelids fluttered, but she remained still.

Then her tail wagged, and her eyes opened. The growl she emitted came out strong and he knew what came next. He jumped up to give her room to shift. Seconds later, she was in her gloriously naked form curled up on the bed.

Jackson returned to her side. "Hey, how do you feel?"

She lifted up on her elbow then glanced down. "Not bad considering."

"You should rest."

"What I need to do is take a shower and then find something to eat. I'm starving."

He smiled. Ainsley was back. He helped her sit up and then held out his elbow to give her some support. She placed her hand on his arm and stood.

"Need help washing?"

"No thanks, but you can keep me company."

"That I can do," he said.

She headed into the bathroom. "Tell me what happened before I arrived," she said.

"When I got there, Connor and the men who had been guarding the stones were being attacked by about seven wolves. I jumped into the fray and injured one of them, but then more wolves showed up. That's when you arrived."

She was surprised he didn't lecture her about how stupid she'd been for rushing in, but if those two wolves hadn't charged each other at the same time—with her between them—she'd have been fine.

Ainsley stepped into the warm shower. "Ah, that feels good."

"I bet."

"Tell me what happened after I kind of passed out."

Jackson leaned a hip against the vanity. "When you became visible, I picked you up to prevent further injury."

"You should have stayed and fought."

He shook his head. "You are more important to me. Besides, the reinforcements had shown up."

She dipped her head under the water then poured shampoo on top. Once she soaped up and rinsed, she looked over at him. "When I was lying in bed, did I hear you say something super sweet?"

He pushed off from the counter, kicked off his boots, and discarded his pants and shirt. "If you didn't understand all of it, I'll be happy to repeat it every day for the rest of your life." He pulled open the shower door and stepped in.

"What would that be?" she said with a smile on her face.

"That I love you with my whole heart."

"You do?" Ainsley threw her arms around his neck and kissed him. "I love you too."

"That right?"

"Yes. Let me get clean first, and then I'll show you just how much."

"Deal." He tried to snap his fingers, but they were too soapy. "I forgot to mention what Kalan told me. The lab analyzed the blood stains on your pink shirt."

"And?"

"Two patches of blood samples matched the blood on Shamus's body."

She stilled. "Are you saying two of the men I killed were responsible for killing him?"

"It looks like it."

She hugged him again. "That makes me happy, though I'm sad that Shamus was in the wrong place at the wrong time."

"Very sad."

As Ainsley rinsed her hair, Jackson insisted on washing her back. Just him touching her, had her wolf roaring to go.

"That feels divine," she said. "How about we dry off?"

Jackson moved closer. "I'd be happy to dry off every drop of water on your body, or I could just lick it all off for you." He stuck his tongue out and wiggled it at her.

Ainsley grinned and shook her head at him. "How about we just use a towel. I'd like to get something to eat first though."

He lifted one eyebrow and grabbed his cock. "I'll give you something to eat."

Ainsley's eyes widened as her body filled with heat and desire. Jackson's laugh snapped her out of her lustful haze. She grinned, stepped out of the stall, and grabbed a towel. "Did you tell me what happened to the sardonyx? I can't remember."

"I didn't. Rye has it now. To keep everyone safe, he's not going to tell anyone where it will be hidden either."

She sighed. "I love the sense of community here, something the Changelings never appreciated. You're lucky to be part of it."

"They're your Clan now too." He lifted her hair and kissed her neck. "And yes, I am lucky because I found you."

"No, I'm the lucky one," countered Ainsley.

Three months later

AINSLEY WAS SO excited. She couldn't believe that Elana was pregnant! Ainsley was so happy for her. Last week, Izzy had called her and said she wanted to throw a baby shower for Elana, and that she was registered at Wilson's Department store.

While Ainsley went shopping to pick out a gift, her heart ached for a family of her own. Jackson would make the absolute best dad, just as soon as he learned not to bring home his work.

So here she was, seated in Elana's living room along with Teagan, Izzy, Missy, Blair, Rye's sister, Chelsea, and Anna, the woman who worked at her store. The baby shower presents for Elana were stacked up on top of the coffee table, looking so festive in blues and greens.

Teagan stood and the crowd quieted. "I just want it on the record that I was the first to know Elana was pregnant—even before Elana herself knew. And may I add that this was my first premonition that was for a good event."

Elana clapped. "When she told me, all the pieces fell together. I'd been feeling ill in the morning, but it didn't occur to me what it might mean." She patted her stomach.

"When are you due?" Ainsley asked.

"In about three months. The doctor said the baby could come any time in April."

She mentally counted backward. "Is that why you didn't have

anything to drink when you came upstairs to check on how the move was going?"

"Yes. I was three months pregnant, but had only just gone to the doctors. I should have mentioned it to you, but I was still overwhelmed at that time."

Ainsley smiled. "I understand. I'm so happy for you."

The doorbell rang and everyone looked at Elana, who shrugged. "I didn't invite anyone else."

She stood, and when she pulled open the door, Elana sucked in an audible breath. "Brian?"

Izzy jumped up and rushed over, while Teagan stood with her hands clenched at her sides. She definitely looked ready to protect Elana if need be. From what Elana had told her, Brian had decided he didn't want her in his life and had walked out. If he planned to do her harm, he wouldn't get far, not with the talent in this room.

Leading Brian into the living room, Elana had the brightest smile on her face. "Everyone, this is my older brother, Brian." The group murmured their hellos.

His face reddened. "I, ah, brought you a baby gift." It was a large box wrapped in blue and pink striped paper.

Elana took the gift and set it on the table. "You didn't have to do that. Come sit down and join us. I am so happy you came."

"Thanks." Her brother glanced around, and from the way he was avoiding looking at anyone in particular, he wasn't feeling all that comfortable.

Elana sat in her over stuffed chair. "I never expected you to take me up on my invitation."

"My therapist, Dr. Patterson, encouraged me to. The more I thought about what you'd said in your letters, the more I realized how much I wanted to reconnect with you. I've never had a family, and there you were, offering me one. I couldn't say no. So, I packed up my things in Ohio and moved down here to Silver Lake."

Elana reached out and grabbed his hand. "You moved here?"

He nodded. "Well, I'm at the hotel for now until I find a place to stay. I want to make sure my niece or nephew knows he's loved."

Elana pushed up from her seat, leaned over Brian, and hugged him. Ainsley couldn't be more excited for her. After Elana lost her parents, she'd thought she had no more family—until Brian came into her life.

"I can't tell you how happy that makes me feel," Elana said. "In fact, the last tenant who lived above the flower shop recently moved out." She then glanced over at Ainsley and winked. "I'd love for you to live there."

Brian smiled. "You sure?"

"I'll introduce you to the landlord. I'm sure he'll agree once I put in a good word for you."

"That would be great." He nodded to the presents. "Aren't you supposed to open them?"

Everyone laughed. The joy had begun.

Ainsley smiled, but her heart was beating a bit too fast. Brian Stanley wasn't who he claimed to be. He was definitely not Elana's brother.

The End

I hope you enjoyed Ainsley and Jackson's story. Up next is HER RELUCTANT BEAR. It's Brian's story along with Jillian Garner, Dalton's sister. Here is a sneak peek of the first chapter.

Chapter One

WHEN HIRED STRIPPER Sergeant McDirty swiveled his hips in front of the dark haired the bride-to-be, his rotating pelvis failed to match the beat of the sensual music. Given how far the other women's tongues and eyeballs were hanging out, Jillian Garner was pretty sure none of the women even noticed.

Jillian just shook her head. Sure the hunk was hot. Not only did he have a nice smile, he possessed slim hips and had shoulders packed with muscles, but he did nothing for her inner tiger. Not that this was about her. Her college roommate, Renee Williams, and fellow coworker at her law firm was getting married, and Jillian couldn't be happier for her.

As Renee stuck dollar bill after dollar bill down the man's G-string, her older sister Camille who worked Vice at the Los Angeles Police Department (or LAPD for short) shouted, "Go Renee!"

It was good to see the defense attorney loosen up, something Renee hadn't done in the last few years. It wasn't until Richie had entered her life that she'd decided to slow down and smell the roses, so to speak.

As for Jillian, Los Angeles had wound her tighter than any Swiss watch, but she wasn't looking for someone to help her slow down. She was fine the way she was.

"Jillian," Camille said nudging her arm. While Renee wore her dark hair short, Camille preferred her light brown hair shoulder length. She claimed it softened her appearance and made it easier for witnesses to relate to her.

When Jillian glanced up, Sergeant McDirty was thrusting his tiny maroon pouch at her. Oh my. The women, who were packed into Camille's tiny, but modern, living room apartment, clapped and cheered, waiting for Jillian to deposit the two dollars she'd been clutching for the last half hour into his *package*. She was thirty-two, much too old to be doing this sort of thing, especially with a guy who didn't look old enough to drink. For Renee's sake though, Jillian tossed him her best smile and jammed the bills inside careful not to let her fingers touch his skin while at the same time not dislodging the mass of bills already crammed into the tiny space.

"Thank you!" He graced her with his perfect smile and thankful-ly moved on.

Camille leaned over. "Dalia would have loved all the fanfare."

"She absolutely would have." During college, Dalia had been the wild one of the three, but ironically, she was living her dream of studying nature in Oregon. Nature, she claimed, calmed her right down. Jillian sucked in a breath. "Oh, shit. I told her I'd take pictures but I forgot. I've been distracted."

"Haven't we all?" Camille winked.

Jillian chuckled then whipped out her cell. Pressing the camera's video button, she recorded the stripper gyrating and thrusting hips in front of his next victim. Jillian made sure to include the three egg tempera paintings above the teal blue sofa that Camille had painted. One of the smaller ones was of a richly colored iguana feasting on a plump red fruit. The one below it was the face of a wolf whose eyes glowed yellow. The delicate interweaving of the grays, tans, white, and black in his fur blended together to create a striking image. The last picture was as tall as the two together. It was a magnificent scene of a white polar bear with her two cubs floating on a slab of ice.

Jillian continued her slow pan to include several women who Dalia had never met. Even as she recorded the festivities, Jillian felt guilty coming to the party when Dalia had flown all the way in from Portland to attend Renee's bachelorette party, only to have come down with the flu.

Jillian gladly would have stayed home and played nursemaid, but Dalia instead she attend—if for no other reason than to take pictures.

With her eye on the screen, Jillian panned the crowd, making sure to include everyone.

"She'll appreciate seeing Renee so happy," Camille said.

"Definitely." Renee, Dalia, and Jillian had roomed together freshman and sophomore year. "Dalia's here for another few days, so I'm hoping the three of us can get together."

"Renee would love that. She was so disappointed when she found out Dalia couldn't make it."

One of the ladies approached them, or rather staggered toward them, with a big bottle of champagne and refreshed everyone's glass. Good thing Jillian's shifter metabolism could handle this massive influx of alcohol. Otherwise, she'd have to call a cab to drive her home.

Mercifully, around one a.m., the hired hunk said his farewells. While Jillian had enjoyed watching the drunken women paw over Sergeant McDirty, she was increasingly worried about Dalia. Her friend hadn't texted even once to ask about the party. Dalia's fever had come down to almost normal before Jillian had left, but those kinds of things could change in a heartbeat.

Just as she was about to tell Camille that she was heading out, her friend jumped up and rushed over to Renee whose eyes had rolled back in her head. Clearly, the bride-to-be had partied way too hard. Good for her, though she'd be sorry tomorrow when the hangover hit.

Convinced no one would even remember she'd been the first to leave the festivities she helped organize, Jillian slipped out.

Fortunately, her house was only a fifteen-minute drive from there. As Jillian entered her neighborhood, she had to smile at how wonderful the get together had been. Camille, who dealt with crime all day, had been more relaxed than Jillian had seen her in months. Several of the other women at the party also worked in her same law office. Seeing another side of their uptight and ambitious personalities was something she would not soon forget.

As Jillian rounded the corner to her house, what sounded like gunshots came from her house! What the fuck?

Even though she lived was on the outskirts of Los Angeles, crime was rare in her upscale neighborhood. Pressing hard on the accelerator, she sped toward her driveway. As she neared, a man wearing a ski mask dashed out of her house through the front door. He looked straight at her before turning and charging fifty feet down the road. He then disappeared into a maroon sedan and peeled out of there, leaving burnt rubber in his wake.

Her heart raced so hard, she thought she'd shift—something she hadn't done or considered doing in years. She couldn't afford for anyone to find out what kind of freak she was. Hell, the world wasn't ready to learn about shifters, especially her very rare kind of white tiger.

Her focus returned to her sick friend asleep in the house. Dalia! Oh my goddess. Had she been shot? That was the only plausible conclusion, but logic had failed her before.

Decision time: Follow him or check on her friend?

What am I thinking? It's a no brainer. Dalia comes first.

Jillian could only hope that he'd left enough evidence for the cops to find the bastard. If he harmed her friend, she'd do whatever it took to find make him pay.

After cutting the engine, she jumped out of her Mercedes, not even bothering to pull into her driveway. Because it was so late, she used her Wendayan talent to sprint almost as fast as a speeding bullet, hoping no one noticed the super human feat.

The front door sat open. Acid burned in her stomach.

"Dalia?" Jillian yelled as she rushed in. When she received no response, her legs nearly gave way. Mouth dry and pulse soaring, her stomach performed a million somersaults as she ran to Dalia's bedroom. The stench of that man's scent permeated the air and put a momentary block on her working brain. Memories came flooding back even though she tried to force them away. Something other than his scent overpowered her—something terrible. It was blood!

The door to Dalia's room sat wide open, and while the light was off, enough moonlight snuck in through the window to show the devastation.

"No!" Jillian screamed then choked out a sob.

As much as she didn't want to turn on the light, she had to see the extent of the injury. When she flicked on the lamp, Jillian gasped as one knee hit the floor. The side of Dalia's skull had a hole in it, the blood staining her long blonde hair. Jillian's heart stopped for a few seconds. While it appeared as if her friend was dead, she checked for a pulse anyway. Unfortunately, her own heartbeat was near to bursting, preventing her from detecting any signs of life.

Her instincts clicked in, and she fumbled in her purse for her cell to call 911. The words to describe what happened barely formed on her lips, but the operator assured her help was on the way.

This couldn't be happening. Jillian's front door had been locked, and she doubted Dalia would have answered if someone had knocked. Had he busted in? Or was he more sophisticated than that and had picked the lock?

Grief rocked her as tears streamed down her face. It was déjà vu all over again. Twenty-six years ago an unwanted shifter had broken into her home and shot and killed her father. She'd seen the killer then, and she'd sort of seen him now—or rather she'd smelled him again. The stress of both murders made her whole body feel as if a ten-ton truck was sitting on her, breaking her bones into tiny pieces.

The image of the man with the crescent-shaped scar that she'd seen this afternoon at the police station appeared in her mind's eye. Jillian had spotted him when she'd stopped in to see Camille. Because Jillian had helped with the party preparations, she needed to discuss some last minute details with her friend. Halfway through her conversation, the same stench that permeated her house now registered. It had come from the man who'd killed her father. She'd been sure of it. Working hard not to let Camille know what was happening, Jillian had glanced around. Big mistake. The second she spotted the man's crescent-shaped scar on his jaw, she'd almost shifted. Then reason intruded. The man was a cop for goddess sake.

It is the same man, her tiger warned, angry at the quick dismissal.

It couldn't be him, she argued.

She didn't have to be a lawyer to know that memories of a six-year old were never reliable. Because scars weren't unique, she dismissed the thought that was the same man.

You're wrong, her tiger screamed. *You never forget a scent.*

Her tiger might be right. His smell was identical to what she remembered all those years ago. Or had spotting the scar brought up that memory and was fooling her now?

FRANK WHITLAW SLAMMED his palm against the steering wheel. Seconds ago he'd been gloating that he'd finally tied up that loose end. He wouldn't have to worry ever again about a six-year old's memory returning.

He'd jammed the key into the ignition and floored his souped-up car. A quick glance in the review mirror assured him that Jillian hadn't shifted. Even if she had chanced coming after him, she never would have been able to catch him.

How had he been so careless? For years, Frank had watched Jillian Garner—carefully. He knew where she lived, where she worked, who her friends were, and even where her relatives lived. Nothing escaped him. Then this afternoon when Jillian was visiting her friend Camille, he'd walked near, hoping to learn about her—or rather to find out if she'd figured anything out. The moment she glanced his way, recognition crossed her face. Even though barely a muscle moved, hatred had filled her eyes.

That mistake on his part sped up her demise. When he'd picked the lock to Jillian's house, he'd made enough noise to waken any shifter. He expected her to come out and investigate. His plan was to then shift into his wolf and attack. Even though he didn't know her species, it didn't matter. He'd trained his whole to be a fighter. Jillian was destined to die.

He should have questioned why the blonde woman in the bed

hadn't stirred. Even more careless of him was the fact he hadn't detected a shifter signature, and yet he didn't stop to think why that was so. He was slipping, and that really pissed him off.

I'll kill the right woman. Soon.

His thoughts jumped back to the night he'd broken into the Garner house. He never would have killed her father if the straight ass hadn't suspected him of pilfering weapons and drugs from the evidence locker where he worked. Her dad said he was going to turn Frank in to Internal Affairs. No way could Frank couldn't let that happen. The money was too addicting.

As he cleared the neighborhood, his shaking hands stilled. He'd fucked up tonight. Hopefully, the mask prevented Jillian from figuring out who he was. While he might have botched his attempt this time, it wouldn't happen a second. That was a promise he'd keep.

"MA'AM?" SOMEONE ASKED as he placed a hand on her shoulder. She looked up to find two paramedics in navy blue uniforms standing next to her.

She hadn't even heard them come in. Jillian must be losing it since noises never escaped her notice. And how come their faces were so blurry? "Yes?"

"We need to check on your friend," the one with the long face said.

Even though she was still holding her phone, she'd forgotten for a moment that she'd called for help. When she didn't move, the second paramedic helped her up.

Pull yourself together, her tiger demanded.

I'm trying, but it's so damned hard, she retorted.

Both men checked out Dalia, and then the one with the long face stepped over to her. "I'm sorry for your loss."

So she was dead. Why would anyone want to kill her? "Thank you."

Her heart nearly cracked. Or were those her bones, readying her to shift into her tiger? *I want to find the bastard*, her animal growled.

Stand down, she demanded. The last thing she needed was for her caged animal to go off half-cocked. Jillian had spent years steeling her human, making her strong enough to fight her tiger's urges. Right now, she was losing the battle.

Jillian wasn't sure how long she'd stood there, but sirens sounded outside and then the paramedics moved out of the room, leaving Dalia in her resting position. No sooner had they left the bedroom than two police officers came in. One was a shifter, the other was not.

"Ma'am."

Her eyes took a moment to focus through the tears. When the man's face became clear, a giant claw ripped at her gut. No! No! No! It was him. The evil person who'd killed Dalia and her father—or so she believed.

I have to be wrong, her logical side screamed.

No you aren't, her pushy tiger countered.

His foul scent once more seeped in through her nose and triggered that horrible memory as well as the more recent one. Her tiger demanded that she shift and kill him right there, but she couldn't give in. As much as she wanted to rip him apart, she refused to let her anger take over. She'd have to find a way to prove he was the killer first. Then she'd bring him down legally.

Jillian drew on her lawyer calm and studied him. The man was tall, maybe six feet and had weathered skin, close-set eyes, and a weak chin, as well as that two-inch scar on his right jaw.

The instinct to flee was strong, but Jillian had to pretend she had no idea he'd done this heinous act. Because alcohol tainted her breath, she believed she could use that to her advantage, and pretend she'd seen nothing—or almost nothing.

"We'd like to ask you a few questions," the man with the crescent-shaped scar said. He turned to his female partner. "Can you take her statement? I need to call the crime scene unit."

"Sure."

He sounds so professional. Could he be the real killer? her human questioned.

Yes, her tiger immediately responded as she scraped her nails along the lining of Jillian's stomach, probably to show the strength of her conviction.

Focus. Jillian had been introduced to many of Camille's coworkers, but she'd never seen this woman before. Her nametag read Officer Rodriguez. She was human, and stood about five foot five, the same height as Jillian. The officer's skin was a warm honey color, and thankfully her dark brown eyes exuded sympathy. Concentrating on putting one foot in front of the other, Jillian followed her out to the living room.

"Please have a seat," the officer said. "Can you tell me what happened?"

Jillian decided to mix truth with fiction, all the while pretending to possess only human traits—that is, someone who didn't have exceptional hearing or fantastic eyesight. She sure as hell wasn't about to mention how fast she rushed into the house. The only stroke of luck was that the killer hadn't been the one to interrogate her.

"I was at a bachelorette party all night. I probably shouldn't have been driving home after drinking, but it wasn't far." Jillian waved a hand, wanting to keep talking before she received a lecture about drinking and driving. "Anyway, as I drove up, I saw a masked man charge out of my front door." She slurred a few of her words for effect. "He ran down the street and drove off."

"Did you see what kind of car he was driving?" the officer asked with no signs of disgust.

Jillian shook her head. "It was dark, and when I saw him come out of my house, my heart beat so fast I couldn't catch my breath, let alone register what was happening." She'd never be able to explain how she'd caught the first three digits of the license plate, as no human would have been able to see them from so far away. The fast beating heart, however, wasn't a lie. Otherwise, she would have memorized the entire license plate number. "I do remember that it wasn't a truck or a van."

The officer jotted down the information. "What time was this?"

"I can't be sure exactly, but I think I left the party around one, so maybe it was 1:15." That was the truth.

All throughout the questioning, Jillian wondered what the man was doing in the spare bedroom. Was he making sure he hadn't left any evidence? It wasn't like she could mention to the female officer that her fellow officer had killed her friend because he smelled the same as her intruder. Humans didn't have a keen sense of smell.

"Can you describe what he looked like?" she asked.

Jillian had said the man wore a mask. "He was maybe six feet tall. He might have been middle aged because his gait appeared stiff." That was all she was going to say. If the man believed she could identify him, he might come after her.

The officer kept asking her what seemed like the same questions over and over again. Eventually, two more people arrived with cameras and cases. Given they wore overalls and then slipped on paper footies and caps, they must be the crime scene unit. Her house now a crime scene, so Jillian figured it was a matter of time before they asked her to leave.

"I don't want to stay here tonight. I'd have nightmares. Would it be okay if I packed a few things and go to a friend's house?" Her plan to escape town had evolved during the interrogation.

"Absolutely. You can't remain here anyway. Where will you be staying so we can keep in touch?"

The first name that came to mind was Camille's. "Camille Williams. She works at the LAPD."

The officer wrote her name down. "That's perfect."

For effect, Jillian staggered as she left the living room. Unfortunately, she had to pass the guest room before reaching the master, so she forced herself not to look. As quickly as she could, she threw warm clothes into a suitcase. Tennessee, where her brother lived, would be cold in February. She picked that location in part because Jillian wanted to be as far away from Scarface as possible and because her brother could help her figure out what to do next. Her clients might revolt that she'd skipped town, but they would be more upset if she were murdered.

Something niggled at the back of her mind at that thought. Had the bullet that killed Dalia been meant for her?

PACK WARS (Paranormal)
Training Their Mate (book 1)
Claiming Their Mate (book 2)
Rescuing Their Virgin Mate (book 3)
Box Set (books 1-3)
Loving Their Vixen Mate (book 4)
Fighting For Their Mate (book 5)
Enticing Their Mate (book 6)

MONTANA PROMISES (Full length contemporary)
Promises of Mercy (book 1)
Foundations For Three (book 2)
Montana Fire (book 3)
Hart To Hart (book 4)
Burning Seduction (book 5)
Montana Promises Box Set (books 1-3)

ROCK HARD, MONTANA (contemporary novellas)
Montana Desire (book 1)
Awakening Passions (book 2)

HIDDEN HILLS SHIFTERS (Paranormal)
An Unexpected Diversion (book 1) – FREE
Bare Instincts (book 2)
Shifting Destinies (book 3)
Embracing Fate (book 4)
Promises Unbroken (book 5)

SOUTHERN SHIFTERS KINDLE WORLDS
Bear 'N Dirty

WERES & WITCHES OF SILVER LAKE
A Magical Shift (book 1)
Catching Her Bear (book 2)
A Surge of Magic (book 3)
The Bear's Forbidden Wolf (book 4)
Her Reluctant Bear (book 5)

Author Bio

Want 3 FREE books? Sign up for my newsletter.

COPY AND PASTE INTO YOUR BROWSER:
http://smarturl.it/o4cz93?IQid=MLite

Check out my latest interview on You Tube:
youtube.com/watch?v=sQo5pyyVMDI

Not only do I love to read, write, and dream, I'm an extrovert. I enjoy being around people and am always trying to understand what makes them tick. Not only must my books have a happily ever after, I need characters I can relate to. My men are wonderful, dynamic, smart, strong, and the best lovers in the world (of course).

You'll find me most days on my chaise lounge with my laptop and my iced tea(unsweetened!) on the side table. I love to sleep in late and write into the wee hours. I also love FB, so you'll find me on there, too!

I believe I am the luckiest woman. I do what I love and I have a wonderful, supportive husband, who happens to be hot!

Fun facts about me

(1) I'm a math nerd who loves spreadsheets. Give me numbers and I'll find a pattern.

(2) I'm addicted to taking pictures (I taught high school photo for 30 years). I plan to periodically post some of my favorites on my newsletter [so sign up!].

(3) I also like to exercise. Yes, I know I'm odd. Not only do I walk with different women each week, I teach Pilates twice a week at a local rec center, and lift weights the other days.

I love hearing from readers either on FB or via email (hint, hint).

Social Media Sites

Website:
www.velladay.com

FB:
www.facebook.com/vella.day.90

Twitter:
@velladay4

Gmail:
velladayauthor@gmail.com

Google:
plus.google.com/u/0/116041077486216602121/posts

Tsu:
www.tsu.co/velladay